IT'S
MURDER
GOING HOME

IT'S MURDER GOING HOME

MARLYS MILLHISER

ST. MARTIN'S PRESS
NEW YORK

A Thomas Dunne Book.
An imprint of St. Martin's Press

Design by Ellen R. Sasahara

Library of Congress Cataloging-in-Publication Data

Millhiser, Marlys.
    It's murder going home : a Charlie Greene mystery / Marlys
Millhiser.—1st. ed.
    ISBN 0-312-14628-0
        p.   cm.
    "A Thomas Dunne book."
    1. Greene, Charlie (Fictitious character)—Fiction.   I. Title.
PS3563.I4225I87   1996
813'.54—dc20   96-22110
                                                                   CIP

First Edition: December 1996

10 9 8 7 6 5 4 3 2 1

*To Boulder with love and perhaps
a giggle or two.*

I would like to acknowledge the help and suggestions of Virginia Lucy of the Boulder Police Department; of Dr. Mark Sitarik, nurse Sherry Flegg, and laboratory technician Heather Poole at Boulder Valley Oncology; of Carrie Bryan on Dorothy L. and her E-mail recipe for thirty-six-hour goulash; and of two wonderful writers who took time out of their busy schedules— Wendy Hornsby in Long Beach where Charlie lives, and Kathleen Phillips, who walked and talked me through her Boulder neighborhood. All misconceptions and misperceptions are, however, entirely my own.

IT'S
MURDER
GOING HOME

CHAPTER 1

❖

G OD, MOM, SHE looks dead," Libby Greene whispered, with a reverence her mother had never heard before.

Charlie looked away from her own mother long enough to check out the kid.

A guy in hospital greens perched on a tall stool scanned three generations of Charlie's family with disinterest—although his scan did linger on Libby before it went back to *The Boulder Poetry Workshop Magazine.*

Edwina looked even worse than dead to Charlie, her hair hidden by a white paper hat, obscenely fresh and snowy against the dirty pewter color of her skin.

I knew something was wrong. Why didn't she tell me? There's no excuse for this. This surgery was scheduled five days ago.

If a neighbor hadn't called, Charlie wouldn't even be here now. She and Libby had caught a last minute flight from LAX to Denver International and then a van to Boulder. Edwina had been in surgery for three hours by the time they reached Community Hospital, and they'd waited another three and a half.

For this . . .

Charlie knew Southern California had thinned her blood, but the room was freezing. It felt more like a morgue than a recovery room and looked like the inside of a small warehouse. An empty room but for the poet on the stool, the various dripping

1

things attached to Charlie's mother by hanging tubes and a needle. A machine making a bleeping sound, Libby's teeth chattering. Charlie put an arm around her without thinking. Her daughter was so distracted she forgot to pull away.

"Have you checked to be sure she's even breathing?" Charlie asked the poet around the sudden swelling in the back of her throat.

This is not my fault. I refuse to feel guilty. I had nothing to do with this.

"That long on the table, woman her age, they put 'em deep, takes awhile," he assured them in haiku, looking over the top of his magazine at Libby Greene. "She'll be fine. How old is she?"

You mean you don't know? "Which she?"

He blinked and lowered his magazine, even glanced at Charlie. "The patient."

"Fifty-seven, I think."

Libby pulled away from Charlie. "You mean you don't know?"

"Well I can't understand why you'd put someone 'her age' in a refrigerated room after six and a half hours of surgery," Charlie told him, ignoring her kid's incredulity.

The poet/hospital person's uniform had short sleeves, and he didn't show a goosepimple. He was soft and plump, and his ponytail had slipped out of the back of his surgical cap. He leaned over Edwina, looking incredulous too. "Fifty-seven?"

"Listen, jerk, what if my grandma's dead?"

"Not to worry," he assured the luscious blonde, "it doesn't bother the patient at all. We unofficially call this the turgid room. Keeps the patient's blood turgid, you know? You can lose a lot of blood with this kind of thing." He gestured to the array of drips, the machine that went "bleep." "The patient's comfort is controlled and closely monitored."

The patient moaned, shuddered, began an arrhythmic quivering violent enough to rattle the gurney.

"See? I told you she was alive," he said.

"Shaaar-leee," the patient said.

"I think she means you, Mom." Libby moved away from the head of the gurney.

"I'm here, Edwina. You're going to be fine." Charlie leaned an ear close to the top of the trembling almost-corpse.

"Terrified . . . die," Edwina might have said. "Soooo cold. Help, Sharrrleee!"

"Get Dr. Greene a blanket now." Charlie sort of hoped the startled poet would refuse. She'd been this angry before, mostly at Edwina, but this guy was messing with family and she wanted to—

Oh, right, Greene. What are you going to do, sic your kid on him?

"Another," she said when the first flimsy excuse arrived.

"Well, what? You want she should bleed to death?" the male nurse or orderly or whatever demanded.

"She's feeling the cold, scared her damn near to death, and you were reading poetry."

"She's so full of drugs, she's not going to remember shit."

By the time they wheeled Charlie's mother down the hall to her room, Edwina wore seven layers of the lightweight blankets, and her shivering had grown worse. So much for medical experts.

Little by little, over the course of the night, Charlie and Libby removed the blankets as Edwina complained of their weight and the heat.

Libby finally fell asleep in a chair. Charlie was too numb to do even that. She hated hospitals, and her feelings for Boulder were a confused mix she would never sort out. A hauntingly beautiful place, it would always be the scene of her crime.

The horror of what had happened to her mother was something that happened to a lot of women but didn't happen to anyone you knew, and somehow—though you feared it more than most things—it would never happen to you.

And the other woman moaning so pitifully in the next bed,

behind its drawn curtain, certainly didn't look old enough to have had this happen.

"Can't you do something for that woman?" Charlie asked a nurse who came in occasionally to check Edwina's vital stats and the medication and blood bags dripping through clear plastic tubes into veins.

"Oh, don't worry—she doesn't feel anything. We have her on heavy pain killers. Hers was a double mastectomy, poor thing. The moaning and groaning isn't unusual." But this medical expert at least peeked behind the curtain. "You okay, Mrs. Lawrence? She won't remember any of this, believe me," the nurse assured Charlie and turned to go, stopping at Libby's chair. "Your little sister is just beautiful. That hair is—"

"She's my daughter." And how do you know Mrs. Lawrence isn't hurting now even if she won't remember it?

"My, you've certainly taken good care of yourself," was the nurse's parting shot.

She'd no more than stepped out of the room when a belated answer from behind the curtain came drug-slurred but clear enough. "No, not right . . . help."

Charlie dragged herself and the luggage out of the cab and up the walk of the little house she had once called home, wondering if anybody had thought to feed the rats. Fishing Edwina's keys out of her pocket, she glanced idly at the house next door where her nemesis used to live.

It had been a scruffy little place for Boulder, but at least it had been little.

What had come to replace it was a giant stucco box that nearly filled the rectangular lot from side to side and end to end. The only trees left that Charlie could see were those in the grass strip between the sidewalk and curb. She vaguely remembered Edwina complaining about the "abomination" next door, but if Charlie had concentrated on all of Edwina's complaints she wouldn't have had time for personal hygiene.

The first thing she noticed walking through the tiny entry hall was that the windows of the modest sunroom opening off the living/dining room looked out on the blank north wall of the neighboring monstrosity. All that window and nothing to see. Charlie was sure Boulder had laws about blocking off neighbors' sun.

Libby had slept through much of the night on her chair and had even been given permission to use the shower in Edwina's room, which neither she nor Mrs. Lawrence would be up to for a while. Charlie had spent the night demanding pain relief for both women, gladly making a nuisance of herself at the nurses' station. This was the cancer wing and pain was a given here. Mrs. Lawrence's husband was home taking care of the kids, and her mother's plane had been held up.

Anyway, Edwina'd seemed happier by this morning—totally hopped is what she was—which is better than agony, and Libby and Charlie'd had breakfast in the hospital cafeteria. Edwina, Libby, and the day shift decided Charlie should go "home," get some sleep, and come back to spell Libby later in the day.

"Is this where I was born?" Libby asked in the cafeteria, over the mess she'd made mixing potatoes, eggs, sausage, and ketchup into a slurry. Charlie hadn't seen the kid eat breakfast in years.

"Well, it's the same hospital, but it's a lot bigger. I don't think this section even existed then." That incredibly horrible night I thought I would die so you could live.

Charlie had been Libby's age that night, sweet sixteen.

Now she hauled the luggage up the steps to the second floor, which had been her father's study and her parents' bedroom when she'd lived here. Currently, it was Edwina's study and the guest room. The south facing windows of the study faced the north facing windows of the monstrosity next door. It was dark and depressing, but Charlie was too bleakfaced to care at this point.

Edwina, in her drug-drunk stupor, had gushed all over the place about Charlie actually being there. She'd cried. Charlie'd cried. Stone-hearted Libby had at least looked unsettled. Poor Mrs. Lawrence had cried when her busy husband peeked in. Charlie could see why—he was a knockout and here she was without boobs.

Charlie shook out and hung up clothes, too emotionally wrung to crawl into the double bed. God, even Libby's waterbed was queen-size. Charlie had secretly, if fleetingly, considered suicide sixteen years ago when she discovered she was pregnant. The feeling, if not the inclination, returned now. She trudged down the stairs to check out the rats in the basement and call the office on Wilshire, thinking things could get no worse.

She was wrong. She'd no sooner made it to the first floor than the doorbell rang. A middle-aged, overweight, sweet-looking woman in sweats and Reeboks stood on the step. Charlie resented sweetness in women. It made them prime victims in a world where that was their role anyway.

The woman looked unsure, almost terrified, and Charlie guessed her identity. This was all she needed. Another excuse for her to avoid Boulder, Colorado. "You must be Reynelda Goff."

Reynelda relaxed against the door jamb. Even her smile was sweet. "You sounded so angry on the phone, I didn't know if you'd even want to speak to me."

"I was angry at my mom for not telling me. I was just stunned." Charlie stepped back, inviting her in.

Reynelda Goff lived across the street, in the house where Professor Burrows used to live. She'd become Edwina's closest friend, and Edwina had leaned on Charlie to read this woman's novel. As in most college towns there was a novel being written in every other house. Libby was under strict orders not to mention Charlie's profession to anyone.

Charlie was a West Coast literary agent when family ties gave her a minute.

"Did Edwina delegate anybody to take care of the rats?" she asked Reynelda, and started toward the kitchen and the basement stairs.

"She got rid of them."

"She what?"

"Every last one. She had to. The new neighbors turned her in to the city."

Edwina Greene was a biology professor at the University of Colorado, several blocks to the east. Ever since Charlie could remember, there had been retired lab rats living in the basement. It was against city codes, but the neighbors never complained before. Eccentricities were not strange to Boulder, and in the university community they were cultivated.

Charlie made it as far as the step down to the sunroom, which Edwina had added after Howard's death and Charlie and Libby's escape from home. It ran the length of the living/dining room—hardly a long length in this house. The last time Charlie'd been here, this relatively new addition was filled with thriving plant life. Now one dead and two straggly survivors graced the otherwise empty plant mausoleum.

Reynelda sat beside her and matched Charlie sigh for sigh. "Have you read my book yet?"

"I can't believe Edwina took this lying down." Charlie pointed to the pinkish stucco filling the view. "I can't believe she didn't kill somebody over this." Five vertical, evenly spaced black spears with wicked points—she hadn't noticed until now—separated the two lots. They must be eight feet tall.

"Somebody *was* murdered over there," Reynelda said, her voice soft and sweet like the rest of her, "just last month. Good thing your mother wasn't home. Good thing she was with you in Utah then, huh?"

7

CHAPTER 2

————————◆————————

IT WASN'T PRECISELY a murder next door. Just that the man of the house had gone missing, and the police suspected foul play. Probably because there was a lot of blood left behind. And it tested out to be his.

Charlie sat on the step where the walkway to the house met the public sidewalk and tried to breathe. She'd sent Reynelda home, promising to discuss the novel later, and then had to get out of the little house herself. It was too depressing in there.

This was old Boulder, with tree roots humping up the sidewalks, tree seed and bird droppings, ants building funnel houses in the sidewalk cracks.

The hum of traffic held at a distance, the buzz of insects, and melody of birdsong. The crack of hammers, the spit of staple guns as people built houses in the cracks of Boulder.

Actually, Reynelda's novel wasn't that bad and certainly not as irritating and sacchariny as its author. Charlie sent it out to some of the few markets that survived the conglomerate warfare of the free-enterprise system. Unfortunately, it was historical but not a historical romance. (Reynelda said "an" historical.) Women wrote historical romances or they wrote Westerns under their initials or a male pseudonym. There was a lot of talk about history mysteries, but the few out there were pretty much formula stuff set in a different time period than hers.

There simply was no longer a crack in the marketing sidewalk for a story set in the last century west of the Mississippi that wasn't category fiction of some kind.

Actually, Charlie would have liked to get out of the book business altogether and concentrate on her screenwriters, but as mega-corporations gobbled up everything in sight, publishing and film media were fast becoming a confusing tangle, impossible to separate. And the unknowns of the coming electronic media loomed menacingly over it all.

Passages of Reynelda's book began to come back to Charlie—further indication of her exhaustion. She read so many manuscripts and screenplays and proposals and treatments that she tried to delete them mentally to make room for new ones once she'd made a decision or sent them out.

A four-wheel-drive van with darkened windows moved at a crawl past her, toward the cemetery. She watched it sit at the corner for several minutes before it turned east on College.

This may be old Boulder, but in Reynelda's novel it wasn't even here yet. The cemetery at the end of the street, where Libby had been conceived, was pretty much out in the country then. These old trees humping the sidewalk under Charlie's feet hadn't been here either. Just grass and weeds and wildflowers. But somebody had been murdered in Reynelda's book too.

Charlie, you are dealing with everything but the one thing that's important here. Your mother has just had a mastectomy for breast cancer. You were with her a month ago, and she didn't even tell you about the lump.

I knew something was wrong. She kept sighing all the time.

Edwina had been an adviser on a documentary shooting in the Canyonlands of Utah, and Charlie, who was not Edwina's agent, got sucked into going out to the location to help her mother in a contractual wrangle. Edwina, of course, had been the expert on rodents of the high desert plateau. Murder had happened there too. Seemed like murder was following Charlie around, and not just in scripts.

But this time, you keep your nose out of murder and concentrate on what could come up a death in the family. The lymph node report isn't in yet.

❖

"Mom?" A block away from the hospital at the Hungry Toad Bistro and Bar—Libby Greene insisted upon calling it the Horny Toad—she bit into a Kermit Burger in a chewy bun, half of which came away stuck in her braces.

"I know it's been a long day honey, but it's straight home to bed from here, I promise." Charlie couldn't believe anybody could be this tired. She could remember eating here before, but then it had been a barbecue place. Obviously an old building, with bare brick inner walls and even a round plastered up hole where there had once been a stove pipe.

"I'm talking about Grandma. Something weird's going on."

"Your grandmother was born weird, Libby. I've tried to explain—"

"Mo-om, will you shut up and listen to me?"

"Might as well, everyone else is all ears. Can't you lower your voice?" The stock ceiling fans and dimmed track lighting that had taken over from the no-longer-trendy ferns. Stock antique advertising signs—*Borax Extract of Soap, Old Dutch Cleanser*—and pseudo Old West bar belied by rows of wine goblets hanging upside down above it, TV screens in the corners. Stock music—old enough to irritate Libby, loud enough to annoy Charlie.

"You didn't notice Grandma's ears?" Astonished incredulity this time.

"Grandma's ears?" The stock assortment of self-conscious yesterday's yuppies, showing their age among the ever young student population waiting on them and the thirty-somethings with children. A few ancient hippies salted the crowd. Speaking of salt, Charlie pushed away the rest of the sinfully delicious shepherd's pie that could have used a little more of it and took a sip of merlot, watched huge empty buses pass each other on Broadway through the front windows. Why those busses in a small city swimming in BMWs? "I—uh—no, I didn't. What's weird about Grandma's ears?"

"They're pierced. Grandma had her ears pierced."

That night Charlie lay next to her daughter in the upstairs guest room, neither of them wanting to use Edwina's bed nor willing to discuss why. If they even knew.

Libby's breathing came evenly with sleep. Charlie stared, exhausted and wide awake, at the tree branch and leaf shadows blowing on the ceiling. There were too many things she didn't have the strength to question. Or was it the courage?

They'd stayed at the hospital until late, until the nurse assured them that Edwina would sleep through, not know they were there, would need them aware and cheerful the next day. The results of the blood tests would come later, but the lymph node reports should be in tomorrow. The nurse would call if Edwina woke and asked for her family.

One of the questions Charlie had been unable to ask was why her mother's mastectomy had taken six and a half hours, why Edwina had tubes draining from her abdomen as well as her chest.

Charlie could have sworn she hadn't slept, but it was suddenly daylight and the house was empty. Libby's note explained she'd taken Howard's Jeep to go to her grandmother and let Charlie sleep because she knew how tired she must be. Besides, there was not one diet Coke to be had in the house.

At least the kid was thinking about someone else for a change. Cancer in the family sure made a difference in some people's behavior.

Charlie's head was thick with just enough sleep to prove she hadn't had nearly enough. Her mouth felt like she'd had a cou-

11

ple of bottles of the red zinfandel the night before instead of a glass. She staggered down to the shower only to remember there was no shower in the ground-floor bathroom, just the tub. So she staggered down to the one in the basement.

There was not really a bathroom in the basement—Simply a showerhead sticking out from the wall not far from an emergency toilet, sitting in the open near the washer and dryer. The hot water heater and furnace completed the decor now that all the rat cages were gone. But the mustiness of stale bedding and the sharp ammonialike odor of rat waste lingered.

Charlie could remember how the rats used to stop their cage antics to stare at her, how chilled she felt the minute she stepped out from under the hot water, how she worried her freshly shampooed hair would smell of rat when she went to school.

"Why do they do that?" she'd asked her mother more than once. The rodents always climbed the side of the cage as if trying to communicate with her, or burrowed deeper into the shredded paper as if to hide from her, or paced any side of the cage Charlie was on until she left the room.

"Just cage antics," Edwina told her. But she added once, "You do seem to get them stirred up though. You don't come down here and tease them when I'm gone, do you?"

The presence of a rat retirement home in her basement had been a constant source of embarrassment to Charlie, but she'd never tormented the animals. It wasn't the rats' fault they were there. So Charlie had picked on Edwina instead.

This wasn't the first time Charlie'd been caught at the head of the basement stairs in nothing but one of Edwina's skimpy bath towels. But it did rate right up there on the embarrassment scale. The stairs ended at an entryway landing and the back door. To the right was a small hall leading to the kitchen and made smaller by the presence of an upright freezer. Charlie was so startled she nearly lost what there was of the towel.

A tall, well built, and somehow familiar-looking guy stood between the screen door and the inner door, holding back one and in the process of pushing in the other.

Dark brown hair with glowing red highlights, cut short at the neck and ears but full and healthy on top. Even deeper brown, soulful irises floating in cream-colored whites. Thick, silky eyelashes.

Two police officers, one of each sex and both in summer uniforms, stood behind him ready to enter. The woman took a weary breath and rolled her eyes. Her cohort looked highly offended. Leave it to Charlie Greene to be able to offend even a cop. But the guy in front was the one having an incredible struggle with his cool.

Charlie wanted to duck behind the freezer, but all she managed was to say, "Kenny?"

"We—uh . . . rang the front doorbell but nobody answered." The guy had turned into a real hunk. He was even wearing a suit.

"Kenny Eisenburg?"

He finally blinked and handed her an envelope. "Search warrant."

Kenny Eisenburg had been best friends with Charlie's next-door nemesis. He may have developed miraculously, but he brought back nothing but memories she longed to ignore—another reason to stay away from Boulder.

When Charlie stepped out of the bedroom with real clothes on, Officer Darla was searching through Edwina's desk. "Just what is it you're looking for?"

Officer Darla was compact, with eyes too large for a blunt face. "Well, for starters, maybe you can tell me if you've already searched this house."

Charlie couldn't exactly put her finger on it, but something told her Officer Darla wasn't a Boulder girl. Something about her told Charlie she was born and bred in the real world. The stony expression suggested big city.

A syndicated columnist once referred to Boulderites as the "fuzzy folk." And years ago another columnist, working at a Denver paper, insisted upon referring to Boulder as "Brigadoon." Edwina had been outraged. Charlie thought "the fuzzy folk of Brigadoon" fairly apt. But nothing fuzzy about this woman.

"I *have* been wondering what happened to the rats. I've been at the hospital so much there hasn't been time to look in the freezer."

Officer Darla was not amused. "Why don't you ask your mother? And why is it she's in the hospital?"

"I wouldn't trust any of her answers. She's lit on morphine. And she just had a mastectomy for breast cancer."

The involuntary hesitation of a blink-in-progress gave the officer away. Charlie wondered if the mere mention of prostate cancer had the same effect on men.

"I need to know if you searched your mother's desk before I got here, Ms. Greene." She looked Charlie up and down as if just as unimpressed with her dressed. "Because it certainly looks like somebody did. And we found the lock on her back door broken just now."

CHAPTER 3

C HARLIE TRIED TO fluff-dry her hair in the breeze on Edwina's back step as she and Kenny Eisenburg checked out the door's very dead deadbolt.

"Why didn't he just break the window and reach in?" The wood around the deadbolt had been hacked away and then sawed. "This had to make at least as much noise as breaking glass and would have taken a lot longer."

"Sometimes burglars are even dumber than cops." He had a dimple that showed only when his expression was being wry. "And quite often they're high on drugs." He whispered without moving the dimple. "Where're the rats?"

"I haven't been here long enough to find out. But the lady across the street in the old Burrows house said Edwina had to get rid of them because the neighbors complained. Why the search warrant? What's going on, Kenny?"

"Neighbors again." And they both stared back at the woman on the redwood deck next door. The deck was huge, stretching almost to the alley. The wicked-looking spears extended to the alley too and along it across the back of the lot.

No sign left of the tire swing where Kenny Eisenburg and his chum, Lance, had tied up Charlie and left her until Edwina found her, gagged and struggling and furious, several hours later. No sign of the launch pad—a concrete floor for either a destroyed building or one never built—where Lance sent live

15

grasshoppers into space, tied to bottle rockets or torched ants with a magnifying glass that concentrated the sun's rays. Lance's father was an engineer at the National Bureau of Standards labs out on south Broadway and considered his son perfectly normal.

The woman next door now was somewhere around Charlie's age, thirty-two. The woman looked anxious, frightened, like she was the one being threatened with a search warrant. Then again there had been a murder over there.

"Could you tell if your mother's papers had been searched?"

"Her desk was a mess, but then it usually is. It's just that . . . well I've been gone a long time now, and I don't get back here often, but I don't think even Edwina, as strange as she's gotten, would dump her pencil trays in her file drawer." It had looked as if someone emptied all the drawers on the floor, sorted through their contents, and dumped everything back helter-skelter.

You never thought she'd pierce her ears either.

"So what's the search warrant all about, Kenny?"

"You know how there've always been stories about this place, the rats and all."

"Edwina's just eccentric. She's not dangerous, unless it's to my blood pressure. Hell, she's a college professor. And this is Boulder."

The boy who had become a cop shifted from one foot to another just as his eyes shifted from the woman on the deck next door back to Charlie. He must lift weights in his sleep. He'd sure come a long way from the scrawny kid who'd played the trumpet in the Boulder High band instead of first string on the football team.

"Don't tell me the new neighbor decided Edwina killed her husband and fed him to the rats? Or buried him in the basement?"

Actually that wasn't too far off the mark. When Edwina returned from Utah, the deed had been done, so she wasn't a suspect. At least not directly. But there had been bad blood between

Charlie's mother and her new neighbors. Edwina had refused to let the distressed widow search the house. The day before yesterday, she'd refused to let the police do it too, insisted they have a warrant.

"I mean, like—if she didn't have anything to hide, why would she do that, Charlie?" Detective Kenny looked down at her with sincere questioning and then reddened. He was either remembering his nasty boyish pranks or Charlie's altogether inadequately covered in a towel at the top of the basement stairs. Or one fateful night sixteen years ago.

"If I knew I had breast cancer, I'd act strange too. My mother had the biopsy only last week."

That must have been one horrible week. What had she gone through? All alone. Too proud to call her only family.

Charlie was by now mentally staggering under the weight of guilt and the horrendous happenings and the unwanted memories of Boulder. She figured she'd about reached her limit and that's why she was feeling silly.

When Kenny Eisenburg suggested his little crew make another, more intensive search, Charlie tossed it off with a giggle and a flap of the hand. "Why not? Just tell me if you find the rats."

But the minute he was out of sight, she dropped to sit on the step rather than double over the pain stabbing her abdomen from the inside.

Where were the rats? The backyard didn't look freshly dug. Why would anybody search Edwina's house? Where was the body of the man next door? Why would Edwina have her ears pierced? Why had the city allowed the travesty on that lot? Why would Edwina's surgery take six and a half hours? How long before Charlie would simply come unglued?

Kenny and party left, finding nothing they admitted to. She'd called for a cab to take her to the hospital and was about to call the office in Beverly Hills when the phone rang under her hand.

"Charlie? Is that you? I can't believe it. This is Heather." After an expectant pause, Heather continued, "You know, from Boulder High?"

When Charlie was at Boulder High, everybody but Charlie was named Heather or Jennifer or Jason or Mike. But there *was* something familiar about the twinkly giggle. "Uh hi, how did you know I was here?"

"You won't believe this, but I'm sitting waiting for a table at Nancy's and the person I'm supposed to meet calls and cancels? And I remember my mom saying that your mom was admitted to the hospital? She'd taken a neighbor to the same surgeon's office or something? You know, when your mom was there? She said your mom was diagnosed with breast cancer. I figured you'd be home. And it's like karma or . . . Charlie, I know it's late, but have you had breakfast?"

Charlie didn't want breakfast, but she had an incipient ulcer that demanded regular feedings. "I've got a cab coming any minute to take me to the hospital."

"I'll have a table soon. Nancy's is right on the way if you come down Ninth. Do you remember it? It's west on Walnut between Canyon and Pearl . . . well, the cab driver'll know. Even just a cup of coffee? You need friends at a time like this. I'd love to see you, and I'll order so it will be ready when you get here. And then I'll take you to the hospital."

"Okay, but it'll have to be a fast breakfast—one egg poached, an order of toast, and milk."

Even with the irritating twinkle, Charlie couldn't remember which this particular Heather was until the cab dropped her off at the improbable white picket fence. It surrounded an elaborate, oversize fountain in front of a blue Victorian cottage with fish-scale shingles for siding. A blonde with long crinkly hair, waving and smiling from a table under a grape arbor, brought back a flood of memories, some worse than others.

Heather Tynne, oh shit.

Remember our agreement not to swear? You're not only a mother now but a role model.

Yeah, but Heather Tynne. Fudge.

"Charlie, it's so good to see you, I can't believe it. I'm so sorry about your mom." Heather and Charlie embraced and sat across from each other just in time for their breakfasts to arrive. "Potatoes come with your egg. They're sooo good here and you need the extra strength now. This is my treat."

Charlie noticed Heather's breakfast was a simple bagel with half the cream cheese scraped off. Maybe Charlie could talk her ulcer into skipping lunch.

Heather's hair had brunette roots, her eyes were huge and makeup enhanced, her smile broad and lips thin. Like her face came in different parts. She wore casual business attire—not casual enough for Boulder.

"So how's your daughter?" Heather was one of those people who could smile and talk at the same time. As Charlie remembered, that wasn't all she could smile through.

"Sixteen and a royal pain. What about you? Did you marry, have kids? What do you do for a living?"

"Divorced. My daughter just had her first birthday last week, and I'm in real estate. You know, Charlie, I could get your mom a fabulous deal on her house? The market is just booming, and that's a good neighborhood."

"Seems to be getting pricey around here. What could she replace it with? And why would she want to move?"

"She wouldn't want to stay here. She could get something much nicer in Denver for the money. Like a condo where she wouldn't have to worry about the yard and upkeep on an old house." Heather's smile was so broad it showed her entire upper gum, presently smeared with cream cheese. "Especially now

19

that she's . . . maybe she'll move out to California to be near you. I mean with the cancer and everything."

Charlie choked on her toast and took a deep swig of milk. "Seems like kind of a long commute, doesn't it? You realize she's still working."

"Working." The cheesy smile lingered only on the mouth part.

Charlie seemed to remember hearing that this old classmate flunked out of CU—which according to Edwina is damned difficult—and went off to Europe for a while to work for some hotel chain. Charlie remembered for sure that Heather had been a cheerleader at Boulder High, an aspiration of Charlie's squashed by the conception of Libby Greene.

And how about Heather's presence at that conception? one side of Charlie's brain asked the other. Or her conscience asked her psyche or whatever. It was all a mystery to Charlie.

It's not that you didn't remember her. It's that you blanked her out. That, I think, is a form of denial.

"Charlie?"

"I'm sorry, what did you say?"

"Just that I didn't realize Mrs. Greene still worked. I guess I thought she'd retired by now. She's widowed, right?"

"She's a tenured biology professor at the university. She can walk to campus from the house, so I can't imagine why she'd want to move. And a great many women survive breast cancer." Charlie pushed away her plate. Not even the potatoes seemed tempting. "And yes, my father died shortly before Libby was born. Heather, the lymph node reports are due in today. I have to get to the hospital."

"Oh, my God . . ." All the parts of Heather Tynne's face joined forces to express astonishment. "I just recognized the guy sitting over by the fountain? He's looking this way. Don't turn around. We still pride ourselves in Boulder for not embarrassing visiting celebrities. I just read an article in the *Boulder Camera* about it . . . how sophisticated we are, you know? I think he's

20

with Goldie Hawn, and there's another guy."

"Yeah well, I'm from Hollywood and we stare at anybody we feel like." Charlie turned and stared into the last pair of eyes she'd expected to see in Boulder, Colorado. "Double fudge."

"No, it's Mitch Hilsten. Oh my God. I don't believe it."

CHAPTER 4

C HARLIE LEFT HER breakfast mostly uneaten and left the patio at Nancy's with a sputtering Heather Tynne throwing cash on the table and racing after her. Of course, to leave Nancy's you had to leave by the front porch and down a sidewalk bordered with flowers and the cutesy picket fence and the goddamned patio again.

Jesus, the guy with Mitch Hilsten and Goldie Hawn was a dead ringer for Jack Nicholson. But before dropping Charlie off at the hospital, Heather recovered enough to point out, "Well, your mother might like to move in to a condo or something. You know interest rates are going up and she'll lose out if she doesn't hurry."

Charlie gave her a noncommittal grunt and wave and waited for the Realtor to drive out of sight before turning from the hospital and heading for the shopping center across Broadway. What she wanted was coffee. What she'd better get down fast was a thick shake. She made it to the Dairy Queen without dying, but it was a close call. The traffic in Boulder was beginning to resemble that in Southern California.

Sucking on the cool cloying sweetness coming with great resistance up the straw, Charlie walked around the block before chancing the hospital. With its parking lot, Boulder Community had gobbled up most of the block it had once shared with tennis courts and modest homes. It stood bloated beyond her memory's recognition. Howard's Jeep sat in the parking lot.

By the time she finished half the shake Charlie felt bloated too, and she crossed a concrete side yard filled with huffing machinery in boxy houses that kept the swollen main building alive, to toss the rest in a Dumpster. Huffing and puffing staff getting their nicotine fix pretended they didn't see her. Or maybe they pretended she didn't see them.

She found the halls of the cancer floor ominously abuzz and wasn't surprised to find that a celebrity was visiting Edwina Greene's sick bed.

The superstar, Mitch Hilsten.

Charlie very nearly turned around and walked out, very nearly left her mother and daughter to their own devices in a family emergency. Just when you think things can't get any worse.

Mitch Hilsten had been in Utah too, narrating the documentary. For some reason he'd taken to Edwina. And he'd caught Charlie at the wrong time of the month.

When she entered Edwina and Mrs. Lawrence's room, the superstar was autographing prescription pads for Christsakes. Libby stood in the background, her mood plainly ugly.

One of Charlie's worst fears was that her illegitimate daughter might face her off about a lover. Which Charlie hardly ever had, being too busy and engrossed in her work and burned too early in life to trust guys no matter how cute.

This guy was gorgeous. She had so hoped he and Libby would never meet.

"You look like shit," Mitch Hilsten confided in the parking lot as he posed like a male model in front of the mountain backdrop.

"Thanks. Thought you'd be on location for the flick of the decade. If you're checking out Colorado, *Phantom of the Alpine Tunnel* was set somewhere on the other side of the mountains."

"I know. We're shooting in Canada anyway."

Phantom of the Alpine Tunnel, after the usual Hollywood craziness, was actually going into production and was based on a best-selling novel by an author Charlie had handled when she was a struggling New York literary agent. Unfortunately, the author was now dead and neither she nor Charlie hit it big with that one. At least Charlie's agency got to help broker the deal among publisher, estate, and studio, and one of Congdon and Morse's star clients was lined up to play the female lead.

Mitch Hilsten thought he'd snagged one of the two male leads that opened up at the last minute, through subterfuge and sex while simply being the nice guy he really was, in the Canyonlands of Utah. He had the most beautiful back Charlie had ever seen.

"Maybe this"—the man with the beautiful back gestured toward the staring hospital windows—"is the answer to that personality change you noticed in Utah. Change in your mother, I mean."

Charlie'd assumed, as had most people there, that it was simply that mysterious thing called menopause.

So much for her psychiatric expertise.

A good breeze, searing and dry for so early in the summer, blew the pollution around and around the bowl-shaped Boulder valley. A kid of about forty-five came screaming down the concrete toward them on Rollerblades, trying to hang onto a kite the size of a 747.

"Hey, Charlemagne Catherine Greene, you're crying." Hair, skin, clothes—Mitch was the color of rich sand, except for dazzling teeth and pale blue eyes that held expressions you couldn't learn from simply living. Acting people learned mega suck-your-heart-out controlling expressions. "You know that?" He held out his arms.

Charlie leaned against his beat-up Bronco instead. "Do you always drive this stupid car? When are you going to get a decent car?"

"I know how you must feel. Christ, breast cancer has got to be every woman's nightmare. And it's your mother we're talking about here, but—"

"I used to think Libby was every woman's nightmare."

Don't talk to him. He's a guy.

"OhgodmitchwhydoIfeellikeit'smyfault? I mean breast cancer . . . Edwina." Even saying the words b—— c—— made her choke up, like saying "Mom" always had. Gays could talk AIDS easier. Maybe they had better control, or more practice. Charlie realized she was leaning against Mitch instead of his stupid car.

And I'm such a horrible selfish shit my own mother didn't think she could tell me she had b—— c——.

Charlie pulled away from the armed superstar. "Wait a minute, how did you know she had surgery? How come you're here?"

"She called me. I just bought a condo in Boulder anyway and it's a few weeks before I report to location so—Charlie?"

"She called you? Edwina called *you?*"

"Sharlee, I love you. I'm so glad you came—" Charlie's mother's pupils were the size of basketballs. "I never thought you would."

"I love you too, Edwina," Charlie said in a voice under such tight control nurse Wanda across the bed looked up from her chart.

And I have to hand it to you, lady, you can rub me the wrong way even when sick and helpless. How do you do it? "And why the hell did you call Mitch Hilsten, a virtual stranger, and tell him about this, but me, I have to find out from the neighbors?"

Nurse Wanda and Charlie's mother gave Charlie the longest, blankest looks on the planet. Mrs. Lawrence, in the next bed, even tugged her curtain aside to stare.

Charlie and Libby were munching pizza they'd found in Edwina's freezer that evening. They were sitting on the back step because the house was stuffy, staying silent because the weighty matters sizzling on the air currents between them were too powerful—when the new widow next door approached.

The lymph node reports had come back clear on both women, and the surgeon, Dr. Denton, gleefully assured Charlie her mother's beating the odds was a miracle. Edwina had found the lump herself but waited far too long before reporting it. A reluctance to seek medical help ran in the family.

"Does this mean she won't need chemo?"

A small wiry man, maybe in his early forties, Dr. Denton fairly bounced with cheer and enthusiasm. Or maybe he self-medicated. "We'll decide that when the blood tests come back in a couple of weeks. But I generally advise cytotoxic drug therapy regardless, just to be on the safe side."

Edwina, in turn, assured him she had no intention of losing all her hair and being sick, thank you anyway. And, demanding a mirror and tweezers, Charlie's mother proceeded to pluck out all of her eyebrows. Charlie tried to turn this into a lesson for Libby on the dangers of drug use but was stonewalled by the astonishment again.

Enormously effective, Libby's expression said, "What? This from a mother who had a public love affair on network television? Why is he here now if it's over like you said? Why is he here when you should be concentrating on Grandma? How will I ever face my friends again? What's wrong with you?" But since Libby never voiced any of this, Charlie couldn't defend herself.

And so they munched gluey cheese and leathery pepperoni in hostile silence as the neighbor widow crossed Edwina's lawn timidly, like she expected to be shot for trespassing.

They'd left Edwina and Mrs. Lawrence celebrating their wonderful luck and vast good fortune with milk of magnesia and prune juice cocktails and a couple of the second-shift nurses watching some television special Edwina would never have considered had she not been high.

Charlie had even learned why the surgery lasted so long and why the drains in Edwina's stomach. She just couldn't believe it.

Charlie's hearing was uncomfortably acute and, while her brain boomeranged between one disturbing thought and another that was worse, her ears registered crickets, a party growing noisy somewhere up the block, a siren screaming down Ninth Street, somebody's shoes crunching along the alley screened from view by a vine-covered fence and the garage, birds singing or squawking or otherwise complaining, and the rustle of the woman's skirt in the wind as she came to a stop before them.

Her name, if a looped Edwina could be believed, was Jennifer Toland.

"I understand you are the daughters of the woman who lives here," she said. But Charlie could almost hear her thinking, *The crazy woman who lives here, so I suppose you're crazy too. But I'm going to be brave and confront you anyway.* "I'm Jennifer Tollerude."

Well, Edwina was close.

Jennifer's hair, styled short and smart—bangs trimmed to mold a round face—fit her like a shiny black helmet. Shadows under her eyes, more etching deep dimples in her cheeks. Her skirt, sheer and loose, reached to her ankles. Her gauzy summer knit top—the kind that makes you wonder if there's a bra underneath—had sleeves pushed up to the elbows. Sparkley sandals showcased painted toenails.

"I'm Edwina's daughter, Charlie, and this is my daughter, Libby. I'm sorry about your husband."

"I understand you're visiting from California." There was an odd lilt of hope in the otherwise downcast cadence of her words. "Where do you live?"

Charlie didn't want to like the woman or feel sorry for her, but the trembling lips and the obvious fear made it hard to be cold. "Long Beach. But I work in Beverly Hills."

"Don't tell the natives where you're from. California is not popular here. Look what happened to Andy." Her voice choked up.

But Libby asked rudely, "What do you want?"

"Libby," Charlie scolded, and the kid grabbed the last slice of pizza and went into the house. "You think your husband died because he came from California?"

Jennifer took Libby's place, uninvited, everything but her hair drooping. "I was at my wits' end until Kenneth mentioned that you were from California too."

"Kenneth?"

"Detective Eisenburg. We moved here to raise our child in a safe place, in a community that offered beauty and strong moral standards. We watched our friends' children in Riverside going bad. Crime growing uncontrolled. We did our best to be good neighbors, to fit in quietly so our daughter could have a chance. Is that so wrong?"

Charlie glanced at the monstrous house filling the lot next door but kept quiet. She suspected that if she were into houses she'd probably build the biggest she could afford without worrying about its effect on the neighborhood too. This woman's pain and confusion were depressing. Charlie didn't especially need any more of that right now.

"We just wanted to be a part of the community, but the terror started the minute we moved in."

This community was full of retired university staff on limited incomes. Charlie could see how that house and a child could remind the neighbors of their age and relative poverty. There had always been wealth in Boulder, but Charlie didn't remember it being so "in your face."

"Don't you worry about your daughter in Long Beach?"

Charlie worried about her daughter anywhere, but Charlie had grown up in this "community." With rats in the basement, a crazy boy living on one side, and a bogeyman in the alley. Long Beach and Southern California did not seem that dangerous if you were too busy supporting yourself and your kid to watch the nightly news.

According to Edwina, the "damn hippie liberal left" had set the world so free in the sixties and seventies, the young were uncontrollable now and reaching the age of consent before the age of common sense. "And we're all paying the piper on that one."

"We just wanted to live someplace where people lead normal lives," Jennifer said. "And in an established part of town, not a raw subdivision. Some place with trees—"

"But you cut them down."

"We had to to build the house."

"But the house doesn't fit in with the neighborhood."

"It will, once new people move in and upgrade."

But then it won't be the neighborhood you wanted.

"We hadn't unloaded the furniture before a fourteen-year-old boy was shot at the school where Deborah will go when she's old enough. And there was a riot of drunken high-school-aged kids just over on the Hill."

"The Hill," a few blocks east, was your regular campus town near fraternity and student rentals where underage drinkers could blend in and get boozed up at parties.

"And then your mother has dirty rats in her basement—I'm sorry, but that woman is not sane. I don't know what I'm going to do now." She buried her face in a gauzy layer of skirt.

"Mommy?" came a small voice from an upstairs window. "Did you ask her about Missy?"

"Just a minute, honey, I will. We can't find our kitty. Poor kid—moving to a strange place, then Andy . . . and now Missy. That's what I came over to ask you about." She searched Charlie's face in the fading light, and Charlie searched back. She had the strangest sense the woman was lying. Was it just about the missing cat? "But you looked so normal and young and somehow with-it, I thought you'd understand—I don't know."

29

Charlie promised to keep an eye out for a small gray-and-white house cat and felt awful as Edwina's new neighbor stumbled off without the comfort she sought. But there was something about Jennifer Tollerude that didn't quite ring true.

CHAPTER 5

───────◆───────

SURPRISED TO FIND the TV blank, Charlie finally located Libby drooping against one of the post supports that held up the little roof overhanging the front door. Nothing so gracious and extravagant as a front porch for the Greenes. As a child, Charlie had envied friends who lived in houses with such luxuries as porches and patios and especially decks.

Now, a house was simply a place to crash after the exhaustion of work and to shelter her child and a pain in the ass to maintain.

It was twilight time, not yet dark, but the sun had gone behind the mountains a few blocks to the west. The streetlights had come on and the headlights of a car winding down Flagstaff Mountain blinked between the branches of the big trees across the street. Libby stretched and ambled down to the main sidewalk.

"Going somewhere?" Charlie said. Not to the Hill, I hope.

"Thought I'd just wander," the breathy voice dripped ennui. "It's depressing in there without Grandma."

It's depressing in here with Grandma, trust me. "I'd like to come along."

Libby shrugged a non-answer and kept going.

Realizing it was foolish, Charlie took off after her without locking up. Boulder wasn't that safe a "community." Then again,

31

the lock on the back door was already broken. Who knew when the repairman she'd called would show up?

"It's normal to feel depressed at a time like this, honey. But with the lymph nodes free of cancer, Grandma's chances of surviving are very good."

A desperate sigh of resignation. "Can't you ever stop playing mother?"

I'm not playing, damn it. "I've opened all the windows to let the wind blow through," Charlie tried another tack. "It should get to smelling better."

The unspoken question here was, of course, would cancer make Grandma give up her cigarettes? Charlie doubted it, but Edwina certainly had changed her ways recently. Pierced ears at fifty-seven? And she'd done an unsuccessful color job on her hair. The result, after six and a half hours of anesthesia at least, was a streaky brown the color of weak coffee with lots of gray bleeding through.

This was a woman so immersed in her work—not the teaching, because students were the enemy, but the research—she'd never paid attention to changing styles, makeup, or feminine wiles.

But the biggest shock was the reason the surgery took six and a half hours. Edwina was bandaged from her throat to her pubic hair. And now Charlie knew why.

My mother's crazy. Good thing I'm adopted and can't inherit that gene.

Edwina'd had her breast rebuilt at the time of the mastectomy and not with a silicone implant. (Charlie was amazed her mother had bothered with a rebuild to begin with.) The plastic surgeon, Dr. Ringer, who was even more cheerful than Dr. Denton, had swept in a short time after the latter and informed Charlie that he'd performed a stomach flap surgery on her mother. "It's the only way to go."

He'd taken the fatty roll from her stomach and a flap of skin with it to build a whole new boob.

What, she's got a boyfriend? At her age? What's going on here?

"Hey, she gets a tummy tuck plus a breast she won't reject because it's her tissue. Great set-up. And it won't grow cancer because it's just fat. Eight, twelve months, I'll even tattoo a nipple on it." Dr. Ringer watched Charlie expectantly, and his grin did a fade-out when she failed to ask the question he wanted to hear.

"Let me get this straight," Charlie said, instead of: You can tattoo a nipple on a breast? "My mother had two surgeons in there all that time?"

"And a surgical assistant."

"Will her insurance pay for all this?"

"She'll be out of pocket some, but she knew that."

Charlie's mother not only went through extra risk and pain to be beautiful but was willing to pay money for it? This was not the Edwina Greene who had tried to raise Charlie. There was something desperately wrong with the script here.

Libby stopped at a streetlight to examine a wanted poster taped to its pole. "They sure lose a lot of cats in this neighborhood. There's a different one on the stop sign."

LOST, SLEEK SIAMESE WHO DOES NOT ANSWER TO THE NAME OF PICKY. REWARD! CALL 444-6899.

"Yeah, Jennifer Tollerude's cat's missing too."

Libby started off across College Avenue toward the cemetery.

"Why don't we stay on the sidewalks. It'll be dark soon."

Libby stopped in the middle of the street, the growing wind picking up strips of silvery hair and blowing them over her shoulders. "You sure have a problem with this place."

"I just don't want to get on those uneven paths when it's dark," Charlie lied. "All we need is for one of us to sprain an ankle or something, have two invalids in the family."

Libby made way for a passing car and stared pointedly at the peaceful scene on the other side of the wrought-iron fence. A couple with a baby in an infant seat picnicked on a blanket

33

among the gravestones. A lithe young thing with a ponytail jogged along one of the paths, and an elderly man turned to stare at her buns, ignoring the dog practically pulling him over in an attempt to go the other way. And down at the other end of the graveyard, two deer grazed contentedly on cut flowers in a glass jar that sat on the platform base of a monument.

"I can remember when I was little and we visited Grandma, you wouldn't let me come here. Do you hear dead people talking or something?"

God, don't start *that*. "Of course not, honey, I simply meant—"

The supple jailbait put one hand on the metal rim topping the spear-point ends of the fence and vaulted over. These spears were black wrought iron like the spears next to Edwina's house, but only about half as high.

Charlie, being singularly unathletic, had to walk to the corner and through a gate to get to where she had no desire to be.

Columbia Cemetery was not only a historic landmark in what had become the middle of the city, but it was also an unofficial park for the surrounding neighborhood. As children, Charlie and her friends played under its shade trees. Lance Kelso had tried to drown her in the irrigation canal that ran through it.

But this was the first time Charlie had entered it since that fateful night when Libby—

"Mom, you okay?"

"Sure, I'm fine. Why?"

"You look like you just saw a ghost." Libby grinned a mouthful of braces at her own joke and then sobered. "It's okay, you can tell me if you hear dead people talking."

"I do not hear dead people talking. That's total nonsense."

"Sometimes I think I hear voices too. You know, ones I don't know where they come from?"

"Libby, will you listen to me? Dead people don't talk. They're dead."

"It's scary, but it's kind of interesting."

34

Great, finally Libby wanted to open up communications and it was on an absurd subject. Charlie's daughter and several other people who ought to know better had got it into their heads that Charlie had some kind of psychic powers. She decided the kid made such a big thing about this simply to irritate her mother.

And true to form, Libby was heading for the one place in this place Charlie didn't want her to be in, that Charlie really didn't want her to go near.

"What's that smokey smell?" she said partially to divert Libby and because the wind did seem to be thickening with it.

"It's smoke," Libby answered, withdrawing into her remote persona. "There's a brushfire somewhere over in the mountains. I saw it on the news in the hospital."

June was early for fires here, but Charlie had noted that the foothills that stopped the town to the west weren't as green as they should be in June. Must be a dry year. Living as she did among the Santa Anas and the colossal brushfires of Southern California, she hadn't paid a lot of attention to Colorado weather. "You watched the news?"

"It was just what was on. Grandma and Mrs. Lawrence were watching it between naps. You were busy playing hot snot, talking to doctors. What's the matter now?"

"Libby, do me a favor? Let's not walk this direction."

"Why not?" Libby stopped only to scan Charlie's expression.

"Because it bothers me, okay?"

The deer looked up from their colorful snack, Libby turned away skeptically, and somebody said, "Two females."

Once again Charlie lay awake beside her sleeping daughter in the too-small bed her parents had shared when she was a child. She listened to the drone of slurry bombers groaning overhead and the thrashing of tree limbs against the roof. The dry wind whirled through the room on its way between windows. White curtains billowed and snapped.

She'd felt this fear and smelled this smoke in Long Beach, but she'd never gone to bed this close to the combustibles, seen the sky redden at night this way.

Get real. Boulder's always been here. Boulder won't burn.

Los Angeles was a figment, fiction, fabrication, fantasy. Doomed on some distant day to fall into the sea. Charlie had read so many proposals and treatments purporting to be the definitive California drowning, she'd given orders to Larry, her assistant, she didn't want to see any more.

Until the last batch of earthquakes, that is.

But Boulder was still reality and permanence. Everything constant about Charlie's life originated here. The girl/woman beside her not the least of these.

In Columbia Cemetery, Libby insisted on walking straight to the very place she'd had her beginnings, the place Charlie had unknowingly sowed her biggest limitation. While the "father" was sowing his wild oats but risking no restrictions on *his* future.

Libby's father was cute and about as smart as a box of rocks. But, at a certain time of the month, the guy involved had less to do with Charlie's desires than the moon or her own hormones, and at that tender and invincible age, protection didn't even figure into the equation. Thus Sleeping Beauty here and the abrupt end to Charlie's girlhood.

There's a tombstone in Columbia Cemetery under which a legendary outlaw, Tom Horn, is buried. He was hanged in Wyoming for killing a fifteen-year-old boy in a dispute between the ranchers and the sheepmen. Tom Horn was a hired gun working for the ranchers. It was sort of like the war against the influx of new settlers in Boulder now, the newcomer fighting it out with the established. But *then* the established had the money.

Anyway, Charlie and Libby's sort-of father decided to "do it" after a few illicit beers on that grave, which was tantalizingly close to the street so they might be discovered by the police and really wig out their staid parents. (Parents were the enemy, but— like Edwina's students—you needed them to survive.)

Tom Horn figured prominently in Reynelda Goff's novel, a fact Charlie learned from her assistant or she wouldn't have bothered to read it at all, knowing the type of people her mother hung out with.

Libby had gone straight to the grave of her beginnings, and Charlie followed helplessly, half-expecting Tom Horn to raise from the shallow indentation extending out from a modest gravestone and pull a gun on her for being a harlot. But that wasn't the worst part.

Libby stood *there* and said, "Well, now we know what happened to one of the lost cats."

And again, Charlie had heard someone say, "Two females." Was Tom Horn speaking from the grave? *Did* Charlie hear dead people talk?

Libby turned away from the little body on Tom's grave, tears filling dark eyes she'd inherited from Charlie. They looked improbable with the shimmery hair. And you rarely saw those eyes tear. "He's the same color as Tuxedo."

He wasn't really. Tuxedo—Libby's cat and Charlie's burden—had a white chest and throat and white feet. This cat was just black and had been eviscerated, but that still wasn't the worst part.

Charlie had swallowed gorge and moved closer. The claw marks in the churned earth were much larger than those of a house cat. More like those of a large dog. They had unearthed something.

Even in the uncertain light, Charlie could identify the bones of a human hand partially clad in stiff, drying skin. And it wasn't a long-dead outlaw rising to the surface to pet a dead cat or shoot an unwed mother either. But it *was* the worst part.

Charlie led her daughter away from the scene of a second crime. Warning the couple with the baby, they rushed back to Edwina's to call the police. They were watching the progress of the mountain fires on Denver TV when Kenny and Officer Darla arrived.

Small fires had spread because of the drying winds and the availability of dried brush and dead falls. Some mountain homes had been evacuated, but Boulder was in no danger at this time. All residents were asked to turn on TV or local radio for instructions if the emergency warning sirens sounded, and to keep battery-operated radios at hand. If Edwina owned one, Charlie didn't know where it would be.

She wanted to leave the windows open to hear the sirens, and she wanted to close them to keep the smokey wind out. She fought sleep now for fear she and her child would burn to death in a wildfire swept unexpectedly into town. Old Boulder's bowl-shaped valley, stopped at this end by the mountains and open at the other, offered hurricane-force winds called chinooks a chance to scrape it out in a swirl of overturned trees, fast-food wrappers, dust, shingles, building materials, and sometimes whole roofs and camper shells.

These chinooks generally tidied up anything hanging loose in the dry winter months when the snow either came in dumps that melted off quickly or stayed up in the ski areas where it belonged. No chinook was predicted for tonight, but as Charlie remembered, they happened rarely when predicted and often when not. Edwina had been able to tell by the smell on the breeze while weather forecasters hadn't a clue.

Leave it to Charlie and Libby to find the body of Andy Tollerude.

After Mitch Hilsten and dead cats and the wildfires and everything else, that was simply too many hits. Any normal person would have folded before lunch the way it was.

Despite everything, Charlie lost her fight and slept.

CHAPTER 6

*T*HE NEXT MORNING Charlie and Libby tried to shower and shampoo at the same time under the drippy nozzle in the basement. The place smelled more of smoke than ousted rats.

They had overslept and were groggy and racing around closing up the house, hoping the repair guy would get there to fix the lock, when Kenny returned.

There was still smoke in the air, but the hot winds had died and the fires were contained. The evacuees were allowed back to their mountain homes to hose down roofs, gather pets and possessions left behind.

"Except for about three houses that went up like matchsticks," Kenny told them over fresh hot bagels at Moe's, another new place since Charlie'd left. Bagels in Boulder had always been tough as hockey pucks when she'd lived here. Moe's was across Broadway from the hospital as well. And a couple of doors down was Vic's, one of those trendy coffeehouses, where Kenny sprung for skinny lattes with nutmeg and a raspberry ice for Libby, who rolled her eyes in disgust but drank it.

They sat at tables outside, she and Libby gulping instead of tasting, while Kenny seemed a little too relaxed for someone who had been up half the night exhuming a body. He had the good grace to show a slight darkness under the eyes, but that was it. He chewed carefully, spoke about the fires in a sensible tone.

Charlie lived in and, truth be known, enjoyed the fast lane as long as it steered her toward work. Charlie was proud to be a Type A achiever. It was her stomach that just didn't get it.

"You didn't want to breakfast with us to talk about the fires," she reminded him.

"I thought you'd want to eat before talking about dead bodies."

"How many did you find?"

"I'm assuming there are three. But we'll take Tom Horn at his word that he's buried deep." The one-time nerd licked steamed-milk foam off his upper lip. "Andy, though, was buried shallow and the cat just left on the surface."

Libby eyed the thirteen or so guys of all ages eyeing her.

The sky was a little too deep a blue, the puffs of white cloud startling in contrast. A sail plane soared in a thermal. A gaudy Remax hot-air balloon bobbed in the heat. A slurry bomber, trailed by a TV news helicopter, disappeared over the dry brown mountain ridge behind the green, irrigated city.

"So why didn't anybody notice the stirred-up grave?" Charlie's stomach turned over, and she gave up on the bagel. "There's all kinds of foot traffic in that cemetery."

She didn't remember there being so many flowers in Boulder. The parks, window and sidewalk boxes, meridians, and baskets hanging from storefronts and private porches were thick with vibrant color.

"Probably because some animal hadn't dug up the bones until shortly before you got there," Kenny answered her without quite meeting her eyes. "It's been so dry, the city's restricting water use and the grass is brittle. Lots of graves are looking rough."

"Didn't look as if that animal had eaten any of the hand or bothered the dead cat." Charlie tried hard to purge that hand from her mind.

"Could have been an animal that prefers fresh meat. At least now we know why all the blood at the murder scene. Looked like his throat might have been cut."

40

"Might? What, you don't know?" Libby said in that way that made Charlie want to kick her in the shins. But the table had a glass top.

"Won't know for sure until we get the coroner's report. Mr. Tollerude was not in real good shape. But you're right, there's always been a lot of traffic around that grave." He glanced at Charlie and blushed again. The fact was not lost on Charlie's daughter, who stopped her bagel halfway to her mouth to study him. "I forgot to mention last night that you shouldn't leave town without telling me. You're not under suspicion, but we might have to check facts about your discovering Mr. Tollerude."

"Kenny, whatever happened to your friend, Lance Kelso?" Charlie changed the subject to warn him off. "Is his dad dead? When did they sell the house?"

"You guys used to know each other?" Libby straightened.

"Yeah, I used to live in your grandma's neighborhood. Uh, Lance has hit it big, Charlie."

"Lance Kelso? You've got to be kidding."

"No, he invented some widget for computers and he's worth millions. Bought his dad a fancy retirement condo on Kuaui. Lance still has a home in the mountains close by. I don't know how much he uses it. Modest little thirty-five-room log cabin hidden back in the trees." The cop's grin was rueful. "I'd always planned it would be me who'd make it big—damnedest thing."

"Yeah, life's not fair." Charlie watched the Remax balloon pass low over the neighborhood to the east of this little shopping complex. Lance Kelso a millionaire . . . why on earth did Charlie pride herself on being able to read people? "The cat kind of looked like it had been laid out like a sacrifice. Do Detectives in Boulder investigate pet murders too?"

"I'm also the resident expert in the department on cults and demonology and crazy stuff." He sounded rueful again. "Third animal mutilation case we've had this summer. All cats. Did you see any other animals while you were there, I mean live?"

"There was a dog on a leash," Charlie remembered.

"And a couple of deers," Libby added.

"Deer, honey, not deers."

"Mo-om. If it's two beers—"

"Sorry, should have known better."

Kenny's gaze shifted back and forth between them. "What sex were the deer? Deers?"

Libby leveled her deadpan and fired, "We didn't ask."

"Some time after Mr. Tollurude left the cemetery and after I talked to you at your mother's house, the officer we stationed at the scene discovered a couple of deer . . . dead . . . chewed up. A doe and her fawn. Usually there's two but sometimes one doesn't make it—the fawns. They looked more chewed than cut."

"Two females?" Charlie asked.

"Did you hear that too?" Libby pushed away a half-eaten bagel and stared hard at her mother.

THEY ARRIVED AT Edwina's bedside to find Heather Tynne conscientiously consoling the cancer patient and trying to get her to list her home.

"Heather, she's drugged. You can't expect—"

"She is the owner of that property, Charlie. And until she's dead, you are only the heir. She needs to make her own decisions for her own . . . Kenny? Kenny Eisenburg? Is that you? I can't believe it. Look at you." The homicide cop went technicolor again and obviously remembered Heather Tynne. He should.

"What?" Libby said to Charlie. "They both live in this little town and never see each other?"

"It's not that little, trust me," Charlie assured this kid, who had spent much of her life in D.C., Manhattan, and L.A. Spent it reasonably comfortably in these places the press reported as so scary. But last night was the first time Libby Abigail Greene had ever slept that close to a wildfire or seen part of a murder victim in a cemetery. And a grandmother high on prescription drugs.

Kenny wanted to speak with Edwina, and Charlie decided Heather couldn't make her mother sign away much of value in front of a cop, so she slipped down to the pay phones in the hospital lobby to call the office on the agency credit card.

"Well, boss, the first order of business is Richard wants to know when you can get back here," Larry Mann informed her, Richard being Richard Morse and everybody's boss at Congdon and Morse Representation, Inc.

"I don't have a clue. What's the big rush this time?"

"Obsidian is offering Monroe four mil to script *Zoo Keepers,* and he won't sign without you dealing."

"This is crazy. Keegan won't be out of prison for two years yet." And that would have to be with good behavior.

"Didn't stop him from doing *Alpine Tunnel,*" Larry pointed out the obvious. "And *Shadowscape*'s cleaning up at the box office. Every agent in town's going to be after him. You gotta keep him happy, Charlie."

"I know. Edwina's lymph node reports were negative, maybe I can get back soon." Kenny hadn't said she couldn't leave town, just to let him know.

Larry gave her phone and fax numbers at Obsidian so she could start negotiations from Boulder. "Richard's not in yet, but he left you a tersely worded message in his own inimitable style: 'Monroe's hot, babe, and so are you. Get your ass back here.' "

Four million. Oh boy. Charlie's commission on that, even after the agency's take, would go a long way toward lowering the national debt at the Greene household in Long Beach.

Charlie's stomach chewed on itself. "What's next on the agenda?"

"Two more things, Liebchen," Larry told her gently as if he could hear her trying to tear the wrapper off a new packet of

Maalox tablets with her teeth. "ICON's offering to option *Hostage* again—same deal as before, but they doubled the pot at the end."

"My answer's the same too, no if/comes." An if/come was a free option on a property, usually for the first six months, to give a producer time to package it—line up a star, director, maybe a writer—and go after the money. And *if* the project is a go and the money *comes,* the owner/author of the property and his agent get some of it. Sort of a no-risk deal for the buyer, but a real trap for an author and his agent who get nothing for a free option while it's shopped around town until it's virtually dead on the market.

The abyss between the incomes of a minute number of star book authors and screenwriters—even with the Writers Guild riding herd in Hollywood—was immense. Sort of like CEOs and grunts at major companies. Charlie didn't have any star authors, but at four million, Keegan Monroe was all alone on one side of that abyss and the majority of her screenwriters were lucky to make forty thousand more than once in five years. The smart ones had day jobs and working spouses.

"Jesus, that's Mel Gibson, Charlie."

"I know. But he can't star in even half the projects they've already got under development." She'd counter with a minimum of a thousand and settle for eight hundred, which was peanuts for ICON, Gibson's production company, but maybe they'd try a little harder if they had to pay. If Charlie did even one if/come, everybody'd be all over her to make it a practice. Her authors were hurting enough, damnit. "What's the other thing on the agenda?"

"Don't forget, you got a book author in town there."

"Yeah, I've talked to Reynelda Goff already."

"No, A.E. called from Omaha yesterday wanting another progress report on the status of his option check from Hunter Productions. He's flying in to Denver today, doing a mystery bookstore, Murder by the Book, and another one in Boulder tonight . . . uh let's see . . . " She could hear him shuffling papers. "Rue Morgue Mystery Bookstore. I told him you were already there."

"Is that guy still on tour? Doesn't he ever stop? And he's been around long enough to know the check will be in the mail for months." Congdon and Morse would hang onto it for another two—it was the law of the jungle. "And what's he doing flying? You can bet this is all on his own nickel. It was bad enough when he quit his day job and drove all over the Midwest to signings he'd set up himself. I didn't see it did him much good either."

"Relax, Charlie, you can only represent them, you can't mother them. He'd like you to come to his signing if you can manage it. He also said you were having fires out there. Is Boulder burning? Sounds more like here."

Charlie assured her assistant the fires had stayed in the mountains and were under control. By the time she got through to Obsidian, ICON, and Keegan Monroe in Folsom Prison, her ear and her feet hurt. And by the time she got back up to the cancer floor, Kenny and Heather were gone and Edwina and Alice Lawrence were walking down the hall.

Very slowly they were walking, and not enjoying it much. They were both wide-eyed and ashen, pushing the wheeled pole stands with the plastic bags still dangling tubes that were attached to their bodies with tape and needles. Edwina had the bulbs at the end of the drains from her stomach tucked into a pocket of a frilly blue robe. The robe was obviously brand new, but it didn't do much for her today.

Pleasant, cheerful staff went about their business as if unaware they were in the middle of a horror show. Libby stood at the far end of the hall, talking to a bald kid in a plaid robe. He had an earring in his ear, eyes bluer than Edwina's robe, and a big smile on a gaunt face like he was unaware too.

"Hi, are you Edwina's daughter?" a softly sympathetic voice said behind Charlie. She turned to find a slender woman in the doorway of Edwina's room, head cocked slightly, blinking rapidly, a hand gesturing toward the painful progress of the two patients and their gear.

Charlie nodded and found herself loaded down with flyers and pamphlets and stapled sheets of printed matter.

"I'm Twyla Clark, and I'm inviting you to the weekly counseling sessions we have for the families of cancer patients. We meet here at the hospital, and with group therapy we work through some problems, allay fears—so many comforting things can happen when we share problems of this magnitude."

"My daughter and I live in Long Beach," Charlie handed the paper load back to the woman, "so we can't very well commute for counseling."

"You're not going to go off and leave her like that?" The sympathy turned to confusion. "What family does she have here?"

"None. Don't you ever counsel the patients?"

"Well yes . . . that's another group. And I do one-on-one also. Edwina won't talk to me. It's so sad, I even live on the same block she does."

"She's not the counseling type." She'd rather drive her daughter nuts. "She'll be okay once she goes back to work."

"Frankly, I don't think either of you are aware of the seriousness of the situation. Nothing will ever be the same. I've had a mastectomy for breast cancer and I know." She straightened her little chest and two points showed where they were supposed to in someone half her age. Modern medicine again. "My husband left me, I lost all my hair, and was sick from the chemotherapy. I was in counseling for two years. Everything changed in my life, right down to my bras. Going to work won't solve any of that."

"She's a widow and all rebuilt."

"Already?"

"She's even going to get a nipple tattoo in a year. What did you do for work, I mean. Before . . ."

"I was a wife and mother and very involved in the community. And now I counsel for cancer," she said proudly and went to speak to Alice Lawrence's mother, who'd arrived late last night.

"Mom?" charming Libby had reached Charlie's end of the hall unnoticed. "That detective guy?"

"Eisenburg. Detective Eisenburg." Charlie was still watching Edwina. How can they turn people loose like that alone after six and a half hours of surgery?

"He wants us to go to Juanita's with him for dinner tonight. Grandma and Mrs. Lawrence say it's the best Mexican in town."

"Sounds good. Want to go?"

"Mom?" Libby stepped between Charlie and the agonizing view and asked the dreaded question that was the *really* major reason Charlie never wanted to bring her to beautiful Boulder. "Is he my dad?"

CHAPTER 7

JUANITA'S WAS unabashedly Mexican as opposed to South-western, from the menu to the exuberantly garish decor. It was also packed, with a line out the door, and impressively noisy. They were served in the lounge where the walls were blatantly red except for the one behind the bar, decorated with glass bricks instead of booze bottles. Kenny explained that this had once been a paint-and-glass store.

They munched warm fresh-baked tortilla chips dipped in zingy salsa and watched each other with suspicion. Libby didn't believe Charlie's insistence that this man was not her biological father. Charlie was scared to death he'd slip and give away the identity of who was. And Kenny was probably nervous about the tension at the table. Men often sensed these undercurrents between women but seemed rarely to understand them. Charlie wished she didn't have to.

"So, uh, you and Mitch Hilsten an item or what?"

"Barely friends at the moment."

Libby pretended to choke on a chip, Kenny couldn't meet Charlie's eyes, and Charlie changed the subject. "Can you tell us more about the ritualistic-like killing of that cat? I mean, it's like we've landed in the middle of more than just Andy's murder."

"Probably some fraternity guys having a hoot at my expense, but the *Camera*'s decided to run with it so I have to too. There're cats missing all over town—cats do that, but nothing like in your mom's neighborhood."

"Aren't there cults in Boulder?"

"Oh God, there's everything in Boulder, Charlie." Detective Kenny Eisenburg must be off-duty because he was drinking a margarita—the real way, with macho-coarse salt on the rim. His head nodded with the rhythm of the salsa music, reminding her of her boss, Richard Morse, who was always keeping time with his own internal rhythms. "It hasn't changed that much since you left, just gotten worse."

I've been gone so long, Kenny, and my knowledge of Boulder was so superficial. "If there are cults around, why jump to conclusions and blame the frats?"

"Okay, it's easier, I know. And this won't be popular with the *Boulder Daily Camera* or my boss, but cult people are most often gentle, weird, and mislead but not really cruel. They live in a fantasy world that's more comfortable for them than the harsh realities of this one. They may talk violence of some kind but don't really want actual involvement in it."

"What about the Branch Davidians? That was a cult. Stockpiling guns and explosives. Sure has the possibility of violence. And that cult burned, don't forget."

Libby rolled her eyes, moaned, and directed the waiter, delivering her combination platter, to the next table which was occupied by two kid-guys dressed in sloppy shorts and greasy hair. They would have been nerds in Edwina's day, dorks in Charlie's.

"She's recently developed a taste for dweebs? That's not it anymore. What are they called now?"

"I don't know. But, Jesus."

"Right."

"They've been giving her the eye since we walked in. I didn't think she noticed." Kenny wrinkled his forehead and it brought the shiny hair down to meet his brows.

"She notices, trust me. And I notice when she does."

The soft moist eyes across the table met hers, and he reached for her hand. "Hey, dweebs or whatever are the latest rage. She'll mature out of 'the latest rage.' We did, I notice. But to be honest with you, Charlie, I'd rather work mall patrol again than deal with raising a kid these days."

The waiter brought him the Snapper Veracruz and Charlie the Chicken Mole and a basket of corn tortillas.

She relaxed slightly. Any cop who'd worked the Boulder downtown mall had seen enough social experimentation to have a clue about what Charlie faced in her home on a daily basis. "She likes to be the center of attention."

"Don't we all? But you're right about the militant religions. The self-righteous tend to arm themselves against the big bad evil. But I don't see them picking on cats. They're more likely to go after liberals and 'foreigners.' Frat guys watch kinky cable channels and videos that give them crazy ideas. Bunch of them probably yucking it up at some frat house right now about the silly stories in the *Camera*."

"In the summer?"

"Okay, grad students then. I tell you, Charlie, this is being blown way out of proportion. Hell, we got an unsolved murder and suspicious fires still burning west of town, and I'm supposed to be looking for Satanists?"

"Couldn't the murder and cats be connected? It all seems to be happening in the same neighborhood. And you think grad students knocked off Andy Tollerude?"

They sat in a large old-wood booth, Charlie mixing beans and rice and mole sauce with shredded lettuce and fresh cilantro into a mess and scraping it up with tortillas. The burned chocolate flavor of the mole contrasted perfectly with the bite of the cilantro.

"I doubt very much they're connected. Charlie, relax, you'll have plenty of time to get to the bookstore."

"I am relaxed." Keegan Monroe won't sign without me. What if he goes with ICM? I have to get back to L.A. "I'm totally relaxed." I just live at a faster pace than you do.

Kenny pointed out the "classic symptoms." She wolfed her food. She talked so fast he could hardly understand her. "You'll get an ulcer one day."

Charlie put down her tortilla and made a concerted effort to wipe her hands and sit a while before taking a slow sip of her sangria.

"I'll bet you're a sinkie at home, huh? That's somebody who—"

"Who eats leaning over the sink, I know." And she did sometimes. Saved doing dishes. "What about the break-in at my mom's? Can you tell me anything about that?"

"Only that the lock on your back door's been fixed. Checked it myself before meeting you here."

"That's another thing in that neighborhood. Something's got to be connected somewhere."

"Coincidence is everywhere. Even in your old neighborhood." He gave her a hesitant smile and said quietly, "You ever think of moving home, Charlie?"

"Boulder hasn't been home to me in a long time, Kenny. My work is kind of specialized."

"Lots of screenwriters in Boulder. We even have a two-day conference on screenwriting going on up at Chautauqua this weekend. Happens every summer. You could work here, Charlie."

Lawrence, Kansas, probably does too, but it doesn't mean I can work there. Or Keegan Monroe either. "You kind of have to be where the action is, Kenny, and able to respond quickly—"

"Hey, your superhighway thing, World Wide Web, faxing, modems—anybody can work anywhere these days." His smile grew even lazier when he started the second margarita. "Aren't you going to ask me?"

"Not with Hollywood or New York until we can teletransport instantly. Ask you what?"

51

"Whether or not he's married," Libby said at Charlie's elbow and startled them both. "Mom, you work so much, your social skills are decomposing."

Libby was off to crawl the mall with Larry and Harry Dweebsville, so Charlie could have the Jeep. The three would take in a late movie on the Hill, then the boys would deliver Libby home. Charlie could visit Edwina after the bookstore "thing."

One introduced himself by "How's it goin'?" and a big grin. The other just grinned.

"I've spent more time with Grandma than you have, and I need a break," Libby said defensively as Charlie refused to hide her impression of these sudden new friends. "Could I borrow a twenty?"

Charlie fished out a twenty and a five. "You're not home when I start to sweat, I call 911 and make your life miserable for six months."

The dweebs hooted. Libby narrowed her eyes and set her jaw, and they all flounced out.

Kenny was furious. "Do you know what kids her age do at night on the mall? And the Hill's even worse. I may not be a parent, but I'm a cop and I could tell you things you—"

Probably much the same things we did. "Look, I don't know if you're married. But I know you don't have kids—"

"It's parents like you who cause so much grief for—"

"Kenny, she's sixteen. She had a summer job lined up and lost it to come here because of her grandmother's cancer. She had to make a difficult decision, and she wanted that job. She's aching to be free, which means having money of her own—it's like wings for a bird. And she had to give up the job. Kenny, don't you remember how it was? A little?"

"You didn't even want to know if I was married. That's usually the first question I get." But he'd softened some.

That's because you're gorgeous. And you know you're gorgeous. You graduated from Dweebsville and I'm happy for you, but I got a kid to raise, Kenny, and I've got a job I love. "My guess is you're divorced and no kids are involved?"

"Well, she had kids. They weren't mine. Did you ever marry after—"

"No. Look, I've got to get to the bookstore and then back to the hospital. Thanks for the dinner and—" He still had most of his second margarita and half his dinner to eat. Charlie made a point of leaving half her dinner on the plate, but she didn't figure a guy his size did. "Well, not right this minute."

"One more thing I need to ask you, Your Busyness, and I'll let you rush on your way." But he was laughing.

"I'm sorry, Kenny. My life is so frantic right now, and I have to get back to L.A., and I don't know what I'm going to do."

"You don't have to get back tonight."

"No." Charlie snagged a passing waiter and ordered coffee, sat back in the booth. "What's the one more thing?"

"Where's your mom's computer? I mean, I'm sure she has one at the university, but wouldn't she need one at home? Or even a typewriter or something?"

Juanita's was just off the open downtown mall to the west on Pearl Street and convenient to the Rue Morgue Mystery Bookstore only another block west.

Charlie was late even so and slipped in just in time to hear her author expounding on how he wrote his books in longhand on yellow legal pads and had his wife type them up for him at night when she got off work.

"That way," A.E. said, "I can write anywhere, anytime, and not have to worry about power failures and computers going down. And my writing is much better because of the time taken to mull and consider and weigh each word. Seems to me computers turn out more junk faster. I'm my own self-contained little unit."

"What if your wife dies?" asked a man leaning complacently

against a wall of books. He wore a Rue Morgue T-shirt and suc-
ceeded in combining a smirk and a grin with a mustache.

Any wall space not concealed by shelved books sported flam-
boyant posters of book jackets ablaze with scenes of mayhem,
daggers, guns, gravestones. Tombstones, shadows, bats, and lots
of cats.

Besides the guy leaning against the books and the woman behind the desk at the back of the store, those assembled to hear
her author numbered seven, five of whom were gray-haired
ladies and one of those was another of Charlie's authors,
Reynelda Goff. Small world. Small store. But packed with mysteries stacked on tables crowded between the walls of shelved
books and paperback dumps.

The mystery was blessed with its own best-seller lists, bookstores, newsletters, book clubs, critics, reviewers, fanzines, dis-
cussion groups on the Internet, and fan conventions all over the
country. Its own writers organizations, and its own editors within
major publishing houses in New York. Some agents even specialized in the genre. Major newspapers, including *The New
York Times,* gave it separate review space. And most of this due
to fans, secondhand bookstores, collectors, and librarians who
refused to allow the genre to languish when publishing grew
tired of it. Many of those fans were gray-haired women like
those listening politely to A.E. Mous expound in all innocence
on his dependence on his wife.

Charlie tried to wend her way unobtrusively through the tables and dumps to the empty chairs, praying A.E. would not announce that Bernice (Mrs. Mous) worked as a checkout clerk for
minimum wage and grueling hours at a chain grocery store.

But just as Reynelda Goff smiled entrapment and patted the
chair next to her—there was no dearth of empty ones—her author recognized her.

"Charlie? Is that you?" He clapped his hands like a gleeful
child, and all turned to stare at her. "This, I'd like you to know,

is my agent. I signed on with her in New York but she's in Hollywood now."

The man in the bookstore T-shirt turned his smirk/grin and attention to Charlie. She felt like she'd walked into a trap.

CHAPTER 8

S TRANGE THAT A.E. should have been talking about computers just after Charlie had discussed them with Kenny Eisenburg. Perhaps he was right about coincidence. She thought Edwina used a computer, although she couldn't remember seeing one around the house or Edwina talking about it. Then again, Charlie hadn't been home in years.

"Edwina visited us mostly," she'd explained to Kenny, embarrassed.

She was also embarrassed now as Reynelda Goff took a hold of her wrist and pulled her down in the chair next to her. "And she's my agent as well."

At that, Arthur Edward grimaced at his agent and widened his eyes in horror. Ruddy, short, balding, and cocky—except for the paunch held up by his belt buckle, he appeared as ageless and durable as always. He was Charlie's first author when she went to Wesson Bradley in New York. She was definitely not his first agent. She'd helped keep him barely afloat, which was about the shape he'd been in when she took him on. He would always hold a special place in her heart.

"Heart you can't afford in this business, Charlie," Richard Morse, her boss, would have said. "It'll get eaten alive, babe."

The woman who'd been sitting behind the desk joined them. Typically Boulder, she wore blue jeans and another store T-shirt and a smile as wry as Kenny's. "I've read Rey's book in manuscript and it's wonderful. I hope you can sell it to a publisher." Her voice was gentle, her handshake no-nonsense. "Hi, I'm Enid Schantz, and the guy with the attitude is Tom. We get the occasional editor, but rarely agents."

Arthur Edward's grimace turned condescending as he gazed upon sweet Reynelda and informed his tiny audience that his last book before this one was under option to Steve Hunter, the producer of *Dead Flies.* The two young gentlemen sat up straight and clicked their ballpoints to the ready.

A.E. Mous opened a copy of his new book and proceeded to read the least appropriate chapter for this group—a scene involving a sadistic phone caller.

Perils of Penelope was A.E.'s first departure from what he did best—which was your down-at-the-heels P.I. with a hitch in his self-esteem and a shrink trying to help him with his alcohol recovery program and assuring him that the bitch he'd divorced really was one and the shrink was usually a woman who fell in love with him anyway kind of book.

They were all seated in a cozy circle with Tom Schantz stationed behind A.E., Tom still staring with curiosity and perhaps recognition at Charlie, over the face of Edgar Allan Poe emblazoned on his T-shirt. Edgar appeared to smirk too. Why did she sense that neither he nor Tom felt Mary Higgins Clark to be in any great danger from this author? The two intense young men were furiously taking notes, though.

The ladies listened without expression, except for one—the oldest of the group by far, with a walker parked by her chair. She scrunched up her forehead under sparse white bangs and turned from the waist to squint at A.E.

"Why didn't she just hang up?" the lady snapped the minute he finished.

"Because she was all alone and afraid," A.E. explained painstakingly, sending a quick glance to Charlie that said, *See what I have to put up with?*

"Of what? He can't come through the phone line and get her.

Why didn't she just tell him to jerk off and hang up?"

"Mom!" The gray-haired lady next to her shrugged helplessly at the room in general. "I'm so sorry."

"Dumbest thing I ever heard." Mom rocked herself up out of the deep easy chair and balanced against the walker, motioning Tom Schantz away when he moved to help her. "I've been getting calls like that off and on long as I can remember, young man, and I've told them all where they could stick their dirty little minds. Lived alone for the last forty years, and not a one of them showed up at my door offering to do anything about it either. You can't tell me the foul-mouthed young women of today are going to get all whiny over a nasty phone call. Take me home, Margery."

More than aware of her own mother, and wondering what was happening to old ladies these days, Charlie tried for some form of damage control with, "Well, she couldn't know that he wasn't on a cellular right outside her door."

But poor Margery, who was probably more Edwina's age, followed her mother out, staggering under a load of books, *Perils of Penelope* most likely not among them.

"I have all your books, Mr. Mous, and I'm glad that Mr. Hunter is going to make a movie of *The Corpse That Got Iced.* But my favorite Scratch Diamond book is still *Dead Men Don't Need Jell-O.*" Another gray-haired lady with a sharp look in her eye pulled a *Perils of Penelope* off the stack of books waiting to be signed and handed it to him, slipping a paper towel under the heel of his hand so it wouldn't smudge, and further identifying herself as a savvy collector by, "Just your name and the date, please."

That was the only book he sold on the spot, but when A.E. sat signing books for the store's mailing list, Charlie asked Tom Schantz if he had any relatives in Long Beach. "My daughter's best friend is Lori Schantz. It's sort of an unusual name."

"I don't know of any, but I just remembered where I saw you before. In a *National Enquirer,* I think it was. Something to do with Mitch Hilsten, wasn't it?"

"You can't believe everything you read, especially in the *Enquirer.*" But Charlie knew her burning face gave her away.

"He's in town, you know. Was in here today, looking for a book on Satanism. I sent him to the Boulder Bookstore."

"Hey Charlie, what do you hear about those German rights?" her author asked importantly.

"I should know in a couple of days," Charlie answered, with no clue as to what he referred to. Fragile egos, these writers.

"We're taking A.E. out to dinner. Would you and Rey like to join us?" Enid Schantz asked.

"I've had dinner, but thank you. I have to visit my mom in the hospital. Do you want to come with me, Reynelda? I know she'd love to see you." And then back to Enid but quietly, "Does he need a place to sleep tonight, do you know?"

But it was sardonic Tom who answered behind Charlie, "We have a guest room for authors who get no backing from their publisher. He'll be fine."

"Can't you get him a better publisher?" Enid whispered.

"I'm trying." Charlie was always trying. The truth was few writers were showered with promotion money. A.E. was lucky to be publishing at all in the popular but crowded mystery market. And sweet Reynelda didn't have a chance in hell.

Reynelda didn't wish to visit her best friend in the hospital. "She's going to need a lot of moral support later and someone to talk out this terrible thing with. I'll be there for her then, I promise."

Charlie came away with the impression that either the woman would love to have dinner with bookstore owners and a published author or she couldn't face the hard stuff on the cancer floor at Community Hospital, best friends who conned daughters into representing first books notwithstanding.

Charlie was in the basement shower the next morning when the phone began an incessant ringing. She hoped Libby—who had tried to sneak into their bed very late, smelling beery but not of sex—would wake up enough to answer. It took Charlie another second to realize she was hearing the phone because it was ringing in the basement with her. She dashed out from under the water and grabbed the receiver hanging next to the stairs, wondering when Edwina had sprung for another phone.

"Yes, is this Mrs. Greene? I'm Lucinda Evers from the CBCP and I'd like to know if I could send you our newsletter and if I have your correct address?"

"This is her daughter. She's in the hospital and I don't think she's up to joining anything right now. Thank you anyway."

"Oh, but I understood she'd been discharged. Miss Greene the CBCP is the Coalition of Breast Cancer Patients and I—"

A chilled Charlie looked longingly at the hot water doing nothing for her over on the other wall. "Do you know where we could get some nursing help for her? I have to get back to work."

"No, that's not our purpose at all. We're here to help the patient in other ways and to raise funds to lobby Congress to do something about this terrible disease. And we have organized to convince women to stay away from hormone replacement therapy. You realize many more people die of breast cancer than AIDS."

Charlie hung up without committing her mother to anything and finished her shower. Edwina tended to disapprove of having the government throw money at anything except research related to her specialty at the university. It was beginning to seem like everybody wanted to help Edwina except right now when she truly needed it.

The next time the phone rang, Charlie was at least out of the basement and on the first floor. The air smelled faintly of smoke again.

"Listen, Charlie, you got to get back on the double," Richard Morse croaked in her ear.

"Relax, I talked to Keegan yesterday and Obsidian and ICON. I'm doing the best I can from here. The lymph node reports were clear, so I'm sure I'll be back soon." Not to mention Libby and I found a lost dead body in somebody else's grave.

"From there doesn't cut it, babe. What, she's in the hospital, right? She has doctors and nurses, right? What does she need with you? Can't you come back for a few days until she gets home?"

"It's going to be the weekend, Richard, what good will it do now?"

"Weekend, shmeekend—things are moving fast here. I spent the night in the office, to give you an idea. I'll pull some strings, get you on a flight back today. Leave the kid there."

"I'm not leaving Libby here and I'm coming back to Boulder to be here when Edwina comes home."

"Thought you didn't like her. You're always bitching about her. Oh, okay. But be packed and ready."

Richard did have a mysterious source of instant airline tickets even when all flights were apparently booked—it was either some form of clout or it was illegal. Charlie didn't really want to know.

Libby, never a very nice person first thing in the morning, met Charlie with the killer squint when she woke the kid.

"Shower and pack our stuff and stay by the phone. Richard's getting us tickets out of here and I'm running to the hospital to say good-bye to Grandma." Charlie threw on a loose, cool dress and slipped into sandals.

"We can't leave her now. What did we rush here for in the first place if we're going to jerk out on her?"

"There's an emergency at the office."

"There's an emergency here. I gave up my job for it, remember?"

Charlie tried to wrestle not-completely-dry hair back into one of Libby's barrettes. Why did her daughter have to decide she had a conscience only at the least convenient times?

So she can hassle you with it, that's why.

"Honey, Grandma has three shifts of nursing care. Around

the clock. She has doctors stopping by daily. When she gets home is when she's going to need us. Right now I'm needed in L.A." It's our living damnit, can't you see where we'd be without it?

Nurse Wanda beamed at Charlie when she rushed into Edwina's hospital room. "Here she is, and just on time. I was about to call you. Aren't you lucky, Mrs. Greene, to have such a caring daughter?"

Charlie leaned one shoulder against the corner wall of the bathroom, trying to catch her breath, the changes in the room more than she could deal with.

Mrs. Lawrence's bed was empty and stripped. Edwina was sitting in a wheelchair, sort of dressed but without her metal pole on wheels. She wore a drunken smile, and the one eye that didn't track right was really off course.

"But you can't—I mean after all those hours of surgery—it's got to be too soon."

Nurse Wanda handed her a vase of cut flowers that Mitch Hilsten had brought to Edwina. "The doctors released her not more than an hour ago. And she's been here four days. We usually get them out in three. Don't worry, I have written instructions for all her medications and how to empty the drains and treat the incisions. It's scary at first, but you'll make out just fine." She handed Charlie a sheaf of papers and prescription forms and put a plastic vomit bowl filled with bandages and Q-Tips and lotion and tissues in Edwina's lap, picked up the overnight bag, and bustled Charlie's mother out into the hall. "I'll help you get her down to the car."

CHAPTER 9

M OM," LIBBY WHISPERED, "look at this."
They were in Edwina's room, the Levolors pulled. Edwina was sleeping, and Charlie and Libby were trying to unpack her things quietly. Libby stood at the dresser and pulled out a black lace push-up bra with Victoria's Secret written all over it.

Charlie put her finger to her lips, then motioned Libby over to the closet door where Charlie had thought to slide in the overnight bag. But there was no room. Bright-colored blouses, slacks, even gaily flowered dresses, packed the hanging rail and the floor was solid with new shoes, sandals, pumps, Keds of all colors.

Libby pulled out a flowing black lace peignoir and put it back, tears welling in dark eyes to tip out on long gray lashes.

They tiptoed into the living/dining room and then into the tiny kitchen. For some unknown reason, a long-ago builder had put double French doors on that bedroom. Perhaps for a separate dining room or study but, whatever the intention, the result was lack of privacy for the occupant.

Charlie, whose room it was when she lived here, could remember pounding nails into the wood to hang beach towels over the revealing squares of window, until her mother relented and replaced the towels with curtains that had since been removed. There was no place to feel away from Edwina now.

"She thought she was going to die, huh? It changed her." Libby searched her pockets until she found a Kleenex.

Charlie searched the cupboards for food, knowing for once exactly what her daughter meant. Her mother had hated to shop, relying on mail-order catalogues to buy the same outfits year after year. She had spent her energies raising a daughter, pleasing a much older husband, and working in her lab. Life hadn't cut her much slack either. "I'm going to have to go to the store, honey."

Libby blanched. Interesting to watch fear, stronger than the revulsion and sadness she'd shown at the discovery of death in the graveyard last night, transform a perfect California tan.

Charlie drew her out to the back steps she'd had a hell of a time getting her mother up a short time ago. Edwina was so weak, she'd nearly toppled them both. That was when Charlie noticed the extravagant cemetery fence next door had been completed that morning, spears and cross bars filled in all around.

"Mom, I can't take care of Grandma by myself. Those tubes with the balls at the end and everything. What if she has to go to the bathroom? I don't know about these things yet."

Me too, baby, but you sure don't want to hear that now. "Okay, how about I give you some cash and you go over to the little mom-and-pop store on Ninth, kitty-corner from the cemetery at the stoplight?"

"I know where it is, but I don't know what to buy."

"I'll make a list. That or stay here, while I go." The air between them and the vine-covered fence that shrouded the alley had a density that could be smog, but it smelled a lot like pine smoke.

Charlie determined by phone that the only help available was something called Home Health Care, but not until an evaluation by a social worker, who didn't work on weekends.

Edwina's longtime neighbor on the side opposite the "California Monstrolith"—Emmy Wetzel, the bird lady—accompanied by Reynelda Goff, came laden with foodstuffs in large foil containers meant to be warmed up in the oven. They'd no sooner left than Libby returned with two bags of Greene family type survival fare—salt- and fat-laden, but convenient.

When Larry Mann called from the office on Wilshire, the depressing din of slurry bombers sounded overhead. He reported that Richard Morse had "found" tickets for her and Libby to get back to the real world if they could make it to DIA in two hours. Which they'd better because these tickets were paid for solid already. Charlie happened to be spooning crackers crunched in Campbell's Chicken Noodle Soup into her mother, who was looking less drunk and more hurting by the minute.

"The few neighbors and friends I've talked to are too close in age and experience to this problem to want to get near it. I'll do what I can from here, but I can't leave right now."

"Richard says you should put your mother in a nursing home for the weekend. Charlie, there are caring people in this world. Don't panic yet."

The most caring person Charlie knew was Stew, Larry's partner, whom Charlie adored but who now spent his life and assets Charlie wondered about, caring for sick gay friends, very sick guys.

"It takes time to get someone into a nursing home, and Edwina's health is good—she just needs some help until she can get her strength back. I'll call over to the university pretty soon and see what they suggest. Call Keegan and explain my problem. He's a lot more reasonable than Richard. I'll call him tomorrow." Keegan was allowed one phone call a day. "Then find an excuse to get out of there. Watch your tail, Kid." Larry was often the victim of Richard's rages. Especially when an absent Charlie was the cause.

"You watch your stomach, boss."

By the time Charlie had her mother fed, doped up, and sleeping again, Libby had reheated something from the neighborhood offerings and the little house reeked richly of garlic, onions, tomatoes, and spices.

"It's like lasagne without meat, and it's even good. And bread to heat with it."

They took the lasagna-whatever, garlic bread, and glasses of milk onto the back step, ate quietly, calmed down. Neither had eaten yet today, and it was somehow two in the afternoon.

"If it's, like, eggplant or zucchini or tofu, I don't want to know, okay?" Libby put down a plate wiped clean and stretched her long body.

Charlie felt better too. She'd always thought bringing food as a condolence offering to people too sick to eat was stupid. Maybe it was really meant for the healthy but exhausted people caring for them.

Libby took their dishes inside, and Charlie tried to stretch her optimism, such as it was, to handle the next crisis that must be hurtling her way.

She inspected the repairman's handiwork on the back door and had her hand on the handle preparing to go in and call the university when a sharp crack spun her around. If this were Long Beach or Sarajevo, she'd have thought it a gunshot. Black things glided in a silent rocking motion down to Edwina's back-yard.

"What was that?" Libby poked her head out the kitchen window. Where was the screen? Had there been one?

"I don't know. Run check Grandma. Stay with her for a little bit?" And Charlie picked up a gray feather tipped with black, like Libby's lashes when she mascaraed the ends. Another, so black it glinted blue-green in the sunlight, sailed past her nose.

"Now what?" Jennifer Tollerude demanded from her deck. "We came to get away from wildfires and shootings and . . . I suppose tomorrow there'll be an earthquake." She acted like this was all Charlie's fault.

"I think somebody might have shot a bird." And the minute she said it, Charlie had a fair idea who.

"Wonderful. Doesn't anybody observe ordinances in this place?" Jennifer had to unlock and walk through a gate to the alley and then through Edwina's gate to confront Charlie this time. She dislodged a pin feather stuck in her bangs when she swept them back. Consternation creases etched her forehead, and her eyes were teary. "Are we all going to be killed like Andy?"

Edwina's other next-door neighbor had only to walk around the side of the garage. Emmy Wetzel was short and stubby with a round head, round face, round eyeglasses. The same bottle-beige hair color but the hair was considerably thinner now. She still wore mid-calf-length denim skirts, button-down-the-front cotton blouses with short sleeves, canvas shoes with anklets. Still spoke with the slight German accent Charlie and her friends used to mimic behind her back.

"Mrs. Wetzel, did you shoot a bird for real this time?"

"Come, I show you." Emmy stopped in mid gesture to stare at Jennifer. "I hear they found her husband's body."

"Yes, and I think you'd better show her too. She's finding this a terrifying enough place the way it is." Earlier that day while delivering a dinner of pork and schnitzel, Emmy had shown Charlie a water gun the size of an M-1. It was a yellow and pink plastic thing you pumped to create pressure and was supposed to shoot a hard jet of water a hundred feet.

"Knock a grackle off a tree limb," Emmy had announced proudly. Grackles were apparently the bane of her existence. Emmy had fed wild birds long before it became the in thing. But, according to Emmy, these grackles were taking over the universe and robbing the good birds of natural and man-fed sustenance by the very nature of their numbers and their intelligence. Emmy swore there was no way to build a foil around a feeder that they couldn't outsmart.

The supremely unpretentious two-story frame house next door had housed a widowed Emmy and her son until he left home. She had been on the janitorial staff at the university before her retirement. Devoting some of her excessive energies to feathered guests and squirrels probably helped her survive her son's frequent return visits.

The backyard was much as Charlie remembered, maybe the trees were bigger and shaggier, the grass, garden, and fence a bit more cluttered and overgrown. There were three bird baths and a fountain with a stone bird, wings raised for takeoff, throwing up a stream of water into a large bowl in which a fat robin showered with little concern at their approach. Charlie knew it was a robin because it had a red-orange breast.

She had a neighbor in Long Beach, Betty Beesom, who would have been bowled over by the array of feeders hanging from tree limbs, perched on fenceposts, and topping metal poles. Charlie could remember being awakened in her downstairs bedroom on a summer day when she could have slept in by Emmy's damn birds.

Very quiet here now, though. After the murder. That grackle must have had a lot of feathers. Spots of blood and even more blue-black feathers had landed here. Except for the brave and merry robin and the vomiting birdbath statue there was no sign of winged life. White slashes of recycled bird food decorating everything proved this was not normally the case.

"Grackles are black," Charlie said.

"Yeah," Emmy said.

Jennifer let out an exhausted sigh.

"A water gun did not do all this," Charlie said.

"No," Emmy answered. "This devil grackle, he take a worm right out of the mouth of a baby robin. I shoot him with the water gun and he jumps two feet and steals another worm from another baby robin."

"So you go get a real gun," Charlie said.

"Yeah." Her tone made it obvious that blowing away the

enemy bird had been a deeply satisfying experience. She pointed at the imaginary transgressor and cocked a finger, making an implosion sound with her mouth and tongue rather than an explosion one. But the meaning was all too clear.

"Every person in this town is demented and dangerous," Jennifer said, back in Edwina's yard. She looked to be past crying, into numb.

"You've been through a lot," Charlie said, finally finding the sympathy this woman needed so badly. "It's natural to overreact."

"Okay, everyone in this neighborhood then."

"You came here expecting *Father Knows Best* and *Leave It to Beaver*."

"Yes."

"That was my mom's generation, and she says it never existed in the fifties either. You know what I'm going to do? I'm going back to California for a reality check the first chance I get."

"You know what I'm going to do?" Andy Tollerude's wife was a tad shorter than Charlie or they'd have been nose to nose. Jennifer may have been exhausted and in shock, but she'd been eating onions. Charlie could hear the perfect little teeth click sharply on the consonants. "That old woman probably shot my husband too, and I am going to call Kenneth."

CHAPTER 10

*C*HARLIE GREENE SAT back in Edwina's deep old bath-tub. It brimmed with exotic bath crystals that her not-at-all-exotic mother bought on one of her crazed shopping sprees. Charlie's doctor had told her to do this when life got out of control.

She sipped a glass of red wine so expensive she couldn't pronounce the name or even the vintner. Charlie's doctor had expressly told her not to do this.

The wine had been delivered with more flowers and a case of diet Coke. The flowers were for Edwina, the wine for Charlie, and the Coke for the youngest of the clan. All compliments of Mitch Hilsten.

If the phone rang, she wouldn't answer. If Edwina awoke and called for her, she'd yell at Libby to answer the call. If the wild-fires reached this roof, she'd finish off the wine and sink below the bubbles. Why, in her sudden haste for luxury, hadn't Edwina bought some large bath towels?

Charlie stretched one leg, then ankle, then toes. What was it about Jennifer Tollerude that bothered her so? Other than the fact the widow had called out the cops on poor old Emmy? Was Jennifer really in mourning, or was she just terrified?

Actually, hiding a body in a graveyard wasn't a bad idea. They should have just buried Andy deeper. Did Jennifer really think Emmy could have murdered him with her gun? Hadn't Kenny told her Andy had been killed with a knife?

Inexplicably, Charlie felt herself relaxing. She stretched the other leg and its appendages. She always cracked up at wine snobs describing how wine tasted, but this was good stuff. "Light but still rich, not bitter but smooth, not peppery but a little spicy. Just right."

She raised her glass to the soap dish and stretched out her lower spine. "But it won't get Mitch Hilsten anywhere, so there."

"Mom, who are you talking to?" Libby's voice came worried from the other side of the locked door.

"Myself. Go away."

"Grandma's still sleeping."

"Good."

"Are you okay?"

"I always drink wine and talk to myself in the bathtub when you're not home. Don't worry about it."

"You only take showers, and you're never home when I'm not. You're always at work."

Charlie stretched her upper back one vertebrae at a time—in her imagination at least—and then circled her shoulders like a stripper teasing a crowd of barflies.

Despite what Detective Kenny said, there really could be a connection between the dead Andy Tollerude, the missing cats, the desecrations at Columbia Cemetery, and the break-in at this house. Were the Greenes in any danger?

How would you know until you knew the reason Andy was murdered? By then you'd probably know who the murderer was.

Charlie pointed the back of her head at the ceiling to stretch her neck vertebrae and then rotated her head slowly. No hurry. No panic.

"Mom?" Panic from the other side of the door. "If I have a can from that carton, will that mean I have to like him? Because I won't."

"No. It will just mean you want a Coke and it's there through

71

no fault of your own. And so is the ice in Grandma's freezer. Now go away."

Were Edwina's rats buried in Columbia Cemetery too? Their demise *was* directly related to the Tollerudes.

What about the ritual killing of house cats? And while we're at this, what about the voice in the cemetery?

Now don't start on that. It was just stupid exhaustion, nothing more.

Libby heard it too.

Oh, she did not. She just wanted to hear voices in a cemetery. Kids do that. It's perfectly normal.

Then why did she hear what I did?

She just thought she did when she realized you heard it. But I don't think it was frat guys or grad students behind a tree.

I don't either. Even for Boulder, this is strange. And it doesn't seem reasonable that most of the strange things happening in one neighborhood don't have some connection.

Had Edwina's desk been tossed? Why would anyone break into this house? What did demonology and chewed-up female deer have to do with anything?

And didn't Kenny say there were "suspicious" fires in the mountains?

Charlie was dried and almost dressed when Libby sounded again outside the door. "Mom? Grandma's awake."

The end of Charlie's time-out. She hadn't really come to any conclusions, but she felt better.

Libby's eyes were all pupil. "And there's this, like, humongous cat on the back step. Not the kitty kind. More like the zoo kind."

There was nothing feline on the step or in the backyard when Charlie got there.

"Mountain lion," Edwina said when Charlie went to the downstairs bedroom. "Libby just described a mountain lion."

Charlie stood in the doorway, trying to change scenes without out a script.

72

With astonishing suddenness, Edwina was back. Her speech was clear, her expression sharp. Charlie's mother took a deep drag on a long brown cigarette.

Edwina had always been difficult to deal with, but last month in Utah, she'd shocked Charlie with foul language and violent temper. *Now* Charlie knew that Edwina had known about the tumor even then. *Then* Charlie, who hadn't known, was being tested and had failed.

Charlie called 911 to report the mountain lion and helped her mother drain the bulbs at the end of the tubes embedded in her incisions. Here was another mystery. Why had Edwina undergone a painful and expensive rebuild? Bought sexy clothes? If, as Libby thought, her grandmother thought herself terminal?

But Charlie asked, "What happened to the rats?"

"Turned them loose. Then I went off to Utah. Thought the neighborhood deserved it, even if the poor rodents didn't."

"Not Emmy." Charlie couldn't believe the amount of fluid in the drains.

"Emmy's not scared of rats, Charlie. She used to clean dormitories. I need to get up and walk. Will you help me?"

"What do you think I'm here for?"

"Beats me." Edwina took one last drag, stubbed out her cigarette in the vomit dish from the hospital, and fixed Charlie pretty much with both eyes in a hard look. "I might have to write you back into my will."

"You wrote me out of your will?" Charlie helped her mother to stand, slipped the robe around her shoulders. If you were a rich person, that might be a real threat. You might be back, lady, but you need *me* now.

"No. But I thought about it. We've had mountain lions around a lot the last few years. Mostly because we now have a city deer herd. Descendants of the mountain ones, you remember. Wouldn't know a mountain if it goosed 'em. You can tell the city deer because they're fatter and sleeker. Stands to reason we'd get mountain lions too. I can take it from here."

Edwina closed the bathroom door in Charlie's face but looked peaked again when she dragged herself out, holding onto the door frame to keep upright. She made it to the back door long enough to peer out at the mountain lion that wasn't there. "You could've watered the grass. It's burning up." And then she noticed the funereal barrier. "What's she done now, built a spite fence?"

Charlie left Libby to make tea for her grandmother and went out to the garage for the sprinklers. The garage sat next to the alley but faced sideways. There used to be city codes about the placement of buildings and lot lines that were apparently no longer in force, if the huge house next door was any indication.

When the old garage, originally a carriage house for a previous home that once sat on this lot, was condemned as unsafe, Howard had this one built. Charlie must have been about twelve at the time.

It was a metal shed with a concrete apron in front. And for some reason, city codes demanded the size of the apron be such that Howard was forced to position his garage sideways to the alley. A double garage that had never held more than one car. The rest was storage.

The vine and fence stretching across the backyard hid the apron and the alley and ended at the garage. A gate opened into the alley and a side door into the garage.

With all this at the end of it, the yard was not deep, but it was still spacious compared to Charlie's in Long Beach, a postage-stamp lawn in front and a concrete-and-stone patio in back. Which was fine with her.

A narrow sidewalk led to the gate in the fence, with only a muddy spur turning off it to the garage door. An informal row of chipped sandstone hunks were meant to pave this path but were set too wide apart and covered by grass in places, mud in others.

Mud?

A hose strung from the house lay leaking ever so little but

probably ever so long next to the garage. As if Edwina had removed the sprinkler without completely turning off the faucet on the house. No puddles but definitely soft mud. And the footprint of a large shoe. In the center of the people print was a distinct paw print the size of a dog's, or maybe a mountain lion's. Both sets of prints were left by adults. More mud smeared the wooden gate leading to the alley.

Charlie didn't remember seeing either print when she'd brought Edwina home from the hospital. But she'd been concentrating on keeping her mother upright until she could get her horizontal.

There really could be a mountain lion lurking behind that bush or around Emmy's corner of the garage.

Edwina wants the lawn watered, she gets the lawn watered. Besides, it looks like the animal jumped over the gate.

But Charlie checked out the yard again when leaving the garage, sprinkler in hand. She looked over her shoulder as she knelt to attach it to the leaky hose, wondering where to place it to water as much grass as possible. Her tiny yard in Long Beach had decorative rocks, a palm tree, and a spiky shrub or two. The tree and shrubs needed some pruning and raking up under but she wasn't real sure how they survived.

"You shouldn't be watering," Kenny Eisenburg's voice brought her to her feet and around to face him.

He flashed a smile and held up a plastic bag with a gun inside.

CHAPTER 11

❖

*I*T'S A BLUE drop day. Means no watering. Whenever your grass needs water and turns yellow, it's a blue drop day and you aren't supposed to water."

"Blue drop?"

"Maybe it's yellow or brown. Or red—I don't know. What, you didn't check the *Camera*?" The tan forehead furrowed. How could it have evolved from the pasty, pimply Kenny of adolescence?

Charlie, who hadn't had time to handle anything but ever-emerging emergencies since she'd hit Boulder, hadn't even looked at the local paper. Kenny had promised to try to keep her name and Libby's out of the information on the discovery of Andrew Tollerude.

"Same thing in winter." His whole face got involved when he laughed, but he was still holding a gun in a Ziploc bag between them. "In the winter, if it's cold and a wood fire sounds cozy—it's a no burn, high pollution day. We got everything covered in Boulder."

"Even mountain lions?" Charlie pointed out the prints by the garage. "I called 911 about it."

"Yeah, Animal Control's pretty busy with critters coming in from the foothills to escape the fires." He knelt without his knees touching the ground to soil his suit pants, stood to look at the fence and the gate, and bent from the waist to inspect the indentations in the mud again. He straightened in a fluid, effortless motion—not a creaky joint on the fitness freak. "This could be the culprit that took out those two female deer in the cemetery."

"Why do you keep saying, 'Two female deer'? Why not just, 'Two deer'?"

"Probably because it makes you turn such an interesting color."

"That's Emmy's gun, isn't it? You can't believe she used it to shoot anything more vulnerable than a grackle. You know Emmy from the cookie days. Besides, you said Andy was stabbed."

"This is Emmy's gun, and it was strudel." Emmy Wetzel used to work all day and bake all night, and the guys, who could afford the calories, would gather in her kitchen to carboload. "All I can say about Tollerude's body is that things are looking stranger and stranger. Forget what I said yesterday."

"Are you going to stand here and tell me you won't let me water my mother's dying grass? She's been in the hospital and couldn't see to it."

"It'll live another day. I want to get a caste of that print—the one wearing a shoe. You might ruin it." He pulled out a little cellular and strolled along the wrought-iron barricade, talking official business, Charlie assumed, not really listening. She knew he regretted confiding in her already. She probably wasn't going to get much out of him directly.

He finally put the phone away and turned to study the fence, which was a good two feet taller than he was. "I sure hope she buys a dog instead of an alarm system. Those things are driving us nuts. You Californians put way too much faith in electronics. Most house alarms get set off by dear and raccoons and squirrels and eccentricities in the wiring. We don't have the manpower to answer those calls. So we don't."

"Great, that's all Edwina needs—a barking dog next door." Car and house alarms had become background noise in Long

Beach. You had to learn how to ignore them to survive. Charlie's condo came equipped with one. Maybe you could get used to a barking dog too.

"She drank about half a cup of tea and went back to bed. But she must be getting better, don't you think?" Libby was beginning to want out of here too. "I mean, she's making sense now—seems more like her." Seeing even so small a portion of Andy's body must have made more of an impression on the kid than she let on.

Charlie wanted to ask her mother about the computer and the kitchen window screen, but Edwina was asleep. Charlie wanted to discuss medical insurance with somebody at the university and see if they had any ideas on what she could do about nursing care for her mother, but the office had closed early this Friday afternoon and there would be no one to help her until Monday morning.

Batting a hundred so far, Charlie decided it couldn't hurt to have another talk with Edwina's best friend. She used the mountain lion as an excuse to visit the house across the street.

The roof was weathered shakes, the siding stained rustic, the trim a dull green. Small and dark, with little peaks in the roof line, and carved shutters, the house crouched on a small lot choked with huge trees. When Charlie was a very little girl, the Burrows' house reminded her of fairy tales starring witches who baked children for dessert.

Now, it reminded her of Professor Burrows at Howard's funeral, the look of disgust on his face that she should even attend, bloated and ugly with Libby's birth less than two weeks away. No one ever said, but Charlie knew Howard's friends thought it was her pregnancy that shocked her father's heart into having a fatal attack.

By the time she reached the little porch, she wished she hadn't come. But Reynelda, all smiles for her agent, opened the door before Charlie could poke the bell. The front of the house might be dismal and overgrown, but the inside was a pleasant surprise.

The woodwork was still heavy and dark, but now offset with pale and creamy yellow paint on the walls, many of which had been removed to open up the house to the new addition attached to the back, most of it window with skylights in the roof. Sunny yellow drapes and upholstery, heather green carpet, bordered by the dark wood floors. A few heavy antique pieces in wood and paned glass cabinets along the walls, the rest light and airy.

"I used to think of this house as ugly and sinister. You've made it charming and warm," she told her client.

Reynelda's plump cheeks flushed with pleasure at the compliment. "I wish you could see it when the air's not so smokey. And I'd just had the window washer here."

The windows looked gleaming to Charlie. She could see a pair of legs and an elbow sticking out from a lounge chair on the sandstone patio on the other side of the wall of glass. "What does your husband teach?"

"Ancient religions. Won't you come out and have a drink with us? I want him to meet you."

Charlie had a gin and tonic, Reynelda a martini, and George Goff scotch, all prepared by the hostess on a small serving cart. A deer raised its head from a rock-and-shrub berm at the back of the lot, radar antenna ears swiveling to check out sound signals from all directions. A post card scene.

"Edwina says Boulder has its own deer herd now."

"Several of them," Professor Goff said, fixing Charlie with an unnecessarily hostile gaze.

"My daughter thought she saw a mountain lion on the back porch." Charlie tried to think of what she could have done to offend this guy already. Was it the spaghetti-strap sundress? "And we found a print that could be one in the backyard."

"You've got deer, you've got mountain lions. You've got suckers, you've got con-artists."

"Excuse me?"

"George!" Reynelda Goff spilled gin on her shorts. Her legs were firm but even plumper than she was. "What's gotten into you?"

"So, you are Rey's fancy new agent, huh?" Professor George didn't bother to acknowledge his wife's distress. A tall, painfully thin man, in cotton summer slacks and Birkenstocks, with a short-sleeved knit shirt that accentuated every rib and shoulder bone. "I think you should know I've talked to the English department—"

"George, will you be reasonable? There are many things in this world on which you are not an expert. I'm sorry, Charlie."

"I've spoken with Horace Crumpet, visiting lecturer here." He ignored Reynelda again, his thin voice coming nasally but with authority, at least half of it through his nose. One protruding gold front tooth accented a mirthless smile. "Well, I'm sure you've heard of *him.*"

"No, I haven't." Charlie could imagine the unkind portrayals student mimics would make of his mannerisms.

"That does not surprise me overmuch, young lady. Because *the* Horace Crumpet has never heard of you either. Now what do you say to that?" He puffed triumphantly on a dead pipe.

"Professor Burrows could never keep his pipe lit either."

Professor Goff brought his feet off the lounge and to the sandstone to scratch a wooden match to rekindle his tobacco. Here was Charlie, hoping to con Reynelda into helping out with Edwina, and this guy was making noises like he thought Charlie was trying to con his wife for another reason. Every now and then, life's little absurdities caught her unprepared.

"George, Horace Crumpet is a pompous ass. And Charlie here is a guest in this house as well as my agent and my best friend's only daughter. Finding Andrew Tollerude's body must have been upsetting enough. You watch your tongue, mister."

"Hear me out, Rey. Horace Crumpet, *the* leading novelist of the last decade and probably the next—I'm assured of this by

Dr. Boyington, chairman of the English department—"

"Who does he publish with?" Charlie interrupted, getting defensive for her client now.

"That, young lady, is immaterial."

"No, professor, that is everything."

"Would you please allow me to make my point, finish a sentence in my own damn house?"

Reynelda slammed down her drink and got to her feet. Charlie half-expected her to roll up her sleeves. "It's my house as well, George. And I will not have this."

The deer on the berm stood up too, ears trained on the patio. Two sets of small ears rose with her, one on each side.

"Both men are much published, I assure you. But Crumpet has a *New York* agent." Old George sat back and remembered his pipe again. He grinned around it, then took a drag. The pipe had forgotten him again. "You, on the other hand, are not a New York agent, and Crumpet assures me no novelist will publish without one. That a so-called literary agent from anywhere else is out to make money on unsophisticated, wannabe writers like my poor wife. Now what do you say, Miss Agent?"

The shit hit the fan at the Goff household, and Charlie didn't have time to answer George's question let alone con Reynelda into a nursing job. She abandoned the gin and tonic and escaped around the side of the house as the good professor in sincere bewilderment asked his spouse, "Rey, darling, you finally have the house as you've always wanted it. I've sunk a fortune into it. What do you need with a phoney literary agent? My God, woman, you're fifty-six years old. I'm sure your little book is very nice, but—"

His wife's response was not clearly verbal, but the message got across to the deer, who decided to follow Charlie. Professor of ancient religions, huh? He probably knew a great deal about ritualistic murder. Perhaps the visit wasn't entirely useless after all. And how did Reynelda know it was Charlie who found the missing body? Interesting that her book made more than passing mention of Tom Horn and that grave too.

Charlie turned to make sure the deer didn't get hit by the dark van coming down the street, and wished she could warn them of the mountain lion. But all three ended up safely in Emmy's yard, and the streetlight came on to expose a beat-up Bronco at the curb.

Mitch.

Was there a pattern setting in here? Didn't even unwed mothers deserve a break now and then?

CHAPTER 12

———◆———

"C ONGRATULATIONS, CHARLIE," Mitch Hilsten said, turning from Edwina, who sat in one of the winged reading chairs on either side of the dinky fireplace. "I heard about Keegan Monroe. He must have a hell of an agent."

"That the guy in prison?" Edwina was trying to act normal for Mr. Wonderful, but Charlie could tell by her grip on the chair arm and the controlled tension around her mouth that her mother was hurting. "What's to congratulate?"

"Only for manslaughter," Charlie said from the kitchen, where she organized another set of pain blasters, antibiotics, iron, and mega-vitamins.

"Hey, he wrote the screenplay for *Phantom of the Alpine Tunnel,* which I'm about to star in. He can't be all bad." Mitch tried to put the best face on things.

"Four million dollars," Edwina said to Charlie when confronted with a handful of pills and a glass of water. "And you're here."

Lights came on next door, and the spikes and bars of the fence cast creepy shadows across the sunroom floor.

As in Reynelda Goff's house, the floors here were old dark wood. But covering the center of this one was a faded maroon-and-blue Persian rug. A dining room table covered with books and papers, built-in buffet and glass cupboards at the kitchen end of the room, a love seat and the two reading chairs at this end. Edwina, who was happiest on her research junkets across the high desert plateau of the sunny Southwest, must envy her best friend's sun-filled remodel.

"Charlie?"

"What? Well, I've had a fax of the contract—looks like a sweet deal to me. I don't think there's any question he'll sign. It's just a matter of what. We have to get the legal department's take." Congdon and Morse wasn't successful enough to have its own entertainment lawyers, but Charlie wasn't about to point that out in front of Mitch, who had never heard of the agency when she met him for the first time last month. That crack about her being a hell of an agent was well meant but condescending.

Congdon and Morse used the legal firm in the same bank building on Wilshire in Beverly Hills that housed its own offices. This firm specialized in the deadly snags of entertainment contracts.

"You didn't go over to the Goffs' to talk about Rey's book. You went to see if you could get her to babysit me while you flew back to California to clinch a big deal. You didn't know about this before you left to come help me, did you?"

"No. And I couldn't discuss the book—her husband accused me of being a charlatan because I was an agent offering to represent a book who didn't operate out of New York."

Which God knew had some validity. But agencies on both coasts were handling talent in almost all forms, from authors to circus performers. Charlie was about as confused as everybody else. There was no denying, however, that she'd rather be back there in the exciting thick of it than here in Boulder. "Did you tell Reynelda about Libby and me finding Andy Tollerude?"

"When she came over with the food. Just told Mitch about it too. Why, is it a secret?"

After Edwina gave in and returned to her bed, Charlie and Mitch sat out on the back step, drinking his wine, to avoid Libby's attitude. Enough pork chops and spaetzle and kraut and strudel to feed a tribe of mountain lions was warming in the oven, heating up the small kitchen and forcing them to open the window again. The whole neighborhood smelled like a German restaurant.

"I wonder if American mountain lions are attracted by the smell of German food," she said, making an uneasy association.

"Charlie, it must have been awful for you and Libby to find the body that way."

"Actually, we saw very little of Andy. We weren't the ones who had to uncover the rest. The dead cat was worse for me," Charlie lied. "And I don't even like cats."

"You know, I've got some time before we start shooting. I can stay with Edwina if you need to get back to what's breaking at your agency with Monroe. Weekends are terrible for scaring up social service stuff—you have to go through bureaucrats who don't work on weekends to get to anybody who does."

"I don't know why I keep forgetting to ask Edwina about that screen. The mountain lion could jump right in and eat our dinner and us too. Mitch, you have a life. You can't take on all my problems."

"Rumor is Monroe wants you back there. The bigger agencies are going to try to lure him away."

Charlie and her ulcer were only too aware of that. "Maybe by Monday, she'll be all right alone."

"A lot could happen before Monday, Charlemagne Catherine," he warned. Tonight he wore faded denim jeans and shirt—lightweight, expensive, brushed denim that highlighted his powder blue eyes under the light shining through the screen door behind him. "I've got a debt to pay, you know." He had a voice that could melt chocolate. "This might even the score. Don't throw the thought out before giving it one."

He didn't owe her anything. The infuriating national heart-throb listened politely but only heard what he wanted to.

And right now he didn't hear the rustling of the vines on the back fence, like she did.

Mitch Hilsten had had a string of successes and become so

much a part of the Hollywood icon thing that most people—including Charlie, who did not travel in such exalted circles—didn't realize his career had fallen on hard times, and could not have imagined him having trouble getting work. Mitch had three box-office bombs in a row. Most actors of his caliber had a few bad pictures in there somewhere. (Most actresses were allowed only a few good ones before age forced them out of the running.)

But most stars of his stature had their own production companies these days too, to ensure steady work. Apparently Mitch, divorced father of two almost-grown daughters and himself an active environmentalist, had either been unable to form one or chose not to. He was simply a different breed. Quiet and reclusive in his personal life, he tolerated no admiring hangers-on.

"I'm out of my league here, Mitch." *I don't want to owe you anything either.* "I can't let my mother down. I can't let Keegan down."

The commission alone on that deal—granted the studio sharks will figure out how to screw my client, my agency, and my daughter's college fund, and the government will get in there for half of what's left—it's wonderful for us all and a real boost to my career as well as Keegan's.

Charlie jumped when Libby's voice at the door behind her announced, "They've caught the mountain lion."

"You're watching the news again?"

"No, Detective Eisenburg came to the front door and told me," Libby said in her brat voice. "I told him you were out on the back step with Mitch Hilsten."

"Did he say what they did with it?"

"He *said* they tranquilized it and will turn it loose far away. But I don't believe it. I bet they killed it. He was so big and gorgeous—"

"Honey, in Boulder they probably do save them." Charlie remembered that a woman with a pellet gun killed a deer eating her bushes while only intending to frighten it off. A segment of the town had been outraged, and she'd paid a stiff fine. Before she could relate this to Libby, the screen door was empty and the volume on the TV in the living room went up. At least Charlie could relax about the rustling noises in the alley now. Probably just the deer.

There was a human footprint out here too. What, people can't be dangerous?

Mitch had been a sexual fantasy figure for Charlie since early adolescence, and she'd been stunned and disappointed when he pleaded with her to mention his name to Richard and the producers of *Phantom of the Alpine Tunnel* when Eric Ashton dropped out of the picture just as it was about to go into production. Mitch had top representation at ICM. He never needed Charlie Greene nor Congdon and Morse.

Since Libby refused to have anything to do with them, they filled their plates and went back outside, letting her fend for herself.

"You're not thinking of settling any of it for points?"

"Don't be insulting. Even people at my level know about creative bookkeeping."

"I honestly didn't mean to be insulting."

"It's just like book authors' royalties. Get it up front."

They argued over whether or not book royalties ended up in the accountancy soup, like studio profits.

He remained unconvinced. "You're so cynical you scare me."

It never ceased to amaze Charlie how little book and film people understood, or wanted to believe, the hard facts of the other's business, how closely related their worlds were. Perhaps because it all hinged on dreams. If you were unsuccessful in one there would always be the other to fall back on. The money and the grass would always be greener.

But they had no trouble agreeing on the quality of Emmy's dinner. The spaetzle was plump and rich with a creamy chicken sauce. The chops, thick and moist, had cooked in a brown juice with the taste of horseradish and ginger. They were accompanied by a hot cinnamon applesauce and a baked dish of sauerkraut and potatoes mixed with grated carrots and onions. Charlie had no room for the strudel, but it smelled every bit as good.

"Does Libby's father still live around here?" Mitch asked while eating his strudel.

"I don't know."

"Aren't you curious about what's happened to him?"

"Mitch, I explained. It was a one-night stupid adolescent stand. And it had very little to do with him, believe me. Why are you so fascinated with him?"

"I just can't believe you can have a man's child and have no feeling or curiosity about him."

"Well, believe it." I'll never make sense to you, Mitch. Give it a rest. "I hope that TV isn't keeping Edwina awake."

"All those pills you gave her, the house could probably burn down and not wake her."

"See? I can't leave this weekend. The mountain lion might be caught, but I haven't heard anything about the fires west of town abating, have you? The family home could be in danger. I may hate it, but it's all she has. And so am I. And the house was broken into while she was at the hospital, and there was a murder next door."

"I'm not exactly incapable of protecting her. Probably be better at it than you. You couldn't carry her out of a burning house or knock a burly murderer on his butt and keep him there until your detective arrived."

"Oh, right, I'm supposed to go off and leave you to help Edwina to the bathroom and to empty her drains for her?"

It was the drains that got him.

Mitch did manage to get some spaetzle and applesauce into Edwina though, insisting she must eat to heal. Charlie put away the copious leftovers and loaded the dishwasher, thinking her mother probably needed to sleep more than eat. Libby continued to pout in front of the TV, but she'd eaten well too.

"She's even going to watch some TV," Mitch said brightly. "And her incisions are itching like mad. That's a good sign she's healing."

Actually Edwina was allergic to tape. But you had to hand it to the superstar, he was trying.

Guys were weird.

The reason he owed her nothing is that Charlie's boss heard they were on location together in Utah and decided Mitch would be the perfect replacement for Eric Ashton and that Charlie should approach him for the now-vacant train engineer's role in *Phantom of the Alpine Tunnel.* The situation was supposedly so immediate, desperate measures were in order. With Richard Morse, everything was a crisis. But Charlie had refused.

"Tell you what, you could help me out with Edwina tomorrow and free me to run up some serious long-distance bills." And your enormous debt will be repaid in full, you can whisk your powder blues off to Canada and a starring role that will rejuvenate your career—if the movie's released—and leave me to deal with an already-too-crowded life.

Charlie knew for a fact she couldn't read other people's thoughts, but every now and then she suspected they could read hers. Like now, when the second most beautiful man in the entire world held her by the shoulders so she couldn't slip away from him. "That's it, isn't it?"

"What's what?"

"You like me but you don't need me, do you?"

"What, for the money?"

"No, for the excitement. You have plenty of it in your life now. I can't compete with the excitement of Hollywood."

"You *are* Hollywood."

"But I'm not your job."

CHAPTER 13

———————◆———————

*C*HARLIE NO MORE than got rid of Mitch Hilsten when the lights came on again next door. She was in the process of closing the screenless kitchen window. It was so dry, she'd seen one mosquito all evening, but the smoke was getting obnoxious. She moved to the other window over the sink, painted shut for as long as she could remember, to examine the light show.

When the lights had cast shadows on the sunroom earlier, she was pretty sure it was just the front lights. Now it appeared only the backyard was lit up. But lit it was. As in spotlights strong enough to illuminate a used-car lot.

Great, not only does Edwina get no sun during the day, she gets no dark at night. It was a blessing the bedrooms were on Emmy's side of the house.

It would have been worse but for the wispy veils of smoke snaking around the lights like shredded gauze.

"That lady has problems, doesn't she?" Libby said behind Charlie.

"I guess. But don't forget she lost her husband. Do you suppose those are the motion detector kind of lights? There are some deer in the neighborhood. Maybe they set them off."

Edwina had stayed vertical just long enough to please Mitch and hear reassurances on the news that, unless heavy winds came up, the fires would stay on the other side of the mountains and were slowly being contained. She had no battery-operated radio. Charlie'd pick one up tomorrow when out on agency business.

"Didn't there used to be a screen on the kitchen window? The one that opens?" she asked her mother.

"Should still be one. Charlie, if the fire comes down our side of the mountain, you get my granddaughter out of this house before you worry about me."

"Your granddaughter and I will get you out between us." She left Edwina—protesting that she'd slow them down too much— to take a phone call in the kitchen.

"It's somebody named Lita," Libby whispered, handing her the receiver but still staring out the window over the sink.

"This is Charlie Greene."

"Charlie, you won't remember me, but I'm Lita Kelso. I live behind your mother now. I have a hot dish I'd like to bring over, and I'm a little concerned about what's going on in our alley. I'll start out right away and come through your gate."

Lita Kelso was right, Charlie didn't remember her.

"Are you related to Lance Kelso?" she asked as the apparition swept around the freezer and into the room.

"Very. I'm his mother. But his father and I separated so many years ago, I remember seeing you only as a preschooler. I traveled so much then. Just moved in across the alley two years ago. Oh, and this must be Libby. What a beautiful young woman." Lita's movements were sudden and whirly. Her loose-fitting skirt and overblouse, cut into long separating panels, whirled with her and almost showed what was beneath. Her perfume, strange and heavy, complemented her makeup. Her permed hair was shaggy, long, and preposterously black.

"Are you in a play or something?" Libby asked, displaying incredulity for somebody other than Charlie this time.

"Oh, no, bless you, I've just come from the shop. I had this goulash made up for you. It looks odd but tastes wonderful." She was breathless, and even when she stood still all her bangles, dangles, and beads shuddered. "Emmy said your mother's lymph nodes were clear. Much relieved to hear it. Nasty business, breast cancer. She's tough. She'll be up and going in no time. But before that, I'm nervous about what might be going on in the alley. Bad enough there's fires just over the ridge."

As she put the bowl in the refrigerator, Charlie explained about the mountain lion being captured by the Animal Control officers. It seemed the more they ate, the more there was. "That's probably why you noticed extra activity in the alley."

"Then why is that man still out there?"

"There's a man out there? In the alley?" Charlie reached for the phone.

Lita Kelso swayed the top half of her body from side to side to study first Charlie and then her daughter. The woman's expression waffled between amazement and confusion. "Well, I'll be damned."

"Excuse me?" Charlie said just as the dispatcher plugged her into the police station.

"Think I'll go check on Grandma. Nice meeting you." Libby, the coward, abandoned ship.

Charlie, keeping a wary eye on Edwina's unusual neighbor, reported a prowler in the alley.

"Is it one of you or both?" Lita asked quietly.

She reminded Charlie of what a gypsy must look like. Or maybe just your average middle-aged flake.

"Mrs. Kelso, thank you for the wonderful dinner. The neighborhood has been so generous." Don't happen to know a nurse around here do you? "Why don't you sit down until the police come? Would you like some tea or wine or—"

"Thanks, but don't worry about me. Nobody can hurt me. I'm protected."

"You are?"

"It's you people I'm worried about." She moved close, too close. She had a weird chemical smell. "Do you practice then?"

Charlie backed into the corner of the stove and the window missing a screen. "Practice what?"

"I'll bet you have a house full of cats, don't you?" Lita Kelso winked. "They're the most telepathic of all animals and attracted to people like you."

"My daughter has a cat. It loathes me big time, and I loathe it even more."

"Well, there's your answer."

"To what question?"

Lita shook her finery impatiently. "It knows your feelings toward it and that's why it reacts to you as it does. I'll bet it's made some overtures and been rebuffed."

"I always wondered why he tears up my pantyhose while I'm still in them." Or makes a point to come in from outside to barf on the carpet. Tuxedo practically choked, trying to hold it back until he reached the stairs to the second floor so he could dribble some on each step on his way to her bed.

"You must be very careful. You could be what attracted that mountain lion," Lita warned in all seriousness. You could not insult this woman.

Couldn't possibly be all the deer frolicking in the neighborhood. But Charlie kept her smile frozen in place. Edwina had to live here when Charlie was gone. And there was no reasoning with people like this. They always had a glib comeback that proved they were right regardless of obvious fact. No matter how you wiggled, they'd pin you down with "logic."

"What kind of store do you work in?"

"The Shop of Mystery," the gypsy announced with a flourish, teal and deep blue colors swirling magically. "But I don't just work there, dear. I own it. I'm on the downtown mall."

Charlie relaxed. Books she could talk. "I was just at the Rue Morgue last night. I didn't know there were two mystery bookstores in Boulder."

Lita Kelso laughed and all the colors shifted into new patterns like a kaleidoscope. "The Schantze's are sweet, and their little store is amusing. But they sell murder mystery books. You know, Inspector Asshole solves a murder and big deal. Charlie,

I sell *mysteries*—books, tapes, music, gems, rocks, videos, crystals, T-shirts, advice."

"Coffee mugs and pyramids?" Charlie was very uncomfortable around people like this.

"Coffee mugs and pyramids. Everything, Charlie, to solve the *real mysteries.* The Rue Morgue merely does fiction."

On her way out, Lita stopped just past the freezer. "Again, I congratulate you on your lovely daughter. I always wondered . . . well I did have an aunt with that color hair . . . if Lance—well you *were* friends."

"No, Mrs. Kelso." He's not Libby's father, but he sure knows who is. "I hear he's done very well."

"Oh my yes. Pays the lease on my shop and bought me my house. He's very smart and very generous. Libby could have done worse." The spotlights next door had gone out again, and Lita barely disturbed the shadows when she opened and closed the gate to the alley.

Charlie couldn't remember even wondering about Lance Kelso's mother when he and his dad lived next door. But she must have—everybody had to have at least one.

She must also have blocked a great many memories of those years. There was no stopping their intrusion now that she was back in Boulder.

Wondering how Lance's extravagant log cabin might fare about now, and still at the back door listening for any trouble Lita Kelso might run into, Charlie saw the man in the alley herself.

He moved along the fence next door, on the alley side, setting off the lights again. A tall, swiftly moving figure cut up by wrought-iron spears, giving his brief appearance a strobe effect. Before he was far enough past the spotlights, they turned off again, leaving Charlie blinded.

But her hearing was still fully activated, and the stealthy sound of Edwina's gate brushing parched grass caused her to reach for the inner door and the new deadbolt.

94

Still, she hesitated—what if it was Lita rushing back in an attempt to escape the strobe figure?

She was too startled to do anything, when Kenny Eisenburg leapt onto the step from out of the dark and slipped inside with her.

"You're the man in the alley?"

"Is he still here?"

"Who?"

"Mitch Hilsten?"

"No. Kenny, what's going on? You nearly stopped my heart when you jumped on the step like that. I reported you to the cops."

"I am the cops."

"I know." She was getting a sore throat from the smoke in the air. "Could we just stop this and start over? Why are you here?"

Kenny was here to find the man in the alley that Charlie and several neighbors had reported, to make sure it was the same mountain lion captured as had been in this neighborhood, and to find out if Mitch Hilsten had scored.

"Want to go for a walk?" Detective Eisenburg said coyly.

"If the mountain lion could still be out there?"

"Well, it was captured in Martin Acres, and that's quite a ways from here. But it still could be the same one. Besides, I'm armed. You'll be safe with me."

"You want to go out and breathe all that smoke?"

"No worse than it is in here."

Charlie would have loved to get out of town, but actually getting out of this house didn't sound too bad right now either.

"Listen for Grandma for me, will you?" she said to Libby as they passed through the living room. "And keep the doors locked. I won't be long. We'll be right in the neighborhood."

"What was that look supposed to mean?" Kenny asked when they were out on the front walk.

"The stunned smirk with the eyebrows raised in question?"

"Well, that's one way of putting it. Please slap me up the side of the head might be another."

"It probably said something like, 'Aren't *we* the social animal tonight?' " Charlie started toward the Tollerude house, completely dark now, blocking out a monstrous section of the night. The streetlights didn't penetrate here because of their distance to either side and the thick foliage of the surviving trees in the strip of grass between the sidewalk and curb.

"I wonder what you have to do to set off the motion detectors," she said, stopping in front of the gate.

"Did you ever find out what happened to the rats in your mother's basement?"

"She let them loose before she went to Utah. I expect, with the changes in the neighborhood and the breast lump, Edwina was feeling pretty trapped herself about then. She just might have freed up something inside her with that little act of rebellion. I never can predict what she'll do."

The glow over Flagstaff Mountain showed dull red in the night sky. A lick of yellow flame to the north flashed sparks and was gone.

What would Charlie do with a post-operative mother who could barely walk, if they had to run?

CHAPTER 14

━━━━━━━━━━◆━━━━━━━━━━

T HEY'RE SETTING crossfires. A slew of fresh firefighters
flew in today and are already on the lines. Some homes up
there are in a lot of trouble. But you'll be okay down here,
Charlie."

"Unless the winds come up."

"Unless the winds come up."

Charlie turned back to the darkened Tollerude house, not
as reassured as she'd like. Either no one was home or Jennifer
had installed blackout shutters as part of her defense system.
A shadowy concrete owl lurked on one of the roof ridges.
Might as well have been a gargoyle. "How many stories is this
sucker?"

"Only two, but it's got ten-foot ceilings and a garden-level
basement. That's why the back deck sits so high. Do you live like
this in Long Beach, Charlie?"

"In a way," she admitted. Charlie lived with her neighbors
in what she thought of as a stucco compound with four two-story
condos, or small houses, standing alone but attached by a six-
foot stucco wall. Two sides of each condo formed the outer corners of the compound, with security grates on windows and
doors of those sides and security gates in the wall fronting to the
street and to the alley in back.

In the center was concrete and stone—covered parking and
a small patio for each condo. It had been the closest thing to a

gated community Charlie could afford at the time. "But you could almost fit all four condos in my complex in this house. And we don't have motion detectors. Yet."

"Don't bother. This kind of system only deters amateurs, strangers. A professional can get around it. Most violence is done by somebody you know, anyway. There you'd be, locked up inside with your attacker. Did you know the Japanese voted Boulder one of the safest cities in the world?"

"You sure are a Boulder booster. Chamber of Commerce pay you extra?" Why not worry about the amateurs? Probably a lot more of them. Was Andy Tollerude killed by someone he knew?

"I love this town, Charlie. I don't know how you could leave it."

"Well, you didn't get knocked up at sixteen, for starters."

"That kind of thing doesn't mean much to guys."

"Tell me about it."

Charlie stepped up the two cement steps, put her hands on the wrought-iron gate in the wrought-iron fence, and shut her eyes against the spotlights suddenly trained on her.

"What happens if a deer or somebody's dog or cat or kid wanders into this?"

Kenny pulled her away from the offending fence. "You want to be careful. That woman's so jumpy, she might start shooting next. I still think she should get a dog."

"Doesn't look like anybody's home."

"I wouldn't count on it."

They started back down the sidewalk the other way and when the spotlights behind them switched off the whole night suddenly got darker.

"Whatever became of Marlin?" she asked as they passed Emmy's. "Edwina hasn't mentioned him, and I didn't have the heart to ask Emmy."

"The last I heard, he'd joined the ranks of the aggressive homeless in Seattle."

Marlin Wetzel had been older than Charlie's generation.

He'd pretty much fried his brains on drugs during the seventies. Came back now and then to break Emmy's heart all over again.

"We thought of him too. Do every time something happens in this neighborhood. We're checking to make sure he's still hustling tourists in Seattle."

Charlie kept a wary eye on the red glow to the west, but she had to admit the smoke wasn't geting any worse. If anything, it was letting up a little. "I forget who even lived here," she said as they passed the house on the other side of Emmy's.

"Gordy Frazier. Played tuba in the Boulder High band. Father was with the university. Hogarths own Gordy's house—he's university too. Teaches, English department, I think. Oh, and across the street from your mother's house is Professor Goff, teaches ancient religions. *Camera*'s going to run an article on the weird happenings in Columbia Cemetery on Sunday. They usually interview me for that stuff, but this time they're talking to him. Hope he doesn't stir up anything. We got enough shit coming down the way it is. And I guess they even interviewed your boyfriend."

"I don't have a boyfriend." She stopped to look back up across the street, wondering if Reynelda and George had called a truce. Charlie was surprised Reynelda had stood up to her husband like that. He'd seemed so assured in his position. The house was dark in front, but the sunroom lightened the sides of trees in back.

"So what do you think?" Shadow hid Kenny's face, but his tone suggested intimacy.

"What?" She realized he'd been talking while she was thinking.

"I thought since you have some pretty special problems yourself, I mean. Oh forget it. Hell, you've never even been divorced."

"Kenny, I've never even been married." God, the last thing she needed tonight was to have to talk personal with a cop. "Still no idea who put Andy and the cat there?" They'd reached

99

the corner and stopped under the light across College Avenue from the cemetery.

"Maybe the *Camera* article will bring some results. We can always hope for a snitch or two." Kenny sounded petulant over her lack of interest in whatever he'd been talking about, but he was no more able to take his eyes off the phantom gravestones across the street than she.

And yes, he knew about Lance Kelso's mother. Naomi of the Seven Veils, he dubbed her. Lance's dad either sent her packing early or she packed her bags and left when Lance was small, to travel all over the world. Mr. Kelso was of a scientific bent and didn't want her infecting Lance.

"She was into everything ditzy, but I can remember particularly her studying yoga in India and talking to porpoises and some scandal at Naropa." There was a local sect of Tibetan Buddhists who'd founded an accredited liberal arts college, the Naropa Institute. You could earn degrees in such things as art therapy, dance, psychology, and poetry. But you did not want to hear Edwina's opinion of this school.

"She's probably into channeling by now," Charlie said, "Lita Kelso." It was amazing that Edwina and Lita were even on speaking terms.

"And old Lance had to go get her a lease for a wacko store on the mall." Again that rueful tone. "Hey, you're a big-deal Hollywood agent. Surprised you don't buy your mom fancier digs."

Charlie tried to explain the fallacy of the entertainment industry. The perception was everybody in it made big bucks because you heard only about the few who did. "And women don't earn like guys in any profession."

"All kinds of women out-earn men. I get so tired of hearing that crap."

"In the same positions and at the same levels?"

"Right. What about that Mary Higgins Clark? She's a best-seller."

"Name another."

"Anne Rice."

"Another."

"Well, I don't read romances, so—"

"Those aren't romances. And what you really mean is you don't read women authors. So, name some male best-sellers."

He reeled off a list ranging from Clive Cussler to Stephen King. "Okay, so guys write better. What, so there are no rich Hollywood female agents?"

"Damn few." But there was always the chance of a Keegan Monroe. Question was, was there a chance he'd stay with Charlie?

They started east on College, and she learned that the vintage houses, some tiny and built of stone, were rentals. The Detective Division—Boulder didn't have enough murder for a separate homicide department—had talked to every person in every house in the neighborhood when Andy Tollerude's blood was found all over his front yard. There had been no tissue samples or any sign of a weapon. "Got to know the old neighborhood again."

"So how did they fix up old Tom's grave? No, I don't want to go see," she pulled back as he was about to lead her across the street. Really less squeamish about revisiting the site of the hand and the cat than revisiting the site of Libby's genesis with someone who'd attended it. "Just tell me."

"The Department plans to spread a sheet of sod there, being so fond of outlaws. Want to donate to the cause?"

"I'm in for a ten."

"Don't strain."

"Don't worry. I don't suppose the wildfires could be connected to any of this?"

"I sincerely doubt it, though they're definitely manmade. We're looking into accidental or intentional right now. The brush is tinder dry. Little wind and you've got fire spreading, jumping roads. There's these homes tucked away in the trees.

101

They all got to have shake shingles. And the street bums like to camp up there in summer."

"Where do you live now, Kenny?"

"Out on North Broadway. Inherited my grandmother's house. Got it all remodeled. I'd like you to see it."

They turned up the alley, still walking slowly but not talking now. She figured Kenny was watching. Charlie knew she was listening.

It was very dark here. Charlie's night vision had never been good. Detective Eisenburg took her arm and she let him. A one-lane drive, unpaved and uneven, with dried-up grass and weeds, bordered mostly by fences or hedges varying in height with the lot lines. All interspersed with garages.

Charlie heard any number of unidentifiable sounds, like rustlings and things brushing other things and snappings and boards creaking and—

How about worms turning over and bats yawning? Get real, Greene. And watch out for Romeo.

There were shadows here that looked like puddles deep enough to sink into up to your knees. But the smoke on the air reminded Charlie of how dry a summer it had been, and she pretended to step boldly.

She could remember Lance Kelso upended in garbage cans, going through any junk put out, to find little motors and parts from electronic gadgets and appliances. Skinny Kenny tagging along. And this was the early elementary school years. It didn't seem that long before Lance was into rockets and pipe bombs. The kid was a menace. And now he was a millionaire. Go figure.

A yappy dog got excited on a screened porch on one side of them, bringing them up short long enough to see two green orbs squint and then widen around the side of a van parked in a backyard without a fence.

"House cat," Kenny whispered, but he'd tensed too. "You'd

think they'd keep their cats in, with all those missing."

Tuxedo took the house apart if you didn't let him out at his request. This one hissed and took off for a cat door in the nearest garage.

In Emmy's yard, the fawns lay like lawn ornaments on each side of a birdbath, light from a window tracing their backs, their heads raised and watchful. Their mom stopped licking the leftovers out of a bird feeder and turned toward the alley.

"Only in Boulder," Kenny said fondly.

"Oh, give me a break. I read somewhere there's getting to be more deer in this country almost than people. Now mountain lions, that's a different story."

"Yeah, but like this?"

It *was* a peaceful scene. The deer family statue-still, with no apparent urge to flee the whispering people peering over the fence at them.

A yard light lit the backyard of the house behind Edwina's, no fence or hedge here. Somehow, Charlie would have expected Lita Kelso to have had a prickly hedge with a squeaky gate. Instead, the light—no glaring spotlight, but a soft and welcoming one—showed a shabby yard, haphazard flower beds, two huge blue spruce that threatened to take over the whole yard, hiding portions of a covered porch extending the length of the house. A light in an upstairs window.

Howard's Jeep still sat on the garage apron. Charlie reminded herself to put it in before she went to bed.

They walked on, Charlie not quite ready to be stuck back in that house. She wanted to see the Tollerude house from this angle. But there wasn't much to see in the dark, and she'd be blinded with too much light if she frightened the motion detectors.

They continued on to Euclid and turned back. On one corner, a once-stately home had been turned into apartments, with incongruously modern decks and stairways to outside entrances built to all three floors and a garret. The backyard was a parking lot filled with cars. Across the alley, the house and lot were dark.

They'd taken several steps past the next lots when Charlie let out a strangled sound that would have been a scream if it had given her more notice.

Detective Eisenburg yanked her into the shadows and smashed her against his chest so fast she could only grunt. And that with just one arm. Moonlight made the shadows now, and it glowed on the white of one of his eyes and the gun his other hand held next to his head and pointed at the sky. "What Charlie?"

"Kenny, the Animal Control people? They didn't capture our mountain lion. It's still here."

CHAPTER 15

KENNY?"

"What?"

"You're crushing me."

"Oh." Kenny loosened his hold enough for Charlie to get a breath. She needed it so bad, it made her dizzy when she got it.

"Do you see him?" he whispered through his teeth.

"No."

"Then how do you know he's still here?"

"I just know."

"You just know." He let go of her, wiped his jacket sleeve across his forehead, stuck the gun somewhere under the jacket, and stood with his hands on his hips, sucking in air like he was trying to inflate. "But you didn't see it."

"Cops get scared too, huh?"

"Only the smart ones." You could hear his swallow all the way to Denver. He rolled his shoulders up and back and down repeatedly then rolled his neck to one side, let it fall forward, and rolled it over to the other side, like Charlie had in the bath tub this morning. "You going to tell me what spooked you like that if you didn't see anything? Or are you going to leave me hanging here on my adrenaline ladder?"

"I heard something."

"Where?" The gun was out and the jacket swinging loose.

Even his shirttail had come out of his pants. At least he didn't grab her this time.

"In my head."

He hung there in this seriously strange position for awhile. Finally he let the arm with the weapon fall to his side. "Don't tell me, okay? You heard the patter of lion paws on the alley grass between the tire tracks." He shook his head slowly and then began to nod. "You uh . . . you heard this mountain lion coming up behind us saying, 'Beautiful evening, ain't it?' "

"Oh Kenny, this is so embarrassing."

"Embarrassing? For you this is embarrassing? Hell, I pulled out everything but my dick." He stood looking stupidly at his gun and his shirttail and cracked Charlie up.

She collapsed to the grassy middle of the alley, laughing so hard people in the house on one side turned on their porch light. "See, I've had this incredibly stressful week. And today was worst of all and I'm just . . . I'm just probably hearing things, it's so bad."

His suit jacket came down on her bare shoulders, the warmth he'd fed the lining comforting as it touched her. "Charlie, before you get totally hysterical, tell me what you heard."

"Female."

"That's it? A word? Mountain lions speak English?"

"Maybe a thought?"

"They *think* in English?"

"Of course not. I must be losing it, Kenny. My kid and my mom and my job need me big time right now. I can't lose it yet. Help me?"

He helped her put Howard's Jeep in the garage. Okay, he put it in the garage, but she opened the door.

They closed the double-car door and stood in the dark. There was probably a light switch somewhere, but Charlie didn't remember where.

"I don't believe what age does to people, Charlie."

Me either. Your biceps must be bigger than my thighs.

"I always thought you were so different from other women. I thought you were the coolest."

"Even after that night in the cemetery? Kenny, you were there."

"Yeah, but everybody else freaked. And you kept your cool."

"I did?" Right and *his* sperm. "Is that how you remember it? I remember everybody laughing at me."

"Nobody laughed at you, Charlie. Not even Lance."

"How can two people be at the same place at the same time and remember two different events?"

Careful, you're coming up on that time of the month. You are not in real great control right now.

Kenny laughed and drew her out into Edwina's backyard. "Hey, if you get your period—doesn't bother me."

"I said that aloud?"

"Nah, I heard this voice in my head."

They were laughing again, on the back step, when Libby slugged them with the screen door.

Charlie put an arm around Kenny to keep him from pulling out the first thing that occurred to him.

"Is it Grandma? Libby? Talk to me."

"It said, 'Female.' I heard it. And Emmy . . . come in quick and close the door."

"The mountain lion attacked Emmy?"

"Mo-om, will you let me finish?"

"Sorry, honey." She had to grab her companion with both arms. "Kenny, relax."

"But Emmy—"

"All right, hesitate for a minute then." But she got him in the house and the door closed behind them. "Libby, what happened to Emmy?"

"Nothing happened to Emmy. She's in the living room watching the news with Grandma."

"Grandma's awake again?" Man, just when things start to lighten up.

Libby had gone outside to look for Charlie because she was worried about Edwina.

"You left Grandma alone?"

"I just went out on the front step. You said you'd stay in the neighborhood. But I didn't see you. Then these deers run out in the street, a mom and twin babies, and this van is coming and I go, 'Oh my God, they're going to get run over!' and this guy comes running out from the side of the house and the van stops to pick him up, and the deers make it across the street but Emmy comes running with her gun."

"We confiscated her gun," Kenny said. "She has another one?"

Charlie stood next to the upright freezer on the landing at the top of the basement stairs, Kenny right behind her, breathing on the top of her hair. Libby stood in the doorway of the kitchen, performing with the light behind her. Excitement had replaced the snotty ennui, and she really threw herself into it.

"So what's the matter with Grandma?"

"She has a gas bubble. At least that's what Emmy says."

"So Emmy's chasing this guy with a gun?" Kenny prompted.

"Yeah, she got him too. Right in the back as he was getting into the van. Boy, was he surprised. He dropped what he was carrying and they drove off."

"This guy drops what he was carrying but she shoots him in the back and doesn't drop *him?* I didn't hear any gunshots, did you, Charlie?"

"What did he drop?" Charlie asked.

"I don't know, but Emmy thought he was chasing the deers. But I don't think he even saw them. Anyway, she's bouncing around the yard because he got away and there's this seriously deep growl in the bushes by the step, and I yell at Emmy to get in the house and Grandma goes, 'What's going on out there?' and 'Libby, you get in here' and 'Where's your mother?' And Emmy runs into our house instead of hers, and I grab the gun and shoot the bushes. I don't know why I did that, it just happened—really fast."

"That's when you heard, 'Female'?"

"No, but I saw him, Mom, come out of the bushes." She made a fluid wavy motion with her hand, and Charlie saw a big cat slink into the night. "And then he turned around and looked at me like . . . like he wanted to tell me something."

"I could have sworn I read somewhere that the big cats won't look you in the eye," Kenny said, tickling Charlie's scalp.

"I hope by this time you were inside the house, looking out at him."

"I was still out on the step holding the stupid gun, looking at him looking at me. He was all wet. I got him right in the face, but he wasn't mad. He was the most beautiful thing. It was so cool."

"What kind of gun are we talking about here?" Kenny was beginning to tumble.

"But when I came in and was telling Grandma and Emmy about it, I heard 'Female,' and then I heard you laughing and I thought he meant you, Mom. Like he was going to kill and eat you, and I wigged."

"Keegan, what's the matter now? There's something, I can hear it in your voice." Please God, don't let it be you want out of your contract with the agency. "This is the deal of a lifetime. And it's your kind of story and . . . you've got all this time to do it in," Charlie finished lamely.

"That's just it, Charlie. I thought if I ever was going to have time to write my novel, it'd be now. One good thing that could come out of all this mess."

"Your novel." I should have known. Why didn't I see this coming? I can't believe I didn't see this coming. "Keegan, it's not going to take you nine months to write this screenplay—

probably more like six, the way you work."

"Right, and after I take notes from every asshole and his cousin at Obsidian, I'll have to change everything twelve times and then back again. Least they can't make me watch the dailies."

"Okay, nine months then. You're still going to be in that place a long time, and you're going to want something to do. Take the assholes' money, write *Zoo Keepers,* and when you do get out with your novel written too, you'll be sitting pretty. Keegan, time drags there a lot, doesn't it? If you fill it *all* up with work, it'll go faster. And having this major screenplay credit and having written two in prison will give you an edge on the talk-show circuit when you sell the novel. And may even help us to sell it to a publisher."

"Know what you sound like?" *He* sounded like a man drained and down, not like someone being offered a four-million-dollar contract.

"What?" There were times when Charlie didn't like herself much, and this was one of them.

"You sound like an agent." He started sobbing.

Charlie couldn't stand to see men cry. Or hear them either. And she could see Keegan Monroe now in her mind. In a crummy prison uniform instead of blue jeans and cowboy boots. His limp little mustache. He had been by far her most successful client, even before *Zoo Keepers.* She had no right to do this to him or to anybody.

"Keegan, I'm your friend too. You know that. Keegan, listen to me. You don't have to write anything you don't want to. The money you already have after *Shadowscapes* and *Phantom of the Alpine Tunnel* will be earning interest and see you through when you get out. Write your novel, and I'll see if I can find a really good New York agent to look at it."

The problem was that Keegan, who was dynamite with screenplays, never finished his novels. Literary aspirations, which have no place in Hollywood, smothered his prose, and he rewrote it to death as he went along. "Keegan, did you hear me? You don't have to—"

"No."

"No, what?"

"I don't want another agent. You're my agent."

"I didn't have much luck with your last proposal." You don't do *Zoo Keepers,* and I might not be anybody's agent for long.

"Okay."

"Okay what?"

"I'll do *Zoo Keepers.* But Charlie, I want you to look at the novel—each chapter as I finish it. I won't start the novel until after *Zoo Keepers* is done. Deal?"

I don't know where the hell he came from, but there *is* a God. "You sure?"

"Yeah. And Charlie? Thank you."

For what? Conning you into something you didn't want to do? Are we even on the same planet here? "You're welcome. I'll send Larry up with the contracts Monday, if they're ready. If not, I'll bring them myself later. And I'll come visit you next week anyway, promise."

Charlie had used one of the pay phones down at Edwina's bank and the agency card. Mostly to get away from Mitch Hilsten, who was babysitting Edwina, and from all the people prowling for the mountain lion.

She wanted to leap around the sedate lobby and yell triumphantly—and beat her head on a massive column in total shame, both at the same time.

Hollywood has finally, totally corrupted you.

Oh, get a life. He had to want me to talk him into it or he wouldn't have changed his mind so quickly. I just hope he doesn't change it again before we get that contract signed.

Instead of yelling or beating her head, Charlie called her boss at Congdon and Morse, and Marty Seidman at Obsidian.

CHAPTER 16

C HARLIE STEPPED OUT of the Norwest Bank building—which used to be called something else when she lived in Boulder—having done some banking for her mother and feeling a little less awful about what she'd done to Keegan. Prison *would* be a real drag without something to do. Wouldn't it?

The bank sat kitty-corner from the courthouse on Boulder's downtown mall. Malls of any kind are magnets to teenagers, but Charlie had fonder memories of this mall than the big enclosed shopping mall, Crossroads, a mile or so east of here, where she had walked herself to exhaustion after learning of her pregnancy.

A four-block area of Pearl Street, Boulder's old main street, had been blocked off with brick paving, kiosks, trees, flower gardens, street vendors, musicians, and panhandlers—like outdoor malls everywhere—but this was among the first, and a great success. It was a tourist attraction, a strolling place for the locals.

As Charlie walked it now, partly in nostalgia, partly to escape the guilt she thought she'd left behind at the bank, she noticed an interesting change in the shopping opportunities here. Esprit, Banana Republic, yes. But there were names she didn't see in every city she visited.

Then again, Charlie was no expert on shopping. She hated it. It cost money, it took up time she'd rather spend working, and it was something women were supposed to like to do. Like

112

washing clothes, nursing sick people, being noble, having babies—the list was endless.

Outside on the sunny side of the mall, she found a place offering breakfast until 11:30 A.M., and eggs poached in milk served over an English muffin, with asparagus. Charlie didn't register the asparagus part until it arrived.

In the meantime she enjoyed the passing parade of people and being free of her mother's house. The fires were all but out up in the hills, and Charlie still basked in the stroking Richard Morse laid on her just now. Here, a month ago, she'd vowed to find a job at another agency because of the way he'd wanted her to handle Mitch Hilsten. And now, with Keegan's success, was the time to make the move. But now she didn't want to.

Charlie tried to analyze her reluctance to leave Congdon and Morse and, oddly, could come up with only one reason. Richard Morse. Which made no sense because he was everything she resented in a man. He was no father figure and certainly not a romantic one. He was something of a mentor and definitely a challenge, but that surely couldn't be enough to keep her at the agency. Any kind of loyalty in Hollywood was suicide.

Maybe I'm just not very bright.

Her breakfast came and even the asparagus was good. Seasoned and slightly al dente, instead of slimy and squishy like Edwina used to make it. A street vendor, pulling a cart with racks displaying bright hats, winked at her from under a yellow saggy one as he pulled his merchandise to its licensed spot further up the mall. Lots of shorts, trim brown legs, and running shoes. Almost all the faces white, all the eyes concealed by sunglasses, and all the passing conversations in English.

Would Charlie and Libby be able to go home on Monday? Edwina survived her gas bubble, but the drains were full again this morning. Yes, Edwina had a computer. It was a notebook, and it was at her office at the university. No, she had no idea why anyone would want to break into the house and search her desk. And, considering her condition, it always came back to, was it safe to leave Edwina alone in a neighborhood where there had been a murder and a break-in and a mountain lion? What could Charlie possibly do with her in Long Beach?

She dared another cup of coffee and perused headlines in the section of the local paper left on the table next to her. *Most new homes in Boulder County sold to local residents moving up, not to newcomers from out of town, Realtors say. More mountain lion sightings due to wildfires, experts say. Only in Boulder, is the city really that unique? Yes, says Chamber of Commerce. Most Boulder County families better off than a year ago, merchants say.*

Charlie had to admit her financial situation had been looking up lately too, and before Keegan's latest offer. Thanks mostly to his two previous successes and to the raise Richard gave Charlie when Mitch signed on to play one of the leads in *Phantom of the Alpine Tunnel.* Richard Morse assumed Charlie had an affair with Mitch Hilsten to persuade him to take the leading role—as he'd insinuated she should, and even though she'd refused.

The joke was on Richard because she'd taken his insinuating phone call lying next to Mitch on the "morning after." And Mitch heard about Eric Ashton breaking his contract on his own and asked Charlie to mention him to Richard and the producers at Ursa Major. Charlie turned them both down and got a raise.

Life was totally weird.

Before, she'd worked on a commission basis and only a small salary. Now, she still kept her commissions but was paid better even when her clients weren't. She'd been so poor for so long she didn't trust this new state of affairs. Maybe she should ease up on the purse strings, as her daughter was forever demanding, take a cue from Edwina and buy some new duds. Maybe she should celebrate Keegan's success. Unfortunately he couldn't.

Even when you have money, you hate shopping. You know

you're just trying to stay out of that house a little longer.

But Charlie hadn't walked half a block before she came to the Shop of Mystery and forgot all about new clothes.

She stood there staring at the window display, aware of birds chattering in the trees above, wind rustling leaves, the squeal of brakes muted by distance, the tinkle of wind chimes, the clink of silverware from yet another restaurant with an outdoor seating area in front of it, and the wind flapping the fringe of the umbrellas over the tables.

"Spare some change, oh lovely one?"

Charlie ignored him even when he jostled her.

"Not even a quarter?"

The window displayed your regular assortment of crystals and rocks and jewelry. But directly in the center was a dead cat.

"Aw, come on, lady, how about a dime?"

And perched on a stack of books in a patch of sun at one end of the display was a live one. Orange, long-haired, with a thick tail that cascaded down the stack and sleepy, squinty green eyes.

"Must be nice to be rich."

The dead cat was enclosed in a plastic case. The live one yawned and rolled out a pink tongue.

"Just trying to put some breakfast together."

Charlie stepped through the open door of the shop.

"I got a kid, you know."

From this side the dead cat under glass looked like he was sleeping. And the panhandler looked incensed.

He shook a fist at the window. "Damn pushy broads, think they're such big shit."

What, he took her for a tourist? Charlie was rarely bothered by these guys. Maybe she was more vulnerable in Boulder and the panhandlers could sense it. She thought of Marlin Wetzel.

This guy finally stalked off, and Charlie turned to look over the rest of the store—odd trinkets, "free" clothes with hefty price tags but that freed up your body and your spirit. Lots of feathery fans too and wind chimes hanging from everywhere, kept in tinkly motion by ceiling fans. But the largest selections were of books, tapes, and CDs.

With its location and size, the lease on this shop must be costing Lance a fortune. Predictable floor-length chains of beads hung in the doorway at the back of the room, and Charlie could hear voices there. She could have grabbed half the inventory and run off with it before the beads parted and out walked Twyla Clark, the cancer counselor.

It took Charlie a moment to remember where she'd seen the woman.

Twyla cocked her head to one side in a gesture Charlie remembered. "May I help you?"

Something about the woman reminded Charlie of a Hollywood version of a nun. "You work here too?"

"Oh, that's right, you're Edwina's daughter. How's she feeling?"

Well, she panicked over a gas bubble last night and she's in a lot of pain, but other than that. . . . "Just fine."

"Reality will hit eventually. And I suppose when it does, you'll be gone."

"More than likely. Uh, that cat in the window? How much is it?"

"That's Wiggims. He belongs to the owner and isn't for sale."

"No, I mean the dead one under glass."

Twyla stood blinking. She wasn't dressed in veils or "free" clothing but in tight knit pants and tunic top, beige to match her short upswept hair. Finally, her eyes formed big tear drops and her tight little mouth warped and split in a sob. She rushed back through the beads, whimpering. "That nasty . . ."

What is it with me today? I'm causing a lot of grief here. Charlie went again to look at the glass case in the window and Wiggims stepped down off his books, arched, and walked languorously across the display, which was open on the store side

116

except for a low glass panel. He held his tail high, stretched his neck up to look at her, and made a tentative mewing.

Used to a treacherous Tuxedo, she accepted the invitation with caution, ready to snatch back her hand before he could bite it. She had never related to cats, no matter what Lita Kelso thought.

Purring loud snorts, Wiggims proceeded to prance his whole body to the end of his magnificent tail under her stilled hand and then turned around to do it again.

"Do you throw up a lot on carpets and stuff?"

"Why don't you pick him up? He loves it," a voice said behind her and it wasn't Twyla Clark or Lita Kelso either.

Charlie turned to face Lance the millionaire.

He was even taller than Kenny but not as muscled. He too wore a suit. She couldn't believe those two in anything but dirty Ts and nasty grins.

"I'd know you anywhere from that hair, Charlie." But he gave her a quick head-to-toe-and-back power look anyway.

"Hi, Lance. I'd know you anywhere too." Who could forget the grossest guy to infect the planet?

Wiggims began kneading the back of her tank top as Lance approached from the front. Charlie actually picked up the feline to hold between them.

Lance grinned and wrinkled his nose. "Never did trust me, did you?"

"Never did." She wrinkled back, still trying to tie down the new, mature, grossly wealthy Lance. Did panhandlers dump on him?

"I hear you've become an editor." He looked her over again.

"Agent." Charlie knew her shorts and sandals weren't very professional, but resented his attitude anyway.

"Well, next step is editor, right?" He hadn't fared as well, looks-wise, as his friend Kenny, but Lance had been busy making money instead.

"Not if I can help it."

Fortunately, his mother parted the beads and stalked in on them, just as Wiggims snuggled between Charlie's breasts like a lover demanding to be stroked.

CHAPTER 17

————————◆————————

*C*HARLIE, I WAS just telling Lance about you, and here you
are as if summoned." Lita wore harem pants gathered at
the ankle and slit up the sides. She'd have looked at home on
the back lot of MGM. "And look at you. You loathe kitties, sure.
Wiggims knows better, don't you, puss?"

"Wiggims'd suck up to Hannibal Lecter." Lance lifted the
cat out of Charlie's arms.

She brushed orange hairs off her black tank top, relieved. The
enraptured animal had been just short of faking orgasm. "I apol-
ogize for upsetting your clerk. I only wanted to know the price
on the dead cat in the window."

Lance handed the live cat to his mother. He and Lita resembled each other little except for a certain expression about
the eyes. He had his father's long sharp nose and angular face,
close-cropped sun-bleached hair and a deep tan. If he were a cat,
he'd be a Siamese.

"You have a clerk?" he asked Lita.

"There's a dead cat in the window?" Lita carried Wiggims
over to the display and stood there for so long, Lance became
curious and joined her.

"That's not a dead cat," she said finally.

"Well, it's not a live one," Charlie insisted.

"And it's certainly not stuffed." Lance raised quizzical brows
at Charlie. "What would you want with it anyway?"

"I'd take it to the police station."

"This is not funny. Poor Twyla." Lita set Wiggims down and, selecting a scarf dangling from a display, she covered the offending object, case and all, and lifted it out of the window. "It's neither for sale nor display," she said firmly and carried it into the room behind the bead door.

Wiggims found a flat place where his sun spot had moved and curled up in it.

"Why would you take it to the police?"

"Because we found one just like it on the street in front of our house last night. Emmy chased a prowler, and he dropped it."

Lance offered to take Charlie next door for lunch. Since she'd just eaten, she sipped a diet Coke instead and told him about the odd occurrences in his old neighborhood. "I can't believe Lita didn't mention any of this."

"She mentioned your mother having a hysterectomy."

"Mastectomy—breast cancer." Did he do this on purpose?

"Oh well, anyway, I just got in yesterday. Came to check out my cabin. Fire actually came fairly close. Took the house across the road, but they're down to clean up and watchdog crews, so we should be out of danger." He'd ordered soup and salad and a full sandwich and was going through all three at a great clip for someone so trim.

They sat at one of the sidewalk tables, as she had earlier farther down the mall, the tables cordoned off by a fence of black metal poles to discourage you from seating yourself or walking off without paying your bill. She was facing what used to be street and was reminded of a scene in Reynelda's book describing a summer day on an unpaved Pearl Street, the air thick with dust and flies, the latter raising off plops of horse exhaust when disturbed by women's long skirts at crosswalks.

"Why would your mother keep a dead cat under glass?"

"Rarely interfere in her activities. In fact I'm rarely in town. My home and business are in Vegas. I travel a great deal. The

120

cabin is sort of a retreat." He was lying. Why?

"I suppose you have your own plane and your own pilot."

"Plus a copilot," he said around a mouthful and washed everything down with half a carafe of iced tea. "A Star Ship. Ever seen one? Beautiful birds. Turbo. You like flying?"

"Not really, but my job seems to demand more and more of it. I fly commercial." And usually coach.

"You live in New York?"

"L.A. Lance, I didn't get a chance to tell your mother, but the cat Libby and I found in Columbia Cemetery when we found Andy's body looked a great deal like the one in her window too. And there are lots of cats going missing in the neighborhood. I'll have to tell Kenny about this."

"Eisenburg? He still playing cop? I haven't seen him in two, three years. How's his marriage coming along?"

"Divorced." Here she was sitting at a table on a warm lovely day talking casually with Lance Kelso. Who would have thought it possible, say about sixteen years ago? "How about you?"

"Have a live-in, but technically I'm free." He wiped off his mouth and hunted for food in his teeth with his tongue, regarding her thoughtfully. He'd finished off the entire meal that fast. Even ate the pickle. "And you?"

"Still single and intend to stay that way."

"Thought I heard somewhere you and Mitch Hilsten were—"

"No. Lance, about your mom."

"You think she's stealing cats and eviscerating them? Doesn't sound like her. Seem's inordinately fond of the damn things. She's a total vegetarian. Won't allow meat in her kitchen. Can't imagine her using a knife on any animal. Always thought of her as a harmless kook. Hope this won't cause major trouble for her. She likes it here."

"Well, you better talk to her before you beam up to your Star Ship. I've got more than I can handle with my own mother. Good seeing you." Well, okay, not as bad as I thought it would be. "Thanks for the Coke. I've got some faxing to do."

"Charlie, you ever think about Buddy?"

"No." She knew he'd spoil everything, the jerk. Charlie squeezed out from between the table and the crush right behind her. The tables were packed tight. Everybody likes to eat outside when the weather's nice. "Bye, Lance."

"He's in town. I saw him last night."

"I don't want to hear this." But she stopped by his chair as a waiter blocked her way with a loaded tray and a stand for the next table.

"He thinks about you."

"You know, you really haven't changed at all?"

"And he thinks about the kid. I can set up a meeting. Charlie, the guy's hurting."

"Aw, poor baby. Hey, he wants to pay her way through college, pick up the rest of the orthodontist bill, he can cry on my shoulder."

"He's got a wife and two kids, Charlie, and not a lot of money."

"That's no surprise." She started off when the waiter moved aside for her, but her nemesis grabbed a wrist and brought her up short.

"Aren't you even curious?"

"No. He's another bad childhood experience, just like you are."

"Well, Buddy is. Curious. He's got two little girls, like maybe four and six? Both platinum blondes."

"I hope when they get to be teenagers, they turn his world inside out. What could he possibly do for a living?"

"See, you *are* curious."

"I am not." And she would have made a grand exit, but just then the waiter shrugged at her hesitation and closed her off again.

"He's in show business. He hasn't made it yet."

"I hope Libby didn't get her brains from his family."

"Oh? And you are what? An editor? So, you can just blow him off? Big deal." He not only let go of her wrist, he sort of thrust it off.

That was the moment Charlie Greene decided Keegan Monroe would sign that contract no matter how many times he changed his mind. She was through being Ms. Nice Guy.

But she smiled down at Lance Kelso and kept her mouth shut. He knew she was a Hollywood agent. And he thought she was too dumb to realize Buddy did too.

Old Buddy had probably read the tabloid supermarket papers, or more likely seen last month's flavor-of-the-minute scandal on tabloid TV—Charlie Greene and the superstar who was, at this minute, mother-sitting Edwina.

"Living with his folks right now, until they can get on their feet financially," the devious millionaire said.

"I can't help him, and I wouldn't if I could."

Edwina was actually walking around the backyard on Mitch's arm, holding herself straighter, less hunched over. She was dressed in a pale cream pantsuit. One of the new acquisitions obviously, but not a wise color choice with her post-op pallor.

One sprinkler soaked the front yard and another whirled circles of water drops that sparkled in the sun on Emmy's side of the house. Animal Control officers found no trace of a mountain lion. Libby'd gone for a walk.

"Told her to go to Chautauqua," Edwina said. "There's usually something going on up there."

The street that began at the cemetery and ran past the house ended at Chautauqua Park, five or six blocks up a gradual incline to the south. It had a huge old barn of a lecture hall and a restaurant that only opened in the summer months, a playground, flower beds, large grassy areas for picnicking and Frisbee, gorgeous views, tourist cabins, and trail heads into Boulder's mountain park system.

Charlie figured Libby had walked over to the Hill instead, where something was *always* happening. Charlie was not even going to think about Buddy MacCallister. Unless they'd moved, his parents lived out in North Boulder. There was no reason to think that, in something like a hundred thousand people—not counting tourists—Libby and Buddy should ever bump into each other.

Edwina even wore gold studs in her newly pierced ears. She must be feeling better. Charlie wondered if she dared call for plane reservations for Monday.

Mitch helped Charlie haul ancient lawn chairs out of the garage and dust them off. They sat in the shade of Jennifer Tollerude's monster house.

Charlie described the dead cat in the window of the Shop of Mystery. That got Edwina going about how strange Lita Kelso had always been and what a burden she was to Lance and his father.

Mitch had just begun to explain his studies in demonology and Satanism when Professor Goff and two other men picked their way through the sprinkler at the side of the house and came to stand before Charlie and company.

The professor used his pipe to point at Charlie. "Now *that* is our so-called literary agent, Horace—look like one to you?"

———————◆———————

CHAPTER 18

G EORGE GOFF WAS in shorts today, legs and arms so thin his elbows and knees looked like lumpy growths on diseased trees. The other two men were beefy. The one with a paunch over his belt Edwina introduced as Matt Hogarth. The other, Horace Crumpet, was heavy all over.

"I hope, Edwina, you are satisfied with the trouble your daughter has caused at my house, with this so-called agent business. Rey's locked me out. Had to spend the night in Matt and Clarissa's guest room."

"Kicked you out, did she? Good for Rey." Edwina started to laugh and thought better of it, catching hold of what was left of her stomach.

Mitch rose to his feet with exaggerated slowness. He had the sleeves of his shirt rolled up above the elbow and the top buttons unbuttoned. He put his hands on slim hips and flashed the famous Hilsten smile. He claimed those teeth were insured with Lloyd's of London. Good thing Charlie was immune to that kind of thing, most of the time. Good thing she was leaving soon too.

Horace Crumpet studied Mitch instead of Charlie. "Have we met?"

"I don't think so." Mitch's teeth might be smiling, but his eyes didn't blink. Like in *Deadly Posse.* Oh shit.

But Professor Hogarth diffused the situation by recognizing the movie star, lavishing praise on his performance in *Bloody*

Promises and being impressed that he was a friend of Edwina's. Professors apparently didn't watch tabloid television either.

Prodded by hooded looks from George Goff, Horace Crumpet—the famous novelist Charlie had never heard of—asked her to divulge to which editors at which publishing houses she had sent Reynelda's manuscript. Charlie's problem was that the longer she was gone from the daily lunch opportunities with editors in New York, the more her previous contacts either didn't survive the conglomerate search for best-seller material or they advanced to higher and higher echelons. Which made it difficult for Charlie to sell first novels and why she wouldn't have accepted Reynelda as a client if Edwina hadn't worn her down.

It came in handy now though. She could reel off three major editors at three well-known publishing houses to whom she'd sent the manuscript. Horace Crumpet recognized two of the editors' names; Hogarth, all of the houses. George simply didn't believe her.

"Did you tell Rey this?" he asked Charlie through his nose.

"I've been very busy since I got here." I hadn't planned on telling her at all, just handing on the rejection letters when they came. "It's a good story." It just doesn't fit anybody's list. "Miracles do happen."

"Well, they are major New York editors, George," Crumpet said. The visiting summer lecturer was tall as well as heavy, with a thin fringe of gray around a sweaty bald patch.

"Yes, but how do we know she isn't lying?"

Edwina stood then, way too fast and way too straight. Charlie imagined bandages ripping from sternum to pubic hair.

"My daughter, Professor Goff"—Edwina did not sound like a woman who had turned a multitude of rats loose on an unsuspecting neighborhood, but rather a literary person in pain—"is a Hollywood agent now because of her success as a New York agent for—"

"Wesson Bradley," Charlie filled in and gently tugged her mother back down to the lawn chair.

"That, George, is a very prestigious agency," Crumpet informed Reynelda's husband.

"Yes, but how do you know she didn't lie to her mother as well as to my wife?"

"So, Mr. Crumpet, who is your editor?" Charlie said before both Mitch and Edwina decided to get physical.

"Maureen Saunders was for my last book. I am, at the moment, between editors," he answered with a wrinkling of his brow and a quick nod, as if that were inconsequential and momentous at the same time. A rapid glance at Charlie tried to determine whether she grasped its ramifications.

Charlie wasn't that out of touch with New York.

"You *have* heard of Maureen Saunders?" George Goff said.

"Yes, she was a fine editor." And she's been dead for three years, and her list for five. But Charlie hadn't the heart to say it aloud.

Mitch and Edwina insisted Charlie have dinner with him that night. They could leave the minute Libby got home. There was no longer much danger from wildfire or mountain lions. Figuring she'd be pretty safe because the danger now would be when or whether Libby would decide to come home, Charlie said if the kid was back in time she would. But not to count on it. Then she drained her mother's drains, sponged-bathed what was not covered by tape and mummy wrap—the poor woman wasn't allowed a full bath until the tape was removed—and put her back in sleeping clothes to rest.

She stepped out of Edwina's bedroom to see her daughter and the superstar having a staring match across the living room. You couldn't even count on the kid to mess up when you didn't want to count on her.

Mitch promised to return in thirty minutes. Charlie helped Libby select a neighborhood offering to feed herself and her grandmother and managed a hasty shower and fresh sundress.

"Listen, I'll call from whatever restaurant we go to and give you the number." Charlie used to say that to Libby's sitters. "And whatever nasty thoughts you have right now, Libby, I'm coming home early. So you won't be left alone with this problem for long, I promise."

Charlie left the house under a glare of unspoken accusation to find grocery sacks filling the back seat of the Bronco. They weren't going to a restaurant. He was going to cook for her. She longed for simpler days when a date would order in pizza and you wouldn't feel obligated and trapped.

His new condo was built high on the mountain backdrop that Boulder worked hard to save as a view and a place for wildlife and vegetation. It was on the north side of the city—the almost-out fires were over the ridge and farther south.

From the outside, in the dark, it had looked like a mansion. Instead, it was three attached townhouses with a view.

Mitch's digs were on the south with a great expanse of window, city lights beginning to twinkle below, a sunset sky over the Flatirons shading the clouds and smoke rose and gray.

The Flatirons were a series of rock faces rearing up at the edge of town, as if the soil cover and pine and grass had been sheared off. To early settlers, they'd resembled upended hand irons, the kind you had to heat on a stove top.

The kitchen, dining, and living areas were all one open room about twice the size of Edwina's whole house, a vast deck running along two sides, a breakfast bar big enough to sport eight stools. Charlie climbed up on one and didn't offer to help make the salad. He poured her a glass of wine. She asked for his phone number and called Libby.

"What restaurant is it?" Libby asked when Charlie gave her the number.

"It's not a restaurant, but you can get me here and I'll be home soon anyway."

"Yeah, right. You're at his place, huh?" The accusation no longer silent.

"Libby—"

"See you in the morning." The kid hung up on her.

Sensing her mood, Mitch worked silently, expertly whirling whisk and sauté pans and equipment Charlie couldn't even name.

"Haven't you ever missed having someone to take care of you, spoil you? Someone to just be there when you need them?" he asked finally without looking up from his utensils and food.

"Yeah once. When I had the flu."

He gave her a sideways look of mock suspicion. "Charlie, I'm serious here."

"Listen, that was one bad bug."

Once he had whatever it was in the oven and the salad in the crisper, he poured himself some wine, and they took their glasses out to lean on the railing and watch Boulder get ready for Saturday night. Sort of festive with all the streetlights glowing orange and the houses lit up. But the air still stank of smoke.

"It's Libby, isn't it?" he said finally. "She hates me. She doesn't even know me."

Jesus, will you give this a break? "It's the worldwide publicity about our big night last month. That's embarrassing for a kid."

"Sorry, but she doesn't strike me as all that naive."

"That's one thing she's not," Charlie agreed. "But didn't you ever go into denial about your parents' sexuality? Especially when you were just discovering your own? I did."

"Yeah, but my folks were old. So were yours. You're pretty young to have a teenager."

Edwina was four years younger than you are now when Libby was born.

But Charlie couldn't explain how her attitudes about the generations involved had become skewed away from the norm by early motherhood. It was all too confusing and she didn't like to waste precious energy worrying about that kind of stuff when she could expend it far more satisfactorily at the work she loved.

The only way to survive in this world was to get your priorities straight and cut out things of lesser importance.

In other words, when life gets personal, change the subject.

"So, tell me about your investigations into Satanism. You were cut off this afternoon before you got started." You, who are supposed to be studying the role and getting your head into the mindset of the train engineer in *Phantom of the Alpine Tunnel* instead.

"Why? You'll just scoff and go into boring detail about how illogical I am and how logical you are."

Mitch Hilsten, superhero, macho man on the screen, had a surprising flaw offscreen. He believed in such things as UFOs and psychics. Looking at him, it was staggeringly out of character to imagine him having, say, an intelligent conversation with the likes of Lita Kelso. Charlie would never blow his image to the world, but the guy was a gorgeous flake. "Please?"

"You have to praise my cooking, okay?"

"Promise." That part wasn't hard. Spinach souffle. Crusty bread you had to tear apart. A sautéed rice, mushroom, almond, and strange herb pilaf. And a salad with every kind of leaf but iceberg. (Charlie preferred iceberg lettuce because it was moist and crunchy and took longer to wither in her refrigerator.) But she was all praise—hell, if she didn't have to plan it, buy it, cook it, it had to be good.

The . . . uh . . . strange stuff, on the other hand, was a little harder to swallow.

"What you have to understand first of all, Charlie, is that witchcraft and demonology or satanism are two different things." The pale eyes shone in the candlelight at the one corner of the large table at which they sat together.

Oh boy. "You sure you don't mean three different things?"

"No." He grimaced in thought, and the candlelight picked up the gleam of his teeth. How could anybody eat spinach souffle and not smear it all over his . . . "Listen, I'm just getting into this stuff. It's new territory for me, understand." He put down his fork and picked up his wineglass, staring into its depths. "Witchcraft is based mostly on female principles, even though it's also practiced by males."

Female principles, of course, were symbolized by hearth and fertility and the blessings of love and healing potions and the homey stuff as practiced by illiterate peasants. While Satanism and demonology was historically a practice of educated male priests using forms of magic, albeit illegal, in an effort to control disasters brought on by the elements thought to be ruled by demons.

Charlie nodded as if she gave a damn and crunched an almond sliver. What if Keegan sat down for dinner tonight, looked at the prison slop on his plate, and changed his mind about signing the contract? But she came up with the straight-man feeder line. "So what does it all mean?"

"Well, see, none of these things are bad in and of themselves, and they all have the best intentions behind them but the Church declared them evil because it couldn't control them. Catholic Church. Medieval."

What if Libby decided Charlie was going to sleep with Mitch tonight and it made her so angry she left Edwina alone in the house and walked in the dark over to the Hill and Buddy was there reliving his youth with friends?

"I'm having trouble putting this all together in my own mind, but I guess what I'm getting at, Charlie, is that the wildfires, the mountain lion sightings, the apparent vandalism at that cemetery near you, and the cat sacrifices may all be related."

"And Andy Tollerude's murder?"

"That too."

What if Edwina got sicker and sicker and had to come and live with Charlie and Libby in their cramped two-bedroom condo? What did you do with sick people these days when you left the house to go to work? Edwina didn't seem old enough for a nursing home, and hospitals shoved you out before you knew what hit you.

More to the point, what's that staring at you over Mitch's shoulder?

Charlie jumped up, dumping her wine all over her pilaf. "Mitch, look out!"

CHAPTER 19

T HE BIG CAT lay on the deck beneath the window in a patch of light from inside the room where Charlie and Mitch stood staring down at it, all three of them stunned. The rose had left the clouds, left them oily dark lumps in a sky only a shade lighter. Where the animal's head had hit, some kind of body fluid—Charlie hoped only saliva—had pasted several hairs to the Thermalpane. He'd been at the high point of an arc in his leap when he hit, and the blinking lights of a far-off airplane wandered across the hairs.

Mitch whispered, as if not to disturb their injured visitor. "Tell me exactly what you saw before you yelled at me, Charlie."

"I was looking at you at an angle and saw eyes to one side. I didn't stop to think there was a window between those eyes and us."

"What color eyes?"

"I don't know. Cat color. Mountain lion color."

"They weren't red?"

"No, I'd have noticed that." Don't flake on me now, man. "Then they widened and looked right into me and rose up and came toward us. He must have been standing on that picnic table and didn't know there was a window between us either. Wouldn't he see reflections from his side? I can from ours."

"He looked right into you . . ."

"Right at me."

"That's not what you said."

"I didn't know mountain lions were this big. He's gorgeous. Libby was right. What if he's dead?" She turned toward a door handle, but he stopped her.

"Beauty can be dangerous, Charlie. That cat's deadly, and if he's not dead he's going to have one hell of a headache. That'll make him even more dangerous. What I don't understand is what he was trying to do."

"Jump in here and eat us up, would be my guess."

"It's like you and Libby are an attraction for mountain lions. Doesn't that strike you as strange?"

"Maybe they want to kill us because they're from Colorado and we're from California and they think we're going to move in on their territory."

This was definitely a guy lion. But he didn't have the large head of an African lion. His seemed almost too small for the powerful shoulders and big feet. He resembled a gigantic house cat, lying there on his side as if asleep. Except that his tail was three feet long, and his fur was a lush tawny buff everywhere but his muzzle, neck, stomach, and rump, where it was as white as Mitch Hilsten's smile.

"He's gotta be two hundred pounds," Mitch said in the same tone of voice he'd used as her lover one night a month ago.

Charlie's only thought was that some dork with a gun would kill the fantastic creature. "Oh, wake up and get out of here, baby. You're worth a hundred heros."

It was that incredible tail that moved first, and then just the end of it, a leisurely curling movement lifting it off the deck to fall back, curl again.

Charlie recognized the motion from her experience with the damn cat at home—not when he was waking up, but more when he lay in wait, sort of in anticipation, faking sleep. If she was dumb enough to reach out and stroke the inviting smoothness, he'd allow about two strokes and come alive faster than you could see, curling his whole body around her hand and wrist so he could bite her, rake her with his back claws, and hold her still for the torture with his front claws. Tuxedo was a real sweetheart. How could he be related at all to this splendid creature?

Nothing jerky or sudden in the way this giant kitty came to. Once the tip of the tail decided it could curl, the whole body responded in a prolonged graceful gathering together of muscle and nerves and bone in one fluid motion.

After a bump on the head like that, Charlie would have twitched and snorted and probably thrown up her pilaf before she even knew where she was.

But the mountain lion's head lifted as did the entire tail—one flopping forward, the other rearing—while all four legs bunched together under the body in a pinching movement to grasp the decking and bring the animal to his feet. A trickle of blood on his lower lip splattered red droplets against the window when he gave his head a quick shake, his eyes never leaving Charlie's. His were a tawny beige like Twyla Clark's hair. They flashed a momentary red when caught by the light from within the room as he turned.

With a warning *rouwoo* sound, again reminiscent of Tuxedo but on a far grander scale, he leapt over the deck railing to the mountainside beyond it.

Mitch's whisper came thin from holding his breath. "That was damn near a religious experience."

"Tell me about it." That may be the closest I've ever been to falling in love. "And I am not normally attracted to critters."

"And you noticed the red glare of his eyes?" Mitch picked up a cordless phone from an endtable.

"Do you have to do that? Maybe he'll just go back into the mountains."

"Maybe he won't. That cat was trying to attack, Charlie."

But Animal Control was swamped with mountain lion calls, and there was a black bear reported on Broadway. The dispatcher told Mitch to bring in his garbage, warn his neighbors, and be careful. Like Mitch, his neighbors were the visiting rich, with homes all over the world. They weren't in town.

"Why now?" Charlie asked. "With the fires about out."

"Might be all the firefighters and news helicopters and things still up there. I imagine there's a lot of sightseer traffic too. Cougars, pumas, mountain lions—they're all the same animal, generally have a fairly large territory they defend. I wonder how they'll mix in town with each other, let alone people and traffic and bears."

"The red you saw in his eyes? It had nothing to do with Satanism or whatever, Mitch. It's what certain lighting does to animal eyes."

"He was meeting yours, wasn't he? Cats usually don't do that," he countered.

"I think they do if they want to have you for dinner."

They looked at their own cold dinner. Fallen spinach souffle was not an appetizing sight.

"I have to get home."

"I know." But he was back over at the window where a beautiful death had tried to leap in.

"The dinner was really remarkable. But the mountain lion, I'll never forget."

As she stepped out of his car in front of her mother's house, Mitch said, "Do me a favor? Don't run around outside. Or let your daughter either. Especially at night."

Inside, Edwina was up again, this time in her robe having coffee with Heather Tynne, the real estate woman, and Reynelda Goff, the probably never-to-be-rich-and-famous author. They seemed to think they were having a party and enjoying themselves.

Libby leaned in the doorway of the kitchen with Harry and

Larry Dweebsville peering over her shoulders, and she mouthed, "I'm leaving."

She jerked a thumb toward the alley.

Charlie waved at the party in the living room and made it to the kitchen before the kids made it out the back door.

"I'm just shocked that you even came home before morning. What, you had a fight with the washed-out movie star?"

Charlie took another look at Larry and Harry. "Do you guys have a car? Good. The mountain lions are really coming into town. There was one in North Boulder at Mitch's tonight. The Animal Control office says there was even a black bear on Broadway. All the excitement in the mountains is driving the animals down into town. Promise you will not let Libby walk home alone or anywhere?"

The boys nodded humbly but then glanced at each other like they thought Charlie was the dweeb here. On closer inspection, they probably weren't brothers. What she had taken for plump was really big boned and strapping. It was the silly clothes and grins that threw you off.

"If she is not home, delivered by car in two hours, no matter her attitude, which won't be pleasant simply because I'm insisting on this, I will not bother calling 911. I will call Detective Eisenburg of the Boulder Police Department, who knows you both by sight, as well as the university police, and send them all to your fraternity house—in under five minutes of the curfew."

The three left, yukking it up and mimicking her threats in grand style. Charlie would have felt more helpless if she hadn't caught the one threat that seemed to matter to the boys. Surprising, but the fraternity house seemed more important than either the city or university police. Charlie had been grasping when she even mentioned a frat.

Still, why would sending authorities there make a difference in these kids' attitudes? As Charlie remembered frats, discipline was no threat in the summer. Or anytime really. Fucking up was a treasured rite of passage at this age, and especially if you were a white male whose parents had money.

They probably just rent rooms in a frat house for the summer term, her other voice kicked in after a surprisingly long silence.

Oh, right. I forgot. What if Buddy's on the Hill?

What, that's a worse threat than a mountain lion?

❖

"Oh my God, I can't believe it," Heather said when Charlie joined the party. "You out on a date with Mitch Hilsten. You always did get around, Charlie."

That was probably to be Charlie's epitaph: "Here lies Charlie, who got around." Not who handled one of the all-time big deals in Hollywood, single-handedly raised a difficult teen, and put up with Professor Edwina for most of her life.

Heather announced proudly that she'd brought Charlie's mother a hot bean dish. Which ought to improve Edwina's gas bubble problem to no end.

"Heather tells us many of the old timers in the neighborhood are selling out and moving to someplace safer," Reynelda said. "Because of the mountain lions and wildfires and the murder next door."

"Yeah, like Denver, I suppose. Reynelda, have you compared the crime rates? And Heather, who in the neighborhood is selling out? Give us names."

"Oh, different ones. Are thinking about it. They've talked to me, but I can't give out names. That's confidential." She put down her coffee cup, ran her fingers through shaggy curls, busily gathered her purse and car keys, and smiled brightly. "I have to be going. Lots of work left to do tonight." But she turned at the door. "Oh Charlie, by the way, there was something I wanted to ask you. My friend runs a summer screenwriting conference up at Chautauqua, and one of her speakers for tomorrow canceled on Friday. She brings in screenwriters and producers from Hollywood, but a Hollywood agent would be interesting too."

"No."

"It'd only be for like an hour. Surely one hour wouldn't be too much? She's really in a jam. The students have paid for two full days." Heather Tynne was out the door and gone.

Charlie almost wished a mountain lion would get her, but her car started up out at the curb and drove off down the street.

"Why do you put up with her, Edwina? She's just trying to con you into selling your house."

"Why not? Put up with you, don't I? As I remember, Heather Tynne got around some herself at a certain age." Edwina announced she could get herself back to bed. "You talk to Rey about her book now. She's been waiting far too long."

Charlie wanted to crawl into a hot tub full of bubbles again. She wanted to crawl into bed. She wanted to talk about the mountain lion–cougar-puma she'd seen tonight. She didn't want to talk to this woman about her book.

But they sat on either side of a cold fireplace, in the reading chairs Charlie liked when she was a tot because Howard or Edwina would sit in one of them with her on their lap and read stories to her.

"I'm so embarrassed about my husband's mistrust and hostility, Charlie. He feels threatened. My writing is the one place he can't intrude. He can't belittle it, because I won't let him read it. It's a form of control. I don't think he even realizes it. There's so little in his life he can control."

"Well, it shouldn't have to be you. You're his wife, not his slave. Just because he spent some money fixing up the house doesn't give him the right to belittle you." Do you think he killed Andy Tollerude and buried him in Tom Horn's grave as part of some ritual?

"Actually, most of that was money my mother left me. Another blow to his pride."

"Do you love him?" Charlie couldn't help but ask. He was

such a disagreeable person. Did you maybe help him bury Andy?

"We have a long marriage in common. There's some comfort in that. However, once he retires, if he doesn't straighten himself out, I may take a hike."

CHAPTER 20

<hr>

S UNDAY MORNING, IN spite of mountain lions and black bears, Charlie and her mother took their second cups of coffee and the newspaper out to the lawn chairs in the backyard. They found a spot of early sun that Jennifer Tollerude's house couldn't obliterate, yet still close to the back step in case a roaming critter wandered by.

Libby slept. She'd come home late, but she'd come home safe.

"I'd like to see you settled before I die, Charlemagne Catherine," Edwina said out of the blue, from whence it seemed to Charlie most of her mother's thoughts came.

"Edwina, the lymph nodes were clear. You aren't going to die."

"I'm going to die sometime. Doesn't look like you're going to settle sometime though."

"By settled you mean with a guy." This isn't what I wanted to talk about. I wanted to tell you about the mountain lion last night, but you're wrecking it all. "Look, I have a home, a child, a job. That's pretty settled for these days. There are lots of perfectly happy single women around now."

"That's what my Aunt Ida Mae always said, and look at her."

"You have an Aunt Ida Mae? In Iowa?" That's where Edwina came from originally. "Living?"

"Yes, but don't get your hopes up. She's taking care of my

Aunt Gertie, who has Alzheimer's. Ida Mae is wearing down fast. She's probably close to eighty."

"You have two aunts in Iowa? How come you never told me?"

"We write at Christmas is all."

"Any other surprise relatives you'd like to tell me about?"

"Well, your father had two children by his first wife. I lost track of that family years ago. That's about it, I guess."

Charlie knew about Howard's previous family, but she couldn't believe Edwina had hidden away two maiden aunts from Iowa all these years. Charlie doubted she would understand women her mother's age even when she reached that age herself. "Do you know your friend Rey told me last night that if her husband didn't straighten out by the time he retired, she'd take a hike?"

Edwina peered over the half glasses she wore on a cord around her neck and winked. "Lots more to that woman than meets the eye."

"Just as long as she doesn't intend to take her hike on the proceeds of her writing."

"Thought you liked her book."

"It's just that it's not marketable. It's a great story but it's not—"

"The flavor of the week."

"The flavor of the week. You have to write what's selling at the moment, not what you want to. Publishing's a business." Charlie picked up the front section of the *Sunday Daily Camera.* "Oh well, maybe she'll win the lottery."

It was late June, and the front page was mostly sports. Pictures and headlines—JOHN ELWAY SPRAINS WRIST ON GOLF COURSE—with even more details to follow in the separate sports section, which also carried more pictures and headlines. Basketball playoffs and football games between college and pros, baseball games and gossip, injuries and contracts. Even a bicycle race.

"Who's John Elway?"

"Some football player in Denver. I think he's a used-car dealer too," Edwina answered with little interest.

Charlie could begin to see why few people she'd met in Boulder were even aware of her notorious one-night stand with Mitch Hilsten.

Up in the left hand corner of the front page, above the masthead, was a small picture of Mitch, with the caption MITCH HILSTEN AND SATANISM, SEE ENTERTAINMENT. And next to it a picture of a mountain lion: MOUNTAIN LIONS COME TO TOWN, ARE THEY MAN EATERS? SEE EDITORIAL. And a small item on the lower left hand corner: JOGGERS, CYCLISTS, WALKERS, AND HIKERS WARNED TO EXERCISE INDOORS THE NEXT FEW DAYS UNTIL EXTENT OF WILD ANIMAL ACTIVITY DETERMINED.

Charlie'd had to learn to speed read to get through college, and it didn't hurt for getting through *The Boulder Sunday Camera* either. Since she skipped all the sports news, she made short work of it. The weather for the day and the coming week was predicted to be unusually hot, dry, and windy. Pictures of firefighters boarding planes to go home, and stories of heroism in the face of disaster.

People were living longer with the HIV virus before succumbing to the devastating illness which demanded so much health care it was bankrupting the nation. People without it were living longer too, and care for the aging with Alzheimer's and similar disorders that led to dementia was bankrupting the nation. Crime was slowing down a bit, but the cost of it was rising and bankrupting the nation.

In third-world countries, men in camouflage uniforms were murdering civilians in clothing resembling that which you could find in most American shopping malls. And male senators in both national and state senates were more likely to dump wives their own age for "trophies" if the politicians blow-dried their hair.

The way to stay fit in Boulder was to cross-train and get into running, walking, biking, weight lifting, stepping, and hang-gliding. And to eat raw onions, garlic, cabbage, broccoli, carrots, and kale that you grew organically in your backyard, and fresh fruits and oat bran for breakfast.

There had been ongoing vandalism at Columbia Cemetery before "unidentified tourists from out of state" discovered the location of Andy Tollerude's bloodless body. In fact, it had been going on sporadically for years, and according to Tom and Enid Schantz, proprietors of the Rue Morgue Mystery Store, the reason was simply the old graveyard's proximity to the university.

Professor George Goff, the University of Colorado's expert on ancient religions, however, maintained that "mysterious forces could be at work here, as elsewhere in the world, to right wrongs."

Granted, speed reading didn't give you a complete under-standing of a piece of writing, but the whole coverage of this slim issue looked pretty thin to Charlie. There was much repetition and extraneous filler, as was usual for such topics.

The big news was movie star Mitch Hilsten's take. (Charlie wondered why the paper hadn't interviewed this Elway instead.) The interviewer began, as Mitch had to Charlie the night before, by explaining that the movie star had only begun to look into this particular aspect but had long had an interest in matters of the occult. He had been recommended to the *Camera* by the proprietors of several book, music, and paraphernalia stores that dealt in such things and that he frequented often when in Boulder.

"I can't believe this," Charlie sputtered. "He's letting the whole world know he's a ditz. He'll ruin his image. Mitch—look at this." She waved the entertainment section at her mother but took it back before Edwina could read it. "And you think he's Mr. Wonderful, don't you?"

"I think he's a decent human being. And a very likable one. Can't tell you how few of those I've been running into lately. So he's not perfect. Big deal. You are, I suppose."

"I'm too busy now."

"Libby will be gone from your house in a couple of years. And you will be alone."

Charlie could still remember how delighted Edwina had been to ship Charlie and Libby off to college and day care in the East so she could concentrate on her own life and her work. Charlie had very similar feelings about Libby's leaving home. "I don't want to give up my freedom."

And with that, she went back to the newspaper, which couldn't be any more inane than her mother this morning.

But it was hard to concentrate. This kind of subject bored and irritated Charlie. The sun made her drowsy, the air smelled of some neighbor's flowers instead of smoke for a change. She'd drifted off into a fantasy of Libby graduating from college, dressed in black robe and mortar board and a red tassel, all stunning against the platinum hair and gleaming straight-toothed smile minus the braces. The welling of pride in Charlie, the gratification of accomplishment.

Rustlings in the grass at the side of the house. Charlie got up to check it out—That was a mistake. It was Wiggims Kelso, trying to catch a butterfly. Wiggims decided instantly that Charlie was more vulnerable and followed her back to her lawn chair.

Historically, ceremonial magic or Satanism was practiced by learned men, often priests, as opposed to the pagan rituals of witchcraft, and has always had strong religious connotations and still does in some primitive societies. In Western tradition, these ceremonies were derived mostly from the Hebrew Qabalah and given a Christian veneer.

Its purpose has been mainly to control the powers of nature, which are a product of heaven or hell, either good or bad, angelic or demonic, and sometimes "appeasing the gods of either" will bring an end to the drought, pestilence, famine, flood, volcanic eruption, or whatever.

The orange cat's euphoric delight in Charlie's ankles, his snorty purr, the splash of bathing birdlife over at Emmy's baths, the bird chatter and trills . . . even Maggie Stutzman, Charlie's neighbor and best friend, is impressed with the interview in the *L.A. Times*—"Charlie Greene, superagent."

"Have to hand it to you, Charlie. All that work's finally paying off." And Maggie raises a champagne glass over the table at the Beacon.

"I just got lucky." But Charlie drank to that anyway . . . rustlings in the alley . . . Charlie would not get up to investigate this time . . .

Historically, while witchcraft was often practiced by the illiterate, the ceremonial magician had to be a learned man, and in many centuries and places, learning was the prerogative of the priesthood. "The powerful divine names that define conjuration—Agla, Adonai, Anaphaxeton, Athanatos or Tetragrammaton, Sabaoth, Sother, and Primeumaton—are all words using a mixture of Greek and Hebrew, and are all names for God."

The ceremonies are far more elaborate than those of witchcraft and much more demanding. Ceremonial magicians go to great lengths to purify themselves—fasting, bathing, donning consecrated robes. "He uses pentacles and consecrated tools like the witch but more elaborate ones. He prays in the forms of—"

Charlie realized she'd dozed off only because she was startled awake by the sure and creepy knowledge that she was being watched, the house cat no longer making love to her bare ankles. But her mind's eye was looking into the tawny eyes of the great beast on Mitch's deck. Charlie could swear she smelled him.

CHAPTER 21

◆

Y OU'RE TIRED OUT, Charlie, working so hard. You need
rest, someone to help with life's responsibilities." Edwina
was unharmed and not the least bit anxious.

"What?" Charlie looked around for the mountain lion but
saw only Wiggims seducing Andy Tollerude's daughter through
the cemetery fence next door. The birds still sang sweet innocence, and Charlie had to brush a peaceful bee off her nose.

"You went to sleep reading the newspaper, Charlie. And it's
not even ten-thirty in the morning. You're too young to fall
asleep over the paper. You have too much care and worry, and
that job of yours is too stressful."

Charlie's mouth was dry and her heart pounding. "Nothing
happened? You didn't see a mountain lion? Or hear one?"

"No. And I don't care what the *Camera* says, mountain lions
rarely ever attack people. And in the desert we call them cougars
or pumas." Edwina returned to her paper in disgust.

Charlie started reading again where she'd left off, feeling like
a fool—and there was no one she resented more feeling like a
fool around than the woman next to her.

"The ceremonial magician uses pentacles and consecrated
tools like the witch but more elaborate ones. He prays in the
forms of Judaism or Christianity and at far greater length than
witches do to invoke the power to perform his magic and com-
pel the spirits of either heaven or hell to do his bidding."

Mitch explained. "In Europe, what he did was forbidden by the Church, but not with such brutality as witchcraft, because witches were pagan heretics and mostly women, and he was more often than not a priest of the Church. And he still considered himself a powerful member of the Church even when evoking demons. The terms Satanist and devil worshiper or demonologist are inventions of the last hundred, hundred and fifty years, and came about mostly through cheap, sensational novels, as many of today's misconceptions still do."

Charlie speeded up her speed reading and gathered the connection to the vandalism at Columbia Cemetery consisted of certain odd markings on the ground around certain grave sites, overturned and damaged gravestones, dead animals left on graves, as well as odd lights spotted by passers by, and traces of candle wax and burned grass.

When asked what natural disasters a modern high priest would be trying to assuage or avert, Mitch noted there seemed to be plenty about the area. Wildfires, wild animals, modern business ethics, rape of the land, rape of the poor . . .

"Know what I think? I think I'm feeling good enough that you should see if you could make plane reservations for you and Libby to get home tomorrow." Edwina flew in from out of the blue again. "I am grateful for your help while I was unable to handle things, but you got me back on my feet, and you need to get back to your life and so do I."

You're just doing this to make me feel guilty. "Seems like you're still in a lot of pain. Are you sure?"

"Isn't that what I just said? And if the medicine can't help the pain, I don't see what you can do for it. I'm learning to deal with it. Bring me some more coffee when you come back."

Charlie managed to book seats but at astronomical prices—it being so late—for Monday afternoon. Returning to the kitchen for Edwina's coffee, she met her daughter still half asleep, pop-topping a diet Coke. Libby wore a T-shirt she'd borrowed, stolen, or accepted from some guy that started at her shoulders and came to her knees managing to conceal nothing in between.

"Mom, I need to ask you a question."

"Shoot."

"Did you love my dad?"

"No." Charlie tried to get herself and the coffee pot to the back door but her daughter blocked the way.

"Then I'm not a love child. Like, I'm just a mistake, huh?"

Love child? Where did that come from? "Honey, you're the most precious thing in my life. You know that."

"Yeah, right." Libby stepped aside for her to pass.

"Hey, I've got some good news. I just booked us on a plane out of here tomorrow afternoon. Grandma's feeling better and says we should go home."

"Oh, might know. Just when things were getting interesting."

"What things? Where did you kids go last night?" I can't do anything right.

But Libby skulked off to the shower in the basement in the grip of abject dejection, without bothering to answer.

Little Deborah Tollerude sat on the narrow runner of new sod between the massive deck and the funeral fence, a tiny, almost elfin, child with long dark hair tied back in a white bow. Wiggims stood on his hind feet on her lap, his front legs encircling her neck to bat at the bow from each side. That cat was not normal. The child appeared bewitched.

Libby emerged in shorts and halter to sit on the back step next to them and brush-dry her hair in the hot sun. It snapped and gleamed, growing lighter as it dried. Charlie knew a moment of unaccustomed tranquility. The warmth felt good to the bone. Everyone in her world was safe. Her errant stomach felt soothed. She'd imagined the mountain lion. And they were going home tomorrow. She'd be back on the job by Tuesday.

"What's Wiggims doing to that kid?" Libby stared through the black spear fence as Jennifer Tollerude stepped out onto the deck, still in her bathrobe and slippers.

"How do you know Wiggims?" Charlie asked, suddenly alert and not sure why.

"Who's Wiggims?" Edwina set the paper down in her lap and lit a cigarette. She kept the pack in the same pocket as the little bulbs at the end of the tubes draining bloody fluid from the incisions in her chest and stomach. "Oh, you mean that cat? Belongs to Lita Kelso. Always figured it was her familiar," she added dryly.

Charlie was deciding whether to insist Libby tell where she'd been the night before or mention the dead cat in the Shop of Mystery's window and ask Edwina if she thought Lita Kelso might have some connection to the Satanism thing, when she realized the birds had gone silent.

Then she heard why.

"Male."

It was very clear. It was also clear that Libby heard it when the rubber hair brush bounced off the step and the kid was on her feet, her hands to her mouth. At the same time, Wiggims Kelso shot straight into the air and Deborah screamed. The house cat came down on the run and tore off across the huge deck. Jennifer rushed to her child, who had a bloody scratch on one cheek.

"What's the matter?" Edwina asked.

Her answer came from the alley in the form of a deep-throated *ruowoo*.

"Libby, help me get your grandmother in the house," Charlie heard her own panic through the buzz of shock in her ears.

But Libby'd turned to stone, and her grandmother had started off across the backyard toward the gate, still moving with painful slowness.

"Mom, that was a mountain lion. Get back here."

"I know. I want to see him. I'm not afraid of any cougar."

Jennifer Tollerude stood holding her daughter, as if too stunned to move either.

This was crazy. Before Charlie could sort out her wits from

her muscles and get to Edwina, her mother stood looking over the gate, holding herself erect with both hands on its top railing, showing no hint of what was on the other side.

When she did get there, Charlie absently laid a hand over one of her mother's and was startled at how cold and frail it felt.

"There's no cougar," Edwina whispered.

Charlie didn't see one either.

Unless you live along a creek or next to standing water, a Dumpster, or horse pasture, flies and mosquitoes are little problem in Boulder's high arid atmosphere. A screened-in porch rather than an open deck is often a clue that someone moved in from points East and remodeled before discovering that.

But it was neither standing water nor garbage that attracted swarms of flies to the concrete pad in front of Edwina's garage. As if cued, the promised hot wind moaned down from the mountainside a few blocks away and whispered a dirge in the leafy vines that made Edwina's open wire fence a solid one. It moved on to sough plaintively through the huge pines in Lita Kelso's back yard across the alley.

"Mom, it was the mountain lion. I heard him," Libby whispered behind them.

Charlie and Edwina turned as one to deflect Libby Greene from the sight that attracted so many flies, but it was too late. The granddaughter was taller than either grandmother or mother and saw the body immediately.

"You said mountain lions didn't bother people," Charlie accused the elder Greene.

"No cougar did that, Charlie. There's a bullet hole in that man's forehead. You just can't see it because of the flies."

"Then how do you know?" Libby said, covering her mouth in earnest this time.

"Probably scared the cougar more than it did us."

The man's face was covered with insects, and Charlie wondered about the hole in the forehead too. There was no doubt about the body's gender. But for head hair and a patch of pubic, it was naked. The flaccid genitals lay shrunken and forlorn against an inner thigh.

He lay on his side, arms outstretched in front of him, knees slightly bent. A cloying odor engorged the air and grew in strength with Charlie's every breath.

Libby vomited up her diet Coke.

"Cougars prefer fresh meat," Edwina said dispassionately and turned to her imprisoned neighbor. "Call Kenny Eisenburg fast. Be useful for once."

But Jennifer carefully set her daughter down, gave a little moan, and slid to the deck like a heap of clothes deprived suddenly of the body that wore them.

CHAPTER 22

THAT WAS A stupid thing to do," Kenny told Charlie as official traffic filled Edwina's yard and the alley behind it. Edwina had stuck it out long enough to give a full accounting of what had happened from her point of view and gone back to her bed, obviously not dealing with her pain as well as she thought. "You hear a mountain lion roar in the alley, and instead of helping your kid and invalid mother into the house, you help them all up to the gate to look into the alley? I don't believe this. And I always thought you were so . . ."

"Cool?" Or so good at getting around? "I didn't lead them. I couldn't stop them. How long do you think he's been dead?"

"I'd guess twenty to thirty hours, depending on how he was stored. Takes about six to twelve hours for rigor normally to establish, usually holds for another six to twelve. Then another similar time period for the rigor to reverse itself that far. But it's been hot. Why?"

"I just had the feeling I may have seen him alive down on the mall, but that's ridiculous. How could I tell by looking at him in that condition. Never mind."

"Yes, mind. Who, down on the mall, did he make you think of?"

"Just a rude panhandler outside Lita Kelso's shop. But that man was alive for sure about twenty-four hours ago."

"He wasn't Marlin Wetzel?"

"No, this man was younger. I think I'd know Marlin even now. I didn't really get that good a look at the panhandler. It was just a feeling of recognition with nothing to back it up. This has been a stressful week, Kenny."

"Tell me what else you noticed. Even if it seems unimportant. Especially if it seems unimportant."

Charlie was sitting on the back step, Kenny in a nearby lawn chair. He was dressed in a light sportshirt and Dockers, evidently having planned to take the day off. She could still smell the body, although she knew it to be covered. Deborah Tollerude, her white ribbon-bow hanging loose to one side now, looked down on the whole grizzly scene from her high castle window, mother Jennifer apparently not on duty.

"It's what I *don't* remember, Kenny. I don't remember hearing a car. How did he get there and when? The mountain lion certainly didn't deliver him." Signs of a big cat were evident in the alley this time. It had recently sprayed a corner of Lita Kelso's garage.

"You probably weren't listening for a car, and since it's not an unusual sound from back there, you wouldn't have noticed it. Tell me what you did notice."

"Well, before we all heard the growl, Libby and I heard, 'Male.' "

"In thought-speak."

"Yeah. In English."

"Charlie, a man's dead. This is serious." But he was fighting a grin.

"Okay." She didn't believe it either. She just couldn't explain it. Life was filled with things you couldn't explain. Which didn't mean animals could talk. "Well, he obviously didn't die there, or we'd all have noticed him earlier. Uhhh, he'd probably lain for a while on a rack of some kind and on his stomach because there were white lines across his chest and thighs and his genitals weren't all gorged and swollen."

Kenny put down his pencil and had to bite his lip to keep

from breaking out in unbecoming crime-scene laughter, which wouldn't have set right with the neighbors and reporters on Emmy's lawn on the other side of the yellow tape. "Now where in hell, Detective Charlie, did you come up with shit like that?"

"Kenny, you would not believe the stuff that crosses my desk."

"Any of it reliable?"

"Probably not. Libby and I have plane reservations for to-morrow afternoon. Any chance we'll make them?"

"Probably not. Now think back to when you first looked into the alley. Besides the body, was anything else different? Try to visualize this for me. Take your time."

"There's a really big deal coming down, Kenny. I have to get back." Instead of the alley, Charlie thought of all the empty seats she'd noticed on airliners. Is this what happened to the people who should have been sitting in them?

"Try for me. The sooner we get through this, the sooner you can leave."

Charlie closed her eyes and just let thoughts come, hoping he'd like one or two and let her catch her flight after all. "I remember my mother's hand being very cold on the top rail of the gate and all the flies on his face and wondering how she knew he had a bullet hole in his forehead under them and the weird sounding wind in the spruces in Lita's yard and . . . the black van parked . . ."

"The black van parked where, Charlie? Don't lose it now."

But Charlie opened her eyes. "You know I've been seeing a dark van around the neighborhood on and off all week. And remember when the prowler Emmy chased with the water gun a couple nights ago left the dead cat in the street? Didn't Libby say he'd jumped into a van and was driven off? Oh, and there's something I've been going to tell you, Kenny. I saw a cat in the same condition in Lita's Shop of Mystery on the mall yesterday morning, when I was hassled by that panhandler. She has to have something to do with all this. And all this happening right around here has to be connected. And she lives here."

He was on his feet, and that brought a barrage from the thickening line behind the tape. Minicams rolled and Kenny stood between them and Charlie. "Come show me where you saw this van."

Out in the alley they were shielded from the press, if not all the neighbors, by the garage and the emergency vehicles blocking it. The body was in a bag on a gurney being slid into a waiting ambulance—where it had lain, chalked in outline on the concrete apron. Charlie wondered how much worse the odor would have been if the wind weren't kicking up dust devils and loose paper products from garbage cans, stirring the mix with grit and heat.

Jennifer Tollerude, still in robe and slippers, stood by the ambulance, staring at the chalk marks, her normally shiny cap of hair lackluster and tousled. Officer Darla was trying to talk to her but getting no response.

Charlie walked Detective Eisenburg over to Lita Kelso's garage and pointed out the dried weed–strewn strip of land between it and the neighboring lot. There was no black van there now. "Maybe I imagined it."

Kenny knelt to inspect the tracks where vehicles obviously parked regularly. "Wasn't there a van in the alley here the night you terrified me by hearing a mountain lion think in English?"

"I think there was. But the town's full of four-wheel-drive vehicles." You couldn't see around them to turn right on red at traffic lights or pull safely out of parking spaces—even in Howard's Jeep, which was dated and small by now.

Charlie glanced up to see the deck of the second story of the residence next to Lita's filled with curious neighbors. She walked over to ask them if they'd noticed a vehicle parked on what would be their side of Lita's garage. Several had, and one had noticed it driving off up the alley.

"Didn't an officer question you?" Kenny asked them.

"Yeah," one yelled back. Charlie unofficially ID'd all but two elderly women as summer students. "But she didn't ask us about the van."

"You know, if that van delivered the body, it's going to have a tell-tale odor for a long while," Charlie said.

"Detective Charlie, you amaze me." Detective Kenny grinned without humor and turned on his heel to charge Officer Darla.

Charlie studied the ground he had just studied, hoping not to find anything—he was already unhappy with her and she'd never get home. The ground was too dry to leave patterns of tire treads, but there was a fresh oil leak. Did that mean the van was an old Detroit model? Or did new cars still leak oil? Or maybe it had been injured in a wreck? She touched it, smelled her fingers.

Not oil. What then? Leaky radiator?

Don't start being helpful, or you'll never get back to work.

Yeah but if I read Kenny right and he thought I might be a threat to his self-esteem rather than an easy lay, he'd send me packing faster.

And when exactly did you start reading people correctly?

A shriek that ended in a wail startled Charlie, and she swung around to see Jennifer Tollerude struggling with Officer Darla.

"No . . . no . . . I told them." She lunged as if she wanted to beat on the ambulance, and Kenny grabbed her too. "All wrong . . . I told them. Idiots."

"Charlie? Can you help us?" Kenny called.

Officer Darla and Charlie sat in Jennifer Tollerude's sunroom, where the windows were unblocked by any neighbor's house. They plied her with fruit juice from her refrigerator and wet washcloths from the powder room next to it.

She shivered almost as violently as Edwina had when coming out of the anesthetic. "Your mother had something to do with this. Don't think I don't know it."

"My mother was in Utah when your husband died."

"Oh, you don't fool me. You may be from California, but anybody can hire things like that done."

"Things like what?" the female cop asked, roughly.

But Jennifer lost her juice before they could find a vase or waste basket to keep it off the flowered upholstery of the wicker chaise or Jennifer either. And she refused to do anymore than break into sobs with further questioning.

"Do you think your daughter would look after the little girl here while we take her mother in for questioning?" Darla rested her hands on her hips—hands short and solid like her figure, blunt like her face. No rings, no nonsense. Charlie decided she'd rather tangle with Kenny.

"Libby detests baby-sitting, after several years of woman's work at girl wages. And somebody has to keep an eye on my mother."

"You don't let up do you?"

"I'll stay for awhile," Charlie offered innocently.

Kenny didn't like the idea at all, but things grew too busy for him to have much choice. His parting words were, "Don't snoop, Detective Charlie. That's an official order. I'll get somebody else over here to do the snooping the second I can spare him."

That was exactly what Charlie planned to do, and with an official challenge like that, she had little choice.

CHAPTER 23

———————◆———————

D EBORAH TOLLERUDE allowed Charlie to brush her hair
and tie it back with a fresh ribbon and even to wash out
the cat-inflicted wound on her cheek—but in total silence. Charlie couldn't think of anything to say, either. Poor kid. Her dad
murdered, her cat disappeared, and now they'd taken away her
mother.

And it all happened in a strange new house in a very strange
neighborhood. Charlie's throat ached with wanting to comfort
the child, but she didn't know how to begin.

Deborah's room was all white-painted furniture and flounces.
Dolls, stuffed animals, and floor pillows, most larger than she,
and posed to the best advantage as you entered from the hall.
Muted rose colors, pinks, and off-whites. It looked more ready
to show to a prospective buyer than to play in. The kid's bathroom was bigger than Edwina's kitchen.

"Want to show me around the house? Maybe we'll find something to do until your mother comes home."

Deborah took Charlie's hand and led her from room to room,
somber, noncommittal.

Four bedrooms and a study upstairs. Each bedroom with its
own full bath, the master suite with a dressing room as well. The
study was a "his" kind of place—dark leather desk chair, small
couch, and easy chair. Massive dark-wood desk, its top empty
but for a lamp and blotter. Empty wastebasket in dark leather

to match the furniture, and a corner window with a view of tree-tops and rooftops and the Flatirons. Maybe Andy hadn't had time to really move into it before his death.

"Have you had lunch?" Charlie asked when they reached the head of the stairs.

"Mommy says I'm not supposed to talk to people at your house." But the soft voice cracked and tears spilled out of the kid's eyes. Charlie found herself sitting on the top step, holding Deborah Tollerude and crying right along with her.

As it turned out, the little girl hadn't even had breakfast.

A peanut butter and jelly sandwich and tall glass of milk later, Deborah forgot she wasn't supposed to talk to Charlie. "Are you sad too?"

"You know, I think I just felt so bad for you, I couldn't help crying?" Charlie said. "Now we both have red puffy eyes and look silly together. Suppose that makes us buds?"

The answer was an adult, searching look. "Want to see some more of the house?"

What Charlie wanted to do was go back upstairs and riffle that imposing desk, but with those solemn eyes on her she hadn't the nerve to suggest it.

Formal living room and dining room, separated by a central hall, furnished in heavy square Spanish or French or Italian provincial—Charlie didn't know one from another. A powder room, laundry room, large eat-in kitchen, and sunroom.

And carpeted stairs leading down to the walk-out basement, which was mostly family room with a huge entertainment center and fifty-inch TV. Puffy furniture to lounge on, a gas fireplace—there'd been one of those in the living room upstairs too, and another in the master bedroom. Another bathroom. What, three fireplaces and five and a half bathrooms—for three people?

It wasn't that Charlie was unused to ostentation. Or unaware that it was a relative thing. Her little condo might look ostentatious to someone in a bombed-out building in Sarajevo. Ostentation abounded in the entertainment industry, the wealthy neighborhoods of Southern California.

Richard Morse, her boss, lived in a Tudor-style mansion in Beverly Hills, alone with his Vietnamese housekeeper. Gardeners and cleaning help were hired from outside by the hour. It was just that something like this in her old neighborhood where Lance Kelso had lived in his ratty little house and played his dirty little tricks was disorienting.

Charlie was so lost in thought she thought she must have imagined what the little girl said to her next, two questions together with no wait for answers.

"Was that Mr. Tollerd they covered up and took away in a truck?" And, "Should we play with Missy?" Deborah started off across the room, past the NordicTrack, Exercycle, StairMaster, and weight bench to a door in the far wall.

"You found your kitty? That's wonderful." And if by Mr. Tollerd you mean Mr. Tollerude, why isn't he Daddy?

"Yes," Deborah said sadly, "but I can't get the door unlocked, can you?"

The door had no knob. Just an eye-level keyhole in a round metal plate too high for the child to reach. The lock looked much like the new deadbolt on Edwina's back door looked from the outside. "Honey, do you know where the key is?"

"No."

"Then how do you know Missy's in there?"

"I can hear her." Deborah put her ear to the line separating door from door jam. So did Charlie.

They were searching for a key when Kenny Eisenburg found them in the study, going through the desk.

"I should have known," he said.

"I can explain," Charlie answered.

Kenny had brought his ex-wife's daughter to look after Deborah until Jennifer recovered enough to come home. She'd collapsed under questioning and was now in Community Hospital.

Fran, the ex-wife's daughter, was a gum-chewing frazzle-haired teen in torn shorts, shredded T-shirt, holey tennies, wise-ass eyes, and careful makeup. She took one look at the little girl, blew a gum bubble, popped it, and moved the chew around on her braces until she could grin.

Deborah looked every bit as enchanted by this apparition as she had Wiggims that morning. She barely noticed when Charlie said good-bye.

Lita Kelso met them in the alley behind the house on her way to the gate in the Tollerudes' black fence. She was looking for Wiggims. Charlie wondered if he could be with Missy behind the locked door, but Detective Kenny took them each by an elbow and headed them back to Lita's house, pausing only to nod at an Animal Control officer looking for signs of the mountain lion.

Lita's house was, not surprisingly, as odd as Lita. Like Mitch's condo, the entire first floor was one room, a popular decorating ploy nowadays. But this was an old house and, like Edwina's, built for modest, cramped rooms—thus the five metal posts lined up down the middle of this "great room," obviously in lieu of the original load-bearing wall. Thick unpainted wooden slabs shielded the ceiling and floor from the post ends, opening up a dark house to what light could filter through beautiful old spruces front and back.

The decor was definitely third world. Charlie took a guess at Pacific Island. Nets with shells adorned roughened wood and burlap walls. Stairs along one wall, kitchen along the other. A couch made to look as if it was built inside a canoe, broken open and lying on its side. Chairs with strawlike seats and backs with frames of wooden poles held together by ropes. Woven baskets everywhere, filled with everything from gritty pasta to women's magazines.

Matting that overlapped in places to trip the unwary covered the floor. Four ceiling fans stirred dust and the odor of cat box. A tape played primitive music that, to Charlie's tone-deaf ears, repeated four or five relentless notes strummed on a rusty water pipe and a garbage can lid. The rhythm section sounded like a couple of dried gourds being whipped with a fan belt.

And tripping down the stairs to come to a surprised halt at the bottom came Lance Kelso and Heather Tynne. Everybody stared at everybody until Lance broke the deadlock. "Hey, Kenny, how's it going, man?"

"Just where were you this afternoon, Charlie?" Heather went on the attack. "I was so embarrassed. I couldn't believe you'd pull a no-show like that for something that important. And not even bother to cancel your appearance."

"You were going to make an appearance?" Kenny asked.

"I don't know what she's talking about. But Lita, I wanted to tell you I saw Wiggims just before we discovered the body."

"You discovered a body, Charlie?" That was Lance.

"What do you mean, you don't know what I'm talking about? You promised last night you'd come up to Chautauqua to the screenwriting seminar."

"Did you see where he went?"

"I didn't promise, accept, or acknowledge your order to be there. He was playing with Deborah Tollerude when the mountain lion came along, and he took off heading north across their deck."

"A mountain lion came along? You editors lead such exciting lives."

"Yeah, can you get Brace up here? I got a situation." This from Kenny on the pineapple. "The Kelso place across the alley from the Greene home." He hung the stem back onto the plastic pineapple phone. "Jesus, Charlie, next time you find a body, don't do it on a Sunday. Weekends are too busy already."

Lance Kelso's amusement threatened his superior composure but he managed to wave good-bye without losing his authority. "Kenny, next time I'm in town, we talk. Got a plane to catch."

"Sit."

"You're kidding."

"This is murder one, Kelso. Not even money buys immunity. Not even in Boulder."

"It can eventually ruin low-level careers, though. Especially in Boulder."

"Sit." But Kenny was sweating. Charlie couldn't see any gun in his pants this time.

"I've got to go find Wiggims." Lita wore cheesecloth bloomers over tights today, and gossamer scarfs hid her chest and upper arms.

"Sit, Naomi . . . I mean, Mrs. Kelso."

Lita Kelso or Naomi of the Seven Veils insisted upon serving them iced tea as they waited for Kenny's backup.

"You sure he was all right?" she asked Charlie over the tray of glasses. "What if the mountain lion ate him?"

Charlie had a hunch that's what had happened to most of the missing cats in the neighborhood but said, "He was booking. I doubt anything could have caught him. Do you think you could turn down the noise, uh . . . music? I have a headache."

Unlike the Shop of Mystery, there were no wind chimes here. They would have been more pleasant than the whiny music.

Kenny made everybody but himself take a seat. He paced importantly and then turned on Lita. "So, just what is it you do to these dead cats, Mrs. Kelso?"

"I don't kill them."

"I know. You prepare them for burial or stuff them, don't you?"

CHAPTER 24

❖

LITA AND HEATHER had similar hairdos, one bleached, the other dyed flat black, both that permed shaggy crinkle Charlie couldn't duplicate with her own uncontrollable curls. She envied them that, if not the color jobs. Lita's was thinner after more years of chemical damage.

Lita Kelso had a sideline—she was a kitty mortician. People overly fond of their feline pets, who could not bear to have them cremated, would bring them to Lita.

Kenny Eisenburg had finally received the lab reports on the once-thought-to-be-mutilated animals. They were instead eviscerated, embalmed, and stuffed.

Someone had been stealing the mortal remains before they were stuffed. But, not wanting to attract official attention to her basement sideline, Lita had not reported the thefts. Look at what had happened to Edwina's retirement home for lab rats.

When Officer Brace arrived, Kenny took Lita downstairs so she could show him the mortuary.

Upstairs, her son kept rolling his eyes, sighing, and glancing at his expensive watch. He moved from the chair Kenny had pointed out to the fourth step on the stairs—in the chair his knees had ended up nearly under his chin. Officer Brace came to attention with the movement but didn't pull out his gun or anything else.

"This is not good for property values," Heather said, throwing Lance an uneasy look. She fidgeted a while longer and, the tinkle in her giggle growing scratchy, said, "So Charlie, you didn't show at the seminar because of the body in the alley? Your client Reynelda Goff was there."

"I'll bet she was."

"Everybody waited and waited. It was embarrassing."

Tough titties. "I had no intention of going."

"What, you're too good for the local writers?" Lance leaned back, his elbows on the next step up, with the amused smirk she could remember on a younger, dirtier face. "Too bad you missed Buddy." Apparently he, Heather, and Buddy MacCallister had dropped in on the screenwriting seminar in hopes of ganging up on Charlie.

You bastard. "My offer to be of no use to him still holds, Lance. You're the millionaire, why don't you help him?"

"He's not my responsibility." He was waiting for her anger to surface. She'd be damned if she'd give him the pleasure.

"Mine either."

"He just wanted to talk to you," Heather, the divorcée, said. "You owe him something."

"How do you figure that?"

"Well, you . . . bore him a child," the real estate agent replied in Biblese.

"He's got a wife and kids, he can be their responsibility. Libby and I don't need him." What we need is Keegan Monroe.

"Of course, if you've got Mitch Hilsten all sewn up, I don't suppose you have to be nice to anybody. Even old lovers," Lance baited her. "But that doesn't mean Buddy has no rights to his daughter. Not these days."

Officer Brace was getting too interested in this stupid conversation. "What would he want with her? She doesn't have a cent. She has lots of bills though. He's welcome to those."

Just for revenge she ought to have Libby spend a couple of weeks with Buddy and family. They'd send her back in a hurry.

Of course, Buddy, not understanding the industry, would try to use the kid as leverage with Charlie, force her to use her contacts to get him work. And Libby might get hurt emotionally.

Lance, still amused, sat watching her scheme with herself. Good thing Libby's college fund was in Charlie's name. The deal was, Libby used it for college or she didn't get it.

Kenny and Lita returned, both looking as sober as Deborah Tollerude, and slipped by Lance to climb the stairs to the upper floor. Again, he and Heather exchanged interesting glances. Charlie wondered how Deborah and the bubble popping Fran were getting on, and Edwina and Libby, and the mountain lion and the Animal Control officer.

Charlie also wondered what was on the computer disks hidden in the pocket of her shorts, the odds of getting into Edwina's office at the university and using her computer to read them.

You know you should give them to Kenny.

He won't tell me what's on them for six months, and I need to know now. I know cops. If there's a dead body within a thirty-mile radius, nobody gets to leave town.

Charlie had taken the computer disks from Andy Tollerude's otherwise empty desk.

Lita Kelso and Kenny looked no happier when they came back down the stairs and Kenny warned everybody in the room not to leave town. Charlie could sense his delight in being able to order the millionaire around. She figured Lance sensed it too.

She was about to suggest they storm the locked room at the Tollerudes' to see if Wiggims and Missy were imprisoned there when Kenny whisked her off to Columbia Cemetery instead.

The weatherman was right for once. The wind blew strong and hot. They stood beside the grave of Tom Horn, hired gun and outlaw of the Old West, Charlie reliving the conception of her child. God knew what Kenny was thinking. Charlie and Buddy had "screwed" on this grave. Heather Tynne and Kenny Eisenburg on the next one over.

Charlie'd achieved no satisfaction—orgasm—from the act, Buddy apparently did enough to make half of Libby. But Heather . . .

"What do you see here, Charlie?"

"History." Guilt, embarrassment, remorse, resentment. Oh yeah, resentment, major, total, cataclysmic resentment. "Why?"

Lance had hidden two or three tombstones to the left, at the Adams family grave site—no kidding.

"Did he put you up to it? Or did you put him up to it?"

Kenny knelt to inspect the not-yet-resodded earth above the remains of Tom Horn. "Who up to what?"

"Lance up to witnessing what happened here sixteen years ago. I may not be able to leave town, Kenny, but my memory is just fine."

He stood and ran a finger to tickle down the fine hairs on her arm. "Charlie, that's not why I brought you here. Honestly. I keep forgetting how much that night upset you. Lets just leave it that I'm not proud of what happened. Okay?"

No, it's not okay. Your life wasn't ruined that night.

Your life wasn't either, Greene. Don't be such a whiner. Look what you've got. A beautiful healthy daughter and a dynamite job. She's almost raised and you're still in your early thirties. You'll be way ahead of other mothers on the career track. So you didn't get to be a cheerleader. Big deal.

Oh, thank you very much, Pollyanna.

"I brought you here," said the guy who'd played in the band instead of on the team, "because I hoped we could noodle it out together. Maybe some of that 'stuff that crosses your desk' could help us. I did not bring you here to stir up bad memories of Boulder."

"For instance."

"For instance, why does everything around here happen at

this grave? And don't tell me it's because four dumb kids had too good a time here sixteen years ago."

"Five. Your friend, Lance the jerk—"

"Okay, five. And the mountain lion didn't leave the dead deer here. Other than that—"

Sixteen years ago this grave had been grass covered. Prickly grass, as Charlie remembered well, but grass. Now the churned earth had been raked back in place, but there was still a slight indentation to remind them of Andy Tollerude.

The grave next to it was that of Charlie and Elizabeth Horn. Whereas Tom had a low red granite stone, theirs was gray. They were seven and nine years older than he but died of old age, Charles in 1930 and his wife in 1940. Tom died in 1903 at the age of forty-two. Cousin, brother? If Charlie ever knew the family relationship here, she couldn't remember it now.

In Reynelda Goff's novel, Tom Horn had been framed for the murder of the fifteen-year-old boy in Wyoming, but was a known and feared hired gun and bounty hunter long before that. He was well acquainted with the Hollywood-immortalized Butch Cassidy and the Sundance Kid.

Charlie could remember pouring over grisly, grainy black-and-white photos of Tom Horn's body taken after the hanging. She and a crowd of others had huddled around Lance Kelso on the wooden platform of the school merry-go-round at Flatirons Elementary, the playground of which abutted the cemetery and was visible from where she stood now, next to Charles Horn.

Lance had even tried to sell some dried-up sticklike things resembling emaciated dog turds, claiming they were some of the outlaw's fingers mummified by time and cut off the corpse by the undertaker.

The selling of trophy parts as collector's items was not an unusual occurrence when the executed was a famous outlaw. They'd all learned this from Professor Burrows, who would sit on his front steps and tell the neighborhood kids stories, observing their reactions under shaggy gray eyebrows so long they hung down behind his wire-rims and almost into his eyes. He taught in the school of engineering, but his hobby was the history of the Old West. And his stories were a lot more interesting than Howard Greene's. Her father, who was mostly bald and had little in the way of eyebrows, was a professor of European history, hence Charlie's unlikely name.

IN LOVING MEMORY OF TOM HORN and the birth and death dates were all that was written on the polished red granite stone sitting upright and shaped like a tablet from a Charleton Heston–Moses movie. A concrete funeral urn on a concrete pedestal sat next to the outlaw's marker. The urn was coated with embossed bumps that were chipping away but were meant to be flowers. It held a dying plant that whipped and nodded in the wind rustling the branches of a scraggy pine tree nearby. The wind pricked dry, sneezy impulses from the lining of Charlie's nose and dried up the fluid lake her contacts needed to swim on.

In the heat, that wind was over-ripe with the odor of dog sh . . . poop.

Charlie pointed out hoof prints and other tracks on and around the grave. Two joggers, ignoring the mountain lion scare—one running up Ninth, the other passing them on College.

"How could anybody hold Satanic rites, even in the middle of the night this close to College Avenue, without being seen?"

"Nobody but Lance noticed *us* sixteen years ago."

"We didn't use candles. I think we should come out here tonight and chant and light candles, lanterns, and flashlights and wave them around. See if anybody notices."

"If they do, what does it prove? I'm pretty sure those are deer hoof prints, not devil prints," he said as she bent over to study them. "This place is full of critters. I don't know how the dead get any sleep." He identified raccoon prints, squirrel, magpie, crow, skunk, mountain lion and dog within a very small radius of Tom Horn.

170

Charlie was interested only in the lion print. "How do you know that's not a dog?"

"According to my expert sources in the Boulder mountain park system, a dog has one frontal lobe here." He pointed to the largest pad beneath the toes. "And toenails. The cats have two lobes and keep their nails retracted, so they don't turn up in prints unless there's heavy snow. Hey, you want to hear about cats? Here I am a detective and what do I get to detect? Cults, religious or irreligious, and animal shit. Story of my life."

Charlie noticed the wind whip the tough old plant in the urn until it loosened on one side. She pulled a long matchstick out of the dirt exposed by the uprooting—one of those foot-long wooden matches used to light fireplaces and barbecues. Raw blond wood on the end that wasn't in the dirt, dirt-darkened and damp on the other, the match head used up. "That's funny."

"Probably used to light a candle or a lantern."

"Yeah, but the geranium or whatever looks like its dying from lack of water, yet the dirt's moist."

This time, Kenny pulled out a pocket knife, finally impressing Charlie. People with pocket knives were sure to be useful. He dug deep, removed a small clod, rolled it in his fingers and then smelled them. "Whatever somebody's been putting on that plant, I don't think it's water."

CHAPTER 25

◆

KENNY EISENBURG rushed Charlie up Broadway to his house in his Saab, both of which he inherited from his grandmother.

"Your grandmother drove a Saab?"

"Hey, my grandma was with-it. Of course, if you look close you'll notice there's lots of body work been done on this—she kind of drove longer than she should have."

The old Saab slowed to a crawl, caught behind a mass of black Spandex butts lurching from side to side over high narrow bike seats because the attached bodies hunched so intensely over low handle bars. The process looked positively painful, and this wasn't the first time Charlie wondered if these guys ever had trouble procreating.

She would have been laying on the horn about now, but Kenny seemed to take this delay philosophically for somebody in such a hurry seconds before. World-class athletes came to train in Boulder's thin air in order to build lung stamina that would make them more competitive at sea level. And cyclists to build tiny butts and barrel thighs on the steep climbs as well.

They turned left on a side street before Broadway rose up out of the valley to what used to be called Dog Patch on one side, where Buddy MacCallister's folks used to live, and pricey Wonderland Hills on the mountain side of the road, where Mitch Hilsten had acquired his most recent condo away from home.

Two more turns and the Saab bumped up a long alley, coming to a stop in front of a restored carriage house/woodshed that had become a one car garage/workshop. It and the house that went with it were painted a powder blue like Mitch's eyes and were decorated with glass carriage lamps. On the other side of a high wooden fence, the traffic roared past on Broadway.

"Whoa, this is old."

"Cellar's still got a dirt floor," Kenny said with pride. "Used to be a farmhouse out in the country."

Inside, the walls were thick and real plaster, the floors old wood, the rooms tiny. Except for the kitchen, which had been expanded and modernized, and the master suite upstairs, which *was* the upstairs. A deck had been built off it on top of the kitchen expansion facing west, where a sweep of windows overlooked the deck. Most of the wall below the windows was a home office.

Charlie looked longingly at the computer, not the king-size bed, and fingered the disks in her pocket.

Kenny explained that when his ex and the girls lived here, his office was out in the carriage house.

"In the winter when there aren't any leaves on the trees, you can see the mountains better." He led her onto the deck. Roofs crowded around this once-solitary house, some old, some new, one still in the building stage and naked of shingles.

"Where did you put the kids?"

"The little TV room downstairs was their bedroom. It was crowded." Kathy now lived with a guy who had a bigger house but before that had helped Kenny plan renovations. "You think it's hard to live with teenagers, you ought to try it with your house all torn up."

"Kenny, your house is wonderful. But I think I should get back. You know Libby, and frankly I'm kind of worried about Deborah Tollerude. She thinks her lost kitty is behind a locked door in the basement that doesn't have a doorknob. Wait a minute—you must have searched that house when nobody could find Andy's body. It would be the northeast corner room."

"I was on another case then. I have seen a sketch diagram though. Like, maybe there was a big exercise room down there?"

"All the exercise equipment is out in the family room now."

He unfolded two lounge chairs that had been laid flat against the wind. "Here, sit. I'll be back in a minute."

"I just told you I have to get back."

"Listen, you're the smart-ass that found a dead body in the alley and ruined my Sunday. You can at least let me eat lunch."

He returned with a tray and two lunches. Charlie looked down at her shorts and sandals. What was there about her that made guys want to feed her?

But it was mid afternoon, and the tuna salad sandwich and cold milk were too tempting to pass up, even with the fine lacing of grit incoming on the wind.

"You rushed back here for lunch? I thought it had something to do with the dying plant in the cemetery urn."

"It did. See that?" He pointed to a redwood planter built into the deck railing.

"Geraniums." Charlie knew geraniums, petunias, and lilacs and that was about it. Oh yeah, and roses. Edwina used to have roses growing up trellises on the side of the house now shaded by the monstrolith.

"And the plant in the urn looked just like that, except it wasn't flowering and wasn't as healthy."

"You came all the way here to check out a geranium? They're all over the neighborhood around the cemetery."

"I wanted to show you my house. I wanted to eat lunch. And I wanted to check the dirt around the roots of these healthy plants."

"What do you think was on that plant in the cemetery urn if it wasn't water?"

"My guess is beer, blood, or wine." Kenny Eisenburg ate the other half of her sandwich and relaxed, enjoying himself while

174

she fidgeted, before he dug around in his own geraniums. "And there's one last reason I brought you here."

"Come on, Kenny . . ." Charlie was at the edge of the lounge and poised to take off for the door, but the detective grinned and bent over her lounge. He straightened, holding a computer disk.

"Want to give me the other one? They made a very clear outline in your shorts."

Charlie handed it over. "I was going to give them to you. I just wanted to read them first. I knew you wouldn't tell me what was on them."

"You got these at the Tollerudes', didn't you? They could be evidence in a murder case, Charlie, maybe two. There are penalties for tampering with evidence." He read the handwritten label—something Charlie hadn't had time to do. "Hey, they're even in Word for Windows. I've got that. And would you believe I'm going to let you help me read them?"

"You are? I mean no, I wouldn't believe it."

"You got to stop underestimating cops, Charlie."

But she figured it out when the first menu came up on his screen. The file names were abbreviated as usual and unintelligible to anyone but the disk's owner. Still, it didn't take long to distinguish the fact that rat references appeared a little too often. Files titled "ORDii" and "LEPIDA" and "MIDDEN" made it pretty clear these disks were what had been stolen in the break-in at Charlie's mother's house.

She picked up the other disk to read the label while Kenny began scrolling through documents. GREENE, a date, software type, and barely legible explanations of what type of information might be found on this particular backup disk.

"This'll take all day," Kenny griped, giving up on the first disk and bringing up the menu on the next. More unintelligible directory and file names—

"Wait," Charlie said, hanging over his shoulder. "Back up, no, stop. There—REALEST. Could be real estate."

"So she keeps her investments mixed up with her work files."

"That's a directory, not a file, and I don't think she has any investments. There—CTYCODES. Try that—city codes, what do you bet? I knew she wouldn't sit still for having the Tollerude house block her sunlight without a fight."

But the first file in the directory dealt with Edwina's search for prohibitions against her keeping rats in her basement. She'd evidently been down to city hall or the public library and copied out zoning ordinances for her neighborhood. You couldn't keep any more than three of one kind of pet without a kennel permit, which was not allowed in that neighborhood.

But the rats had apparently come under the chicken ordinance, and chickens were no longer allowed in this part of town—nor horses, mules, donkeys, cattle, and so on—because of the population density. Charlie could remember horses, donkeys, chickens, and geese out in Dog Patch, but on one-and two-acre lots. She could just imagine Emmy Wetzel with a rooster for morning reveille.

The next file, MEETING, contained a series of notes on a neighborhood meeting to discuss a rezoning application. There was no date for the meeting, but Edwina had keyed in her notes a little less than a year ago. The Hogarths, Emmy Wetzel, the Goffs, and Lita Kelso had been there because she'd noted some of their comments and named others Charlie didn't know. They'd met at Flatirons Elementary and heard various explanations from unnamed city officials—Edwina referred to them as CtyOaf One, Two, and Three—of what they could do to keep the size of new construction and remodels within certain limits.

"This doesn't seem to be going anywhere."

"Why don't we ask Edwina what happened at these meetings and what there might be on these disks worth breaking into a house for?" Charlie said.

The trip back in grandma's Saab was faster than the one out. Any Spandex butts on bicycles were damn lucky not to be on the road ahead this time. "She's going to have to talk to me now, and I don't care if she's napping, doped up, or what. This time I want answers. This time we have a body almost at her back door and she's in town."

"You suspect my mom? Kenny, she's hardly in any shape to hurt someone else. And she *was* in Utah when Andy got iced."

He looked away from where they were hurtling and a little old man, bent almost double into the hot wind, made it to the curb only by chance, incredible good fortune and in the absolute nick of time. "Got iced?"

"All that stuff crossing my desk? Makes you talk funny." This was the first Charlie noticed this guy capable of speed.

"Edwina's been too involved with the Tollerudes, Charlie. I was hoping you could shed some light on any information that might be useful before I had to badger a sick old woman."

"She's not a sick old woman. She's just post-op. Perfectly lucid now, and her brain could eat ten of yours for breakfast and still starve."

But to her mother, Charlie said, "Edwina, we've got to talk and now. You want some coffee?"

They settled on iced tea in the tiny kitchen. The wind and grit make it unpleasant outside.

Kenny brought out the 3.5 floppies Charlie had found in Andrew Tollerude's desk drawer. "So, why do you suppose he would be interested in your computer documents?"

Edwina sent Charlie for her little reading glasses and peered down through them at the labels on the disks, then up over them at Kenny. "He couldn't have been dead for a month if he broke into my house while I was in the hospital."

"Maybe it was Jennifer," Charlie offered and, seeing the pain reconfiguring the muscle and veins in her mother's neck, went to the sink for more blasters. Edwina took them but said, "You know what I think I really need? A scotch and water."

"Do you have any here? Like, do you think you should mix alcohol and your medication?"

Edwina lit a long brown cigarette and took a deep drag. She

gave Charlie a hard look. "Like, I think I should mix them. Scotch is in that cupboard above the sink, as you know very well."

Charlie used to serve her friends gin and vodka when her parents weren't home and then replace what was stolen with water. It didn't take Edwina and Howard long to learn to appreciate scotch, which Charlie never figured out how to replicate.

So they went to frat parties on the Hill or convinced somebody's older sibling to buy them beer. Other drugs weren't hard to come by either, but Charlie stuck with beer until she realized it added too many calories to her thighs and helped her to conceive a daughter.

She discovered wine in college and found she could better control it and eating sparsely and life in general. Charlie decided last month to keep no booze in her home in Long Beach after Libby invited the football team in to a party while Charlie was in Utah trying to save Edwina's butt in a murder case. She'd banished booze even knowing Libby could always find it at friends' houses, even knowing at a gut level—quite literally—that her own particular addiction had become her work.

All this reflection touched off by Edwina's throwaway comment about Charlie's obvious knowledge of where the liquor cupboard was located.

"I was looking for a way to stop the building of the California monstrolith," Edwina said, holding on to her middle while Charlie fixed her drink. "There are laws against blocking a neighbor's sunlight, but lots are small and narrow in this part of town. You can't plant a tree anywhere that won't one day shade neighbors too. So it's not that difficult to obtain a variance, particularly if you get permission from your neighbors.

"Nobody asked my permission on anything, and that house was up, roofed, and being moved into before I could fight through the bureaucratic tangle to get a complaint underway. Once a building is up and lived in, nobody's going to insist it be torn down around a family. Andrew Tollerude claimed all the neighbors had been notified of the height and size requirements of his house and no one objected. He called me a liar when I said I didn't get any notification. I didn't kill that man, but I could have."

CHAPTER 26

A NDREW TOLLERUDE had not only built his house between Edwina and her place in the sun and called her a
liar, he'd offered to buy her out for about half what her home
had been worth before he built next door. "Like he said, with
no southern exposure this old house was worthless. Only the
land was valuable now, and the house would have to be razed
and hauled away. An added expense to the buyer who would
want to build a newer, bigger house."

"That buyer would still have to build most of the house in
the backyard to get any sunlight," Charlie said. "And that would
block Emmy's sun."

"Then you buy out Emmy and build a bigger, better house
toward the front of the her lot and shade the Hogarths," Edwina
added to the story.

"Sounds pretty paranoid," Kenny said. "I don't think
Tollerude had that kind of money. And believe it or not, there
are people who don't like sun. Look at Lita Kelso's place, and
remember Professor Burrows?"

"Yes, but you notice that the Goffs have opened up the old
Burrows house. Light and airy is what's in now." Charlie's stucco
condo wasn't in at all. She wasn't there during the sunny hours
enough to care. It would be interesting to know what Heather
Tynne would consider a good price for listing Edwina's house.

"Can't you think of anything Andy or Jennifer might have been looking for on those disks?"

"Not unless they were looking for my financial statements, which are on here." Edwina picked up one of the floppies. "Or my will, which isn't. They were waiting for me to drop dead of old age any minute. Maybe they thought they could convince my heir to sell out. Surprised I'm not the one who's dead."

Edwina had always had the knack for looking twenty years older than she was. Her laugh/squint crinkles were highly evident no matter how joyless her expression. Sun and cigarettes had helped a lot. Charlie remembered both Jennifer and Heather's astonishment over Edwina still being gainfully employed.

"Young people today look at someone like me and assume I'm living off Social Security checks taken straight from their paychecks. Well, I'm not."

"What I don't understand," Charlie said, hoping to change the subject before a generational war got going, "is what real estate has to do with Tom Horn and mountain lions."

Edwina looked totally blank.

But Detective Eisenburg said shrewdly, "It's possible there's more than one strange thing happening here. This *is* Boulder."

Charlie was about to insist she and Kenny go over and check on Deborah Tollerude and his ex-stepdaughter, when they and Libby appeared at the back door, wearing the oddest expressions.

"Mom, we found the missing kitties," Libby said.

"In that locked basement room? Did you find a key?"

"Fran picked it with a nail file. It was awesome."

Kenny stared at Fran who shrugged and snapped her gum. All three girls were chewing, Charlie noticed.

"I think you guys better come over and take a look."

Edwina insisted upon hobbling along instead of staying put, resting, and waiting for a report. Charlie looked over her shoulder to see little Deborah reach up and take one of Edwina's hands. Libby was on the other side of the older woman, and Deborah peeked around at her. "Is this your grandma?"

"Yeah, what do you think?" Libby blew a slimy green bubble and popped it. "You got a grandma?"

"I think so." But the child looked up at Edwina as if she hadn't believed such things as grandmothers existed until now.

Edwina appeared to be enjoying all the attention.

The neighborhood cats had the run of the house because the girls had left the door to their prison open, but most seemed to have stayed in the basement. Either that or the neighborhood had lost a lot more cats than Charlie thought possible.

Wiggims reached up to claw her bare knees, and Charlie picked him up in self-defense. She asked Deborah, "Is your Missy here?"

She needn't have asked, because a lanky gray-and-white adolescent hissed at them from the back of the puffy couch and crawled onto Deborah's shoulder in a proprietary stretch.

"That has got to be Picky," Libby said of the statue-still Siamese posing on top of the Exercycle seat like a living vase. "Hey, Picky! See, he didn't answer." Whoever it was didn't even blink.

But Charlie was once again reminded of her distaste for house cats when a roar sounded from the next room and all the cats took off for the ceiling, including Wiggims, who took a bunch of her skin with him.

Kenny was already in the room when she caught up with him, she still licking blood off one arm. It was disgusting to think of it this way, but it had a kind of salty, satisfying flavor.

There were two mountain lions, both prowling their separate cages. An altar draped in blood-red velvet had a man draped across it as well. Rows of strange white symbols decorated the altar drape, suggesting ancient American Indian hieroglyphs or mosaics from outer space.

"That's not Mr. Tollerd," Deborah whispered behind Charlie.

"Libby, get that poor kid out of here," Charlie ordered. But Libby was busy staring back at one of the caged lions.

"No," Edwina stood next to Kenny, "that's Marlin Wetzel."

Kenny reached for the body's jugular. "He's not dead."

"Probably stoned as usual." Edwina sat on the lower stair of the altar. "Poor Emmy, that's all she needs now."

Marlin Wetzel must have been over forty, but he'd been hard on himself and could pass for a lot older. Marlin had always worn a mustache, but now his lower face was thick with a gray-streaked beard. He was totally recognizable because his nose was so small for his face and pushed up like a pig's, which sounds awful when you describe it but looks kind of cute when you see it. Problem was, it made him look harmless—which he was not. This guy was a nasty piece of work.

He was a dedicated addict and capable of all kinds of cruelty to sustain his dedication. There had been no kid near Charlie's age within a five-block radius who hadn't known that early. Parents learned to stop sending lunch money to school with them, to go in and pay up by the month themselves, never send a kid to the neighborhood grocery with cash but to run a tab. Charlie could remember whole years when she was afraid to venture into the alley. When Marlin was in jail, everybody breathed easier.

That's one of the reasons Emmy was always baking wonderful strudel for them. That and, Charlie suspected, as a plea for them not to hurt him when their time came. But when it did, so did the pent-up rage. She knew of at least twice when the neighborhood teens ganged up on Marlin in the back alley and beat him within an inch of his life. And one more time on the downtown mall on Halloween, which used to be a bacchanalian, adult orgy down there until the destruction began to scare everyone—well, everyone but costumed teens and plainclothes street people from Boulder and serious toughs from Denver.

It didn't matter whether you played football, were in the band or were a cheerleader or a thespian or a budding scientist. If you knew Marlin when he was bigger than you and then found him at a disadvantage, the normal response was to gang up with your buds and beat the fudge out of him while he was down. And for that one triumphant moment, you were united. You were probably getting ready for the corporate world and didn't know it.

Charlie had been in on the Halloween one, pregnancy concealed by a nun's habit, her friends in high hilarity over the irony. (They'd pretty much stayed with her until Libby was born.) Anyway, her little group ran into the neighborhood nerds dressed as a six-pack of beer. The Halloween mall crawl would bring thousands of costumed revelers and as many gawkers to the four-block area, and the crunch was worse than the exits at a football stadium when the game let out.

Stephanie Bullock was the only other neighborhood kid in her group when they bumped into the six pack and were told old Marlin was drugged-out in the alley behind the post office and the nerd pack was trying to get to him but impeded by their bulky and interconnected packaging. Charlie and Stephanie followed the pack to the alley and helped the guys get out of enough of their paraphernalia to beat on old Marlin, the bogeyman. The girls even got in a bunch of hard kicks themselves. And it was funny, as proficient as Charlie was at guilt, that savage act had never bothered her. Kicking on old Marlin had been satisfying.

What, like tasting your own blood?

It didn't bother her now either. She simply marveled that the cute nose hadn't been broken many times over the years.

"Wonder whatever happened to Stephanie Bullock," Kenny said, he and Charlie having the same thoughts. Not surprising, since Kenny'd been one of the six pack.

"Went into aerospace engineering, had a great job down in

Texas and a great future," Edwina answered him. "Last time I talked to her father, she'd been downsized and looking for work. He was sending her money."

"Mom?"

"Get away from that cage, Libby, and get Deborah out of here."

"This lion's been hurt."

This lion was not as big and handsome as the one on Mitch's deck. His cage was in bad need of cleaning, and he had a wound on his neck and a bloody bandage on the floor at his feet. The female in the other cage looked sickly and she too had a sore or a boil on her neck.

"Those creatures need food and water," Edwina said, sagging on her stair.

"And you need to get back to bed. You're doing too much." But Charlie reached for the empty water bottle on the outside of the cage that fed into a small untippable trough inside. The lion lunged, and she nearly dropped it. Libby grabbed the other and they took them to the sink in the corner between a work-bench and the furnace. A large refrigerator hummed meaning-fully on the other side of the furnace. Both lions did their sticky version of a roar.

"I think they're trying to talk to me, but I can't understand what they're saying," Libby whispered.

"Oh, will you stop?" Charlie whispered back.

Fran and Deborah filled some of the small bowls sitting around the edges and took them out to the family room, where the little kitties stayed away from the big ones. They emptied a bag of dry cat food into a few others and took them out too.

"There's probably a deer carcass in that refrigerator, Kenny, if you could find a knife and cut these guys some dinner," she said when he'd finished calling for Animal Control and backup. Old Marlin might wake up and want some revenge with his dope. "You don't want to move those cats when they're hungry as well as angry and wounded."

185

"That's what they were trying to tell us." Libby looked at her mother with something akin to respect. "There was fresh meat in the refrigerator."

Charlie hated to disappoint her and lose that ounce of approval but she could not tell a lie. "It's the bloodstains on the concrete in front of the refrigerator that sort of suggest it. And Grandma told us both they like fresh meat."

"Looks more like beefsteak," Kenny said, pulling packages in butcher wrap from the refrigerator. "But it smells fresh and looks bloody." He threw a couple of sirloins into the cages—steaks that would have cost Charlie a fortune at home and probably did here too.

"Since when does meat from the butcher drip blood on the floor?" Libby demanded. "Can't you ever loosen up and see what's around you? There's no way *you* could have a love child. Oh no, all you have are mistakes."

She stalked out in full rage, and everyone but the gorging mountain lions took notice. Even Marlin Wetzel.

CHAPTER 27

M ARLIN WETZEL SAT up, his squint moving from
Libby's exit to the big cats ripping raw flesh from the
meat-market steaks held between their toenails, on to pause at
Charlie and then Kenny and then level on Edwina.

His swallow rasped so loud, Charlie had to stop herself from
going back to the sink to get him some water too.

Yeah, right. The only thing she'd get *him* was hemlock.

"I'm sick, man," he said finally to Kenny. "I know you?
What's going on?"

"We're waiting for you to tell us. What are you doing here,
Wetzel?"

"Doing my job." His speech was fairly clear but his pupils
looked like Edwina's when she was still on the morphine drips.

"What, sleeping?"

"Feeding the animals," Marlin squinted over at the cages
again. "Eating, aren't they?"

A woman from Social Services came to break everybody's heart
and take Deborah somewhere. Edwina offered to take in Missy
for the time being and practically threatened Kenny with a law-
suit if he didn't locate the little girl's grandmother. "That's where
she needs to be, not among strangers and without her kitten."

Lita was called over to help parcel out the neighbor cats, and

Animal Control was called to take the mountain lions to a wild animal facility for treatment.

Charlie wanted to ask the owner of the Shop of Mystery and Wiggims-the-gigolo why she had been on her way to the Tollerudes' when she found her cat missing. And like, what did she know about the strange altar and the mountain lions and bloodstains on the cement floor in that basement room. And Marlin Wetzel being there supposedly to feed the felines, big and small. But Professor Hogarth and a university policeman found them before she had the chance.

Edwina's office had been ransacked at Ramaley, one of the biology buildings on campus. They wanted Edwina to determine what might be missing, but Charlie put her foot down and her mother didn't argue, which said a lot about how Edwina felt. She seemed to be getting worse, and so did the hot wind and everybody's tempers and the smell of smoke on the air.

Charlie was never going to get back to real life.

"Unless you want to carry her on a stretcher and take responsibility, she stays here and I'll go do what I can. My mother's recovering from serious surgery, and she's had too exhausting a day to go anywhere."

"Her home has been searched too," Kenny added and called in Officer Darla to go to Ramaley with Charlie.

It was Sunday, but summer school was in session and the young and trim and the old and lumpy streaming in and out of Norlin Library were all in shorts and sunglasses. The wind, swirling and scooping the courtyards between pink sandstone buildings with red-tiled roofs, tried to snatch loose papers from books and folders. It tried to blind students with grit, torn leaves, and their own hair.

It was a beautiful campus, even though lawns had grass drying brown at the edges. An inappropriate sheet of mist blown thin from a broken sprinkler head flew at Charlie like wet smoke.

"Edwina doesn't have summer classes anymore, does she?" she asked Matt Hogarth as he struggled against the wind to hold the front door of Ramaley open for the rest of them. The campus cop knew the professor personally and had stopped at the Hogarths when he couldn't raise anybody at the Greene house.

"I don't think so. She's mostly in the research end of things now. She has some graduate seminars during the fall term, I believe," he said wistfully. Industry and government research grants had always freed more hard-science scholars from the mundane teaching of the next generation than it had those in the liberal arts, but it was becoming worse. Charlie could remember Howard holding forth at length on the subject years ago.

Edwina's office was not unlike the one Charlie remembered, this one not as small and cramped. Edwina had moved up in the world—the expanse of paned window on one wall actually looked out on a tree and sky instead of Norlin Library. Bookshelves and long tables once piled with papers lined the other walls. The desk was larger and nicer, but the desk chair still worn to the shape of her mother. There was even room for two comfortable chairs and a small coffee table.

Charlie and Officer Darla stepped over journals and books and computer printout sheets, spiral notebooks and loose papers flung to the floor by whoever had searched the room. Charlie's first thought was, how long before Edwina would regain enough strength to sort all this out? It wasn't the kind of thing someone else could do for her.

Her second was the same as the policewoman's. There was a printer and a monitor. But—and they voiced it at the same time—"No computer."

"Do you know what kind it was?" Darla asked, leaning down to peer into the desk's knee hole.

"It was a notebook. And look, somebody's lifted it right out of the docking device and taken it with them. They've got her hard disk. They've got everything."

❖

That evening, Charlie and Mitch sat out on the back step, drinking wine and eating a neighborhood offering again. The wind had gone down with the sun, and at this high dry altitude, when the sun went down the air cooled magically. It felt wonderful. Heather Tynne's bean dish wasn't bad either. Charlie never met a bean she didn't like as long as it was a pinto. Heather's dish had every bean but and a scattering of tomatoes and all kinds of spices and plump rigatte. Mitch brought one of his extravagant salads and a crusty baguette of French bread.

"I didn't have the heart to tell Edwina about her computer being missing," Charlie told him. "She didn't seem to care anyway. About the break-in at Ramaley, I mean."

"She doesn't look good. And I thought the last time I saw her she looked like she was getting better. When do those blood tests get in?"

"Another week. I was supposed to be going home tomorrow." Charlie tossed off her wine and handed him her glass for a refill.

"You're acting childish." But he poured her more.

"I'm feeling childish."

"Arugula?" he asked for no reason.

"Not unless I get overtired."

"No, the leafy herb in the beans—arugula—there's some in the salad too."

God save the world from men who cook. "I suppose," Charlie said, resigned, "you have a bread machine."

"Yeah, Marla gave me one for Christmas. How did you know?" Marla was one of his two nearly grown daughters. Her father peered into Charlie's face with that mygodshe'spsychic look.

"Seems like most guy cooks are into bread machines lately." Smart guys eat out. And before he could wax poetic on waking up to the smell of fresh baked bread in the morning, she asked,

"Don't you have a cook and servants? I mean you've got houses and condos."

"I have a houseboy in L.A. He sees to hiring people to take care of the house and grounds. But when I'm home and not working we cook together. When I'm out of town I do my own cooking. I enjoy it," said the star of *Deadly Posse,* the guy who shoots from the hip, swears from the spleen, loves from some kid scriptwriter's idea of what girls should want a guy to love like. "Tell me about the body in the alley."

And Charlie did. And about the rest of her meaningless, unrelated experiences and suspicions too. While part of her worried about the return of Edwina's gas bubble even though she'd chosen the bean dish. Charlie had wanted to try Lita the Flake's goulash out of morbid curiosity. Goulash without meat, or is that what she did with the dead-cat innards? Libby and Fran were off to the teen terrors somewhere moms could not go. What was little Deborah doing in a strange place about now? Last time Charlie checked, Missy was sleeping on Edwina's bed. What was Keegan Monroe planning in Folsom Prison tonight? *Zoo Keepers* or suicide or changing representation? What had Kenny Eisenburg done with Marlin Wetzel?

But what Charlie talked aloud about was, trying to relate candle wax on Tom Horn's grave to the body in the alley, the murder of Andy Tollerude, captive cats and mountain lions, break-ins at Edwina's home and office, and the surge in real estate values.

"I can see maybe a connection between crazy nonchurch services in Columbia Cemetery and the weird basement room next door and even Lita Kelso's feline mortuary services. But why would anyone want to steal the cat carcasses before they're stuffed? Wait, maybe Lita did the mortuary stuff in her basement and the services for the dead kitties were held in the Tollerude basement. But what did they need the mountain lions and live neighborhood cats and Columbia Cemetery for? And why would anyone hire Marlin Wetzel to do anything, let alone do it in their own home around a young, vulnerable child? I mean, this town and this neighborhood have always been screwy, but things have gotten out of hand here. And what about the fires in the mountains? Kenny hinted they were purposely set."

"Who's Kenny?"

"Detective Eisenburg."

"You're on a first-name basis with Boulder cops?"

"Mitch, what say we stake out the cemetery tonight? See if anything interesting will happen around the grave of Tom Horn?"

"I can sure think of something I'd rather do."

"I'll go alone then."

"Oh right, I'm going to let you stand around in a dark cemetery with cat snatchers, devil worshipers, mountain lions, black bears, murderers, and homicide cops on the loose. And you oiled to the gizzard with Papinard Eighty-three."

"That sure was a good year."

They convinced Emmy to come over and sit with a zonked Edwina.

"Yeah, good for young people to get away before it is you grow old," she said in blessing, turned the TV on low, and brought out her needlepoint. There'd been no sign of Marlin at her house, and Charlie hadn't the heart to bring him up. She trusted Kenny Eisenburg to have stored the bogeyman someplace safe.

On the way to the cemetery, Charlie stumbled over a crack in the sidewalk, and Mitch caught her arm. "Does oiled to the gizzard mean drunk?"

"Well definitely tipsy. Doesn't wine make you horny?"

"No."

"What does then?" he asked. "Jesus, after one night with you in Moab, I didn't think I'd ever walk again."

"Guilt." And the time of the month. "The hills are burning again, aren't they?"

"Sure smells like it."

CHAPTER 28

———————◆———————

IT'S HARD TO hide anywhere with Mitch Hilsten. Even at night. He didn't exactly glow in the dark—well, his eyes and teeth certainly seemed to—but his voice carried in that indefinable way actors learn, and although he was more reticent than most, actors are not by nature quiet people. Still—"Keep your voice down, okay?"

They sat scrunched behind the Adams family monument.

"I have been." Even his whisper bounced off tombstones and trees and urns now that the wind was dead.

Traffic on Ninth and the thumping of one of those mega car stereos kids use to get even with the world these days, the barking of a dog—all background music here in a land of the dead surrounded so closely by the accoutrements of the living.

"What could Edwina have on her computer worth breaking and entering for?" Charlie wondered.

"Maybe a student stole it to play games on."

"Look, there's that dark van I keep seeing around the neighborhood."

"Maybe it belongs to a neighbor."

"Kenny thought it might have dumped that man's body in the alley this morning." The van turned right off Edwina's street onto College and up the alley that ran behind Edwina's house.

And, don't forget, behind any number of other houses, some of them multiple dwellings, lining both sides of the alley and that van might be about the right shape, but you can't tell much more than dark or light at night.

"There's one way to find out—go find it and take a sniff. We'd know if it transported the body." She was about to get up and blow their cover when she caught a glimpse of a dark figure moving along the schoolyard fence that segregated the quick from the dead.

She nudged Mitch and pointed as the shape bent over to slip through the hole that had been there as long as Charlie could remember. The wire netting was bent back a couple of feet where it met the wrought-iron fence on the street side. They squirmed around to the other end of the shadows of the Adams family monument.

"Can't you scrunch your eyes down a little? They glow."

"They do not glow. Must be the Papinard Eighty-three." He sounded disgusted, but Charlie suspected that had to do more with Kenny than her lack of sobriety.

You hear owls hoot mostly on TV commercials, but it's a real kick when it happens at night in a cemetery with a black-robed character approaching and you hunkering behind a runty tombstone next to a fair-size superstar whose eyes glow.

Charlie crouched tighter into the earth above the Adamses, but that just made the spices in the bean dish fight the Papinard for control of the flavoring on her ulcer-afterburn juices.

The owl was in the tree right above the cemetery urn next to Tom Horn's grave. Every *oooooooow* sent shudders through Charlie's body that broke out as goosebumps on her bare skin, which there was too much of for this place this time of night.

But when another owl answered, her spooky feeling abated. What was there about that answer? Other than it didn't sound much like an owl? Something familiar about it, that's what.

The cloaked figure straightened to look up into the tree and his hood fell back.

"Kenny? What are you doing here?" Charlie stood, her cramped legs and back singing her praises. And something came crashing down out of the tree that wasn't an owl.

And that was not a type of tree meant to be climbed. Fran swiped at scratches on her legs and arms. The other owl grew insistent.

"Kenny, I think I saw the van going up the alley just now." Charlie started forward and nearly tripped over Mitch. "Oh, Detective Eisenburg? Mitch Hilsten."

"Hi, Kenny," Mitch said sardonically, rising to his feet with more grace than either Charlie or Fran.

When you get right down to it, all hunks look alike. Kenny was taller, but both men were well built. Charlie had a brief memory of other guys she'd known. There weren't that many. She had a life. Most had a special physical trait *she* found attractive *they* didn't know about because they couldn't see it.

"Fran, what are you doing here?" Kenny asked.

"We thought we'd catch the weirdos doing their weird."

"We?"

The other owl graduated from insistent to urgent, and Fran squeaked. "We've got to hide. They're coming."

They all scurried from the Horn and Adams families for the deeper cover of heavy shadow that puddled in the center of the cemetery away from street and schoolyard lights, the passing headlights turning onto Ninth from the east and sweeping across the outer graves on that side. This time Charlie ended up with Kenny. In his cloak with him.

She had lost sight of Mitch and Fran and felt a little panicked by the smothery cloak. Kenny stood behind her, leaning against a tree, holding the dark material so that only her face was exposed.

The owl on the other side of College Avenue was suddenly silenced. Charlie hoped it didn't mean Libby had been found out. She began to suspect all this was a joke on the adults present.

Until she realized people moved in and out of shadows in most of the graveyard visible to her.

Charlie didn't see them until they moved, as if they had formed the shadows they'd been standing in and took some with them when they stepped out. All wore hooded cloaks like the one she stood in.

Charlie wanted to ask Detective Kenny Eisenburg where he had come by this one but was afraid to make a sound.

A weirdo passed by quite close. She couldn't see the shape of the face because of the hood. But they were all converging on the same place.

The grave of Tom Horn the outlaw.

A red glow in the sky behind and to one side of Flagstaff Mountain, the sound of her body trying to assimilate Heather Tynne's bean dish, the increasingly damp and musty odor of earth here in the midst of a dangerous summer drought . . .

But other smells and sounds seemed to disappear. The stoplights on Ninth stayed red, there was no traffic, no city sirens, no wind. But for the sounds her body made in her head and the chanting, all the rest was quiet.

Let's not get carried away here.

Yeah, but look at them. All these people creeping in from all directions, and when they get there, the crowd doesn't grow that much. I mean, this is seriously weird.

And you've had some serious wine.

Oh. Right.

You're probably asleep in Edwina's guest room.

The trees didn't move. The robes didn't move. Only the candle flames as one of the figures held a candelabra high in each hand and little points of light pricked the darkness.

Growly guy voices chanted in a low murmur, angry and musical at the same time. The chant rose with the candle flames and still more figures approached, blending into what should have been a bigger crowd.

One of Charlie's contact lenses stuck and she looked up hoping to force it to move. The lights of an airplane heading back to California, like she wished she was doing, appeared to be as stuck up in the sky as she was down here. They were right where they should be on a 747 or something, but they weren't heading west, east, up, or down.

Oh boy. Charlie swore off beans forever. "Kenny, do something to wake me up."

Kenny didn't do anything, didn't even answer.

Why should he? It's your dream.

The man with all the candles knelt to set them on Tom Horn's grave, and when he rose, a long knife in his hands glittered in the candlelight from below, appeared to draw together the many small flames into one large one, then lure that one ever higher as the robed figure raised the weapon above his head. He was facing Charlie's direction, his back to College Avenue and to most of the chanters, who formed a dark semicircle around him.

And still they came, literally melding with the group already there. Charlie looked away to clear her head of dopey stuff, only to realize that there was traffic on Ninth after all. It just wasn't going anywhere. Two cars heading up toward Chautauqua sat stilled in the traffic lanes. They hadn't even reached the red stoplight.

The man with the knife ranted on in a liturgic cadence. Charlie could either make out no words or he spoke a foreign tongue. His was the only face she could see, and then all she could determine was that he was white. The other hooded figures appeared to be looking up at the knife—one of those dramatic kind with metal curlicues at the bottom of the hilt to keep your hands safe from slipping down on the double-edged blade.

When the knife lowered slowly, so did all the heads. It disappeared into the man's robe, as Charlie had into Kenny's, but out came a stoppered bottle. The high-priest weirdo held it at arms length and made a slow circle to show it to the assembled, ranting on endlessly. When he was once again facing Charlie he took a delicate, perhaps symbolic swig—it was so quick—and then passed it to the man closest to him.

Gathering his skirts together, he very literally disappeared into the assembled and was gone.

"Gone," Kenny said behind her.

"Excuse me?"

"Whoever Fran thought she saw coming either never existed or is gone. What, you have a problem hearing somebody talking right into your ear like this?" He gave her lobe a nibble.

The traffic lights on Ninth had turned green. The cars continued on as they'd meant to. There was even smoke on the breeze again. But the area around the grave of Tom Horn was totally barren of people and cloaks and candles.

"Okay, Fran, front and center. What the hell is going on?" Kenny released Charlie from his cloak so fast she grabbed the tree to keep upright.

"Charlie? Are you all right?" Mitch was suddenly in her face. "You look sick."

The plane in the sky was heading on its way to California. Charlie was not.

CHAPTER 29

◆

S IRENS SCREAMED up Ninth Street—two police cars. They didn't bother to stop at Columbia Cemetery because nothing at all had happened there.

An ambulance and fire truck followed in a matter of minutes. Charlie could remember her parents pausing to listen for which way the sirens turned where Ninth ended at Baseline. Shaking their heads if the frightened sounds headed west because in that direction Baseline soon became Flagstaff Road and zigzagged tortuously uphill. One of them would say, "Someone fell off the mountain again."

Now the emergency could well be fire, but then it usually meant a car taking the hairpins too fast. Flagstaff Road had exacted a grisly toll over the years, mostly of high school and college students under the influence.

Fran was trying to explain to Kenny that Libby, hidden behind a parked car across the street, had signaled someone was coming and that's why Fran insisted they all hide.

"So, she must have been wrong." Fran peered around Kenny and called, "Hey, Libby, what's going on?"

Charlie's daughter vaulted the wrought-iron fence and came toward them, a long sweatshirt hiding the fact she had any other clothes on—she was all well-formed legs. She was also wobbly on her feet, her voice breathless and near tears. "I was so scared. Where did they all go?"

"Where did who all go?" everyone but Charlie asked, almost simultaneously.

Charlie knelt over Tom Horn and ran her hand over a dirt clod. It came away with a glob of waxylike goo, still warm to the touch.

The next morning Charlie was back at that grave first thing, studying the earth around it. The slurry bombers and the hot wind were back too.

She could find no major disturbance of the area great enough to account for the crowd of cloaked figures. Only she and Libby had noticed anything weird. Kenny claimed his ex had made his cloak two years ago for a Halloween party, and Charlie couldn't be that sure it was just like all the rest last night, because in the dark that sort of apparel is going to look like its neighbor.

In the privacy of their overcrowded bed, Libby told Charlie she'd seen just two robed figures move toward the cemetery initially. One along the schoolyard fence—that was Kenny—and another appeared a short time later on College from her left, which could have been from Edwina's street or the next two over or their alleys. Because of the dark shadows and dark cloak she hadn't noticed him until he stepped under a streetlight to cross College Avenue.

She'd increased her hoot-warning at this second figure and watched everybody scramble for cover. "But why were we the only ones who saw those other guys coming from all over? And they were sort of rap singing. I could hear it from across the street. Why didn't everybody hear and see them like we did?"

"I don't know, honey, that's got me baffled too, but I'm glad you backed off about it with Kenny and Mitch. We need to know more before we announce to the world we're mother/daughter nut cases. Why did you and Fran pick tonight to check out the cemetery?"

"Sunday night seemed maybe religious and like a good time

to hold a ceremony. And if I know you, you'll finesse a way for us to go home tomorrow, I guess it's today now. We had as much right to be there as you did, and I bet you all were there for the same reason we were."

When Charlie'd left the house a few minutes before, Missy was curled around Libby's feet instead of Edwina's. Charlie's mother seemed to be slumbering peacefully now, but there were signs in the kitchen she'd been up in the night.

And there were signs here in Columbia Cemetery that Charlie, Libby, Kenny, Mitch, and Fran were about the only "crowd" that gathered last night.

Except for the candle wax. She found another blob, this one congealed to a cheesy texture and cool, on the base of Tom's headstone. But Charles and Elizabeth Horn's graves did not look trampled. The geranium in the urn, however, was now legally dead, and another foot-long matchstick was stabbed into the soggy, sticky soil next to it. Must have been used to light the candles that weren't there.

She'd seen no dark van parked in the alley when she'd come down it. On her return, she walked all the way around the block and back up the alley to be sure, stopping at Lita Kelso's lot.

Two ancient hibachis and a round Weber grill decorated one end of the full-length porch, all in need of cleaning. A bag of charcoal briquets leaned against the house, alongside a red cardboard cylinder of those long-stemmed matches. According to her son, Lita was a vegetarian. Charlie wondered if she barbecued tofu and vegetables.

She punched the doorbell again but heard no answering chime, so she knocked on the rough wood of the door. A slatted-wood porch swing lurched drunkenly on its hooks when a gust of wind, redolent of evergreen as well as smoke, slammed into the house and Charlie too. She could remember as a child thinking the world smelled like Christmas trees on hot summer days.

Charlie'd decided the woman had already left for her store on the mall when the door opened and out she bustled, a cloth shopping bag in one hand, the rapturous Wiggims in the other.

"Oh Charlie, was that you? I thought it was the wind knocking that old swing into the house. Didn't pay any attention to it. Is something wrong? I'm on my way to the shop."

"Could you answer a couple of questions before you go?"

A look of uncertainty crossed the shopkeeper's face—and was that fear behind it? But the fluffy orange cat revved up his motor and stretched out his head and neck, eyes half closed with ecstasy at their meeting this way. Fearing the rest of him would follow, the scratches from their last tryst still burning on her arm, she reached out to ward him off.

He took one sniff of her fingers and ejected for the porch rafters with a yowl, leaving his poor mistress's silk sari torn at the shoulder. Lita wore a little red dot on her forehead, crinkly hair wound into a bun on the back of her head. Wispy strands broke out all over, and the cat hadn't helped any. Somehow the effect was more frazzled than Far East.

Wiggims Kelso spat at them from above—this, the most passionately adoring of cats. His eyes glared wide, almost all pupil. Tiny pointy teeth bared in warning, the pink floppy tongue so upset it drooled.

The loose end of Lita's sari hung to the floor, the only shoulder to it torn. It was the colors of peacock tails and worn over a white short-sleeved shell. She'd ornamented the outfit with ropes of fine gold necklace chains. "What did you say to him? I've never seen him act this way."

"I didn't say anything. You were standing right here, you'd have heard it."

"I'm not a sensitive, regrettably, but I have been taught to detect them, and I know you could have easily upset him with some telepathic message. I demand to know what it was."

Oh great, now I'm telepathic. Wasn't bad enough to be psychic. Oh no. "What could anybody possibly say to gross out a cat who lives in a cat mortuary?"

"If you have come over here to insult me and frighten my

beloved Wiggims, you can just turn tail and get off my property."

"All I did was hold out my hand. He took one sniff and went ballistic. There was no message."

Lita grabbed Charlie's hand and sniffed it.

"I just came from the cemetery. What is it you think you smell?"

"Blood." Lita Kelso stepped back into her house and slammed the door. Charlie heard the lock click.

She sat on the porch swing to wait. Lita would have to come out to get her cat, get to her garage, get in the car that would take her to her shop. Charlie might not be sensitive or psychic or telepathic, but she could wait.

From high on his rafter, Wiggims moaned warning, sounding a lot more like Tuxedo now. Charlie gave him the finger— about as telepathic as she planned to get.

What was the connection between neighborhood cats and mountain lions? Her hands did sort of smell. But of blood? Or was it sweat? Metallic? Or simply like they'd been stuck in the dirt of a graveyard urn?

Why *did* only she and Libby see what obviously didn't happen last night around Tom Horn's grave? The grass cover was so dry, a crowd of any size would have left bruised grass, barren earth.

"Don't look at me like that," she told the stupid cat. "I am normal, buddy. *You* never have been."

Wiggims's tail ballooned like an engorged cactus. His ears lay flat. His whiskers vibrated.

From Lita Kelso's porch, Charlie had a different point of view of both Emmy's and Edwina's properties. Where was Marlin Wetzel? Charlie had been too overwhelmed by what did not happen at Columbia Cemetery last night to remember to ask Kenny.

If that creepy ceremony and cloaked crowd didn't happen, what did? How could Libby have seen it too, if you were just having an illusion or dream or something?

We both ate Heather Tynne's bean dish?

No, you and Mitch did, Libby wasn't home for dinner. If there was some hallucinogen in the beans, Mitch should have been the one going goofy last night. He's more given to such things anyway. But it was Libby. She didn't have lunch with you and Kenny either. Other than her diet Coke, she didn't have breakfast at all.

If Andy Tollerude offered to buy out Edwina, would it be as an investment? Had he gone through Heather Tynne or another Realtor or approached Charlie's mother privately? If the two properties across the alley sold, and then the Hogarths maybe, so what? Neighborhoods were revamped daily. In a boom real estate climate like the one Boulder currently enjoyed, the only people to suffer would be those who had no desire to move up or change or move at all. Which probably described a fair number of the neighbors here. Until they were ready to move to a safe retirement community or forced to move to a nursing home—they'd endure most anything. And many of these people had some kind of pension and social security still coming in. Only two things could force them out of here.

Escalating living costs and property taxes. A fear of crime and lack of personal safety.

The first was happening even now, with relatively lavish homes like the Tollerudes' moving in. But add crime and wild animals and Satanic rituals in the heart of this community, and you had a real threat to the personal safety of the middle-aged and just plain aged who lived here.

Lita Kelso never came back out her door. Wiggims Kelso made it abundantly clear that he had no plans to leave his perch with Charlie on the porch below. Charlie's ulcer began to order breakfast, and she noticed a window screen about the size of the one missing from Edwina's kitchen window lying up against this side of Emmy Wetzel's garage.

CHAPTER 30

———————◆———————

THE THREE GREENE women gathered in Edwina's sick-room for a breakfast of toasted bagels.

Edwina claimed not to be sicker, just tired, and she did manage half a bagel with cream cheese, a glass of grape juice, and two mugs of coffee, as well as a whole lot of pills. To Charlie that looked like *some* progress.

She sat on the edge of the bed, Libby seated Buddhist fashion on the rug beside it, Missy Tollerude on a ruffled peignoir, circa Marilyn Monroe, that had been draped over a chair but had slipped to the floor.

Charlie experienced one of those rare moments of peace again. (When she got old, would that be all she'd want to experience? Like, forget the excitement?) Again they were all safe, a patch of sun that was able to sneak into Edwina's east window highlighted Libby's hair and Missy's frowsy coat and the rich color of the old wood flooring.

". . . attention," her mother was saying between drags on her cigarette while staring meaningfully at Charlie.

"I'm sorry?"

"I was telling my granddaughter that you never did pay attention."

Libby put a hand over her face as if her Coke had frizzed up her nose and blinked a warning at Charlie through parted fingers.

205

"What I said was," Edwina continued, "I have learned two things by all this surgery. The first is that you really can become addicted to caffeine. I didn't get any coffee for three days in the hospital and they kept telling me I couldn't possibly feel a headache because I was on so many drugs. Well, I did feel it, and the first cup of coffee stopped it right there. The second thing I learned—"

Libby doubled over, trying to reign in her laughter but making little helpless snorts.

"The second thing I learned is"—Edwina's walleye stared disapproval at her granddaughter—"look, it won't hurt you two to learn a few things before you have to undergo a surgeon's knife someday. Did you know with anesthesia you risk hair loss?"

"Hair loss." Charlie spent a long while crunching toasty bagel, afraid to commit more and worried Libby would choke on the merriment of whatever was going on here. Edwina's hair had always been sparse. Now it was ruined by a bad color job is all. "I don't see that you've lost that much. I mean, it's not like bone loss or ostero-whatever."

"Look at my eyebrows," Edwina ordered. "They're gone. Completely gone."

Libby exploded. Charlie very carefully set her tray down on the nearest table.

"What's the matter with that girl?" Edwina demanded.

What Charlie meant to do was say, "Hey, don't worry about this. It was the drugs, but not like you think."

All she could manage was to slip to the floor and hide her face in her hands like her daughter.

"What is so funny about losing your eyebrows? I'll have you know, my mother—because it was the rage for young women of her time—plucked out all her eyebrows and drew them back on with a pencil so they'd look perfect. This is no laughing matter."

Edwina gave up on politeness and yelled over the hysterics on the floor, "I'll have you know, my mother regretted that act for the rest of her life. When styles changed, the eyebrows would only grow back patchy and awful and she went to her grave with them penciled in like . . . like an uncertain appointment."

Charlie ordered Libby to explain things to her grandmother and pretended to occupy herself with clearing away the remains of the breakfast. But Libby would get halfway through the first sentence and break up.

This was the first time Charlie could remember someone else being the brunt of an inner-family joke. She savored this moment too and as long as she dared. Finally she sat beside her mother and explained.

"I did no such thing. How can you sit there and tell me I purposely—"

"Oh, Grandma, stop. I hurt. I think I broke a rib."

Edwina scooted down off the pillows and blinked at Libby and then back at Charlie, defenseless for once. "I really . . . ?"

"Yeah. It's okay."

Charlie was finishing up the coffee and loading the dishes in the dishwasher when the wall phone rang in her ear. She reached for it, sending up a prayer that it wasn't Larry calling to report Keegan Monroe had refused the contracts. It was Richard Morse himself.

"Richard? What? Is it Keegan?"

"Nah, Larry the Kid's on his way up to Folsom right now with the contracts. I sure hope you make it home this afternoon—I'm getting impressed with your work, babe."

"There's been another murder here. I don't think they're going to let me come home."

"Charlie, comes the day when you got to grow up—you know, grab the cow by the tits? Push your weight around?"

207

"Cow by the tits?" Charlie's boss delighted in anomalies while pretending total innocence of their existence. "What, bull by the horns would be politically incorrect?"

"Hey, you got a book author named Goff there in town, right? McMullins and Braintree both called this morning wanting to discuss the manuscript with you. It's Sarah Sharpe at McMullins and Roger Tedesco at Braintree." He'd obviously never heard of either one of them, but Charlie had.

"You have to be kidding."

This sudden interest in Reynelda's manuscript by two New York publishers was by no means the most surprising thing that happened that Monday, but it was certainly right up there.

Charlie was swiping a sponge around the kitchen sink, the phone held between a scrunched shoulder and her ear, when she noticed the dead ants all over the counter.

"Well I did call you first, Sarah, knowing you'd be as excited about this book as I am, but I have to warn you there's interest in other quarters, as we all knew there would be. . . ."

Okay, the ants weren't all over, they were clustered in three different groups.

"Sarah, I'll run this by the others and the author and get back to you soon as."

The ants were clustered in three different groups around food spatters. How many had she already swiped into the sink's disposal?

"Roger? This is Charlie Greene . . . I know, it's been years. How are you? And Linda? Oh, I'm sorry—I guess I didn't hear about—oh, Joan? Congratulations." When Charlie and Roger Tedesco slaved together as poverty-stricken freshman agents at Wesson Bradly Literary Agency in New York City, he had been happily married to Linda.

"Well no, I'm not surprised. I knew you'd like this kind of story. That's why I sent it to you." Charlie wished like hell somebody would repeat the title because she sure couldn't remember it. She could remember a large portion of the story though, which signaled that the title needed changing. "I know, wouldn't it be so much less complicated if we were the only ones who recognized the commercial appeal of Reynelda's story, but—yeah, I'm afraid so. That's certainly interesting, let me run it by the author and the other houses and get back to you, okay?"

Wouldn't ants know better than to eat poisoned food?

Who said it was a) food and b) poisoned? And why do you think insecticides work?

"Roger, I have to let you go, but I'll . . . Keegan Monroe? Yes, he's been my client for several years. I know, but prison does give him lots of time to write."

Roger picked up on Keegan's success, which might give her some clout as an agent who was not afraid to bargain. She wasn't about to tell anybody in New York that she was as stunned by Keegan's good fortune as he was.

Charlie'd about reached the point of believing in Richard Morse's oft-repeated anomaly homily, that hard work and talent were nice, but nothing worked as good as sheer bolt-out-of-the-blue dumb luck. Maybe she'd start playing the lottery again.

She studied the counter, the sink rim, the window sill above it. No more dead bugs, but there was a small plastic lid on the sill, the kind that protects curious little kids from trying out potent medicines at deadly dosages.

Keegan Monroe had a track record, a series of smaller successes. He was a known commodity. And he was male.

How to explain the sudden interest in Reynelda Goff? Granted, hers was a mystery of sorts and series mysteries by and about and for women were hot at the moment in New York. In Hollywood, male egos still reigned except for weep-o-rama and romance on TV movies—still, two of Reynelda's three main characters were guys, but it was a one-shot, not a series. That should play in L.A. but not New York.

One interview with sweet Reynelda, and the young macho screenwriters would a) start vomiting and b) copy the salient features of her manuscript and disguise them. Bottom line was Reynelda Goff might be marketable as a woman mystery writer, but she'd never play in L.A., baby.

What was it about the kitchen counter that was different? Besides dead ants? What was there about Reynelda's manuscript that set two major publishers after it on the same day?

She called the office again and asked Richard if there'd been anything in the trades about Tom Horn or Boulder.

"No, but there was a news segment on CBS last night about fires and wild animals in Boulder and desecration of a cemetery. Something about dead cats on the grave of an Old West outlaw named Tom Horn. First I ever heard of him. I was just thinking I'd forgot to mention it when I talked to you."

"Richard, the Goff manuscript? It's about Tom Horn and that cemetery."

"Yeah, the Kid told me before he left." Richard was a homophobe along with all his other wonderful traits. Everybody in the office picked up nicknames—Larry Mann was Larry the Kid. He'd apparently made a real splash at the agency before Charlie came to it when he'd auditioned for a Texas Barbecue Sauce commercial and came back to work in costume. Charlie was referred to as Mother of Libby. "Where else did you send it?"

"Pitman's is all. I think I'll give Ellen Harm a ring. She might not have read it yet."

"That's your end of the business, but I knew I put it in good hands." Richard left the writing talent to Charlie, he and the other agents handled the performing talent. "Oh, and babe? This news story last night? It also mentioned Mitch Hilsten was in Boulder, looking into the cemetery stuff. Thought you two were splitsville. Doesn't he have a film to shoot with my little Cyndi?"

"He happens to have bought a condo here, Richard. And there was never anything between us that needed splitting. He reports to location any day now." From love, you split with remorse and hurt feelings. From sex, you walk.

"So you have seen him?"

"Yes, and that's all." Charlie hung up, wishing she hadn't sworn off swearing. Richard Morse knew how to punch her buttons almost as well as Edwina.

While on hold waiting to speak to Ellen Harm at Pitman's, Charlie noticed the row of medicine and vitamin bottles. They all had caps. Embossed on the white plastic lid orphaned on the window sill was the familiar—TO OPEN LINE-UP ARROWS ON CAP & BOTTLE PUSH CAP UP WITH THUMB. The same message embossed on the cap of Edwina's aspirin bottle. The two caps were identical.

Edwina took an aspirin a day to thin or clot her blood or something. When Charlie had taken the medicines in with her mother's breakfast she had included her daily aspirin tablet and the bottle had been about half full. She opened it now and it still was. Two caps for one bottle? She hadn't just used up one bottle and opened another, throwing away the empty and leaving the lid on the window sill, because she'd been doctoring her mother out of the same bottle since she came home.

Ellen Harm had not read the manuscript but an outside reader had and was writing up her take on it and ten others this week, if Charlie wanted to wait a little longer for a decision.

"I'm not at the office but at my mother's home in Boulder. She's just out of the hospital and—"

"I saw on the news about the fires there and the mountain lions. I hope she'll be all right."

"Did you see the report on the strange ceremonies in the cemetery?"

"Yes, sounds like Boulder's getting as weird as L.A."

"Well, Reynelda Goff, the author of that manuscript we're talking about, lives very near that particular cemetery, and her story concerns the outlaw Tom Horn whose grave is the center of investigation right now. This seems to have peaked the interest of McMullins and Braintree in the Goff manuscript. I've been on the line with both this morning from my mother's kitchen, but of course I wanted to check with you first, before I made any decisions . . . you know." Wink wink, nudge nudge.

CHAPTER 31

B Y THE TIME Charlie figured out someone had replaced Edwina's Percocet with the look-alike but far weaker pain killer—aspirin—and called Kenny to find out where the hell Marlin Wetzel was, she had the potential for an unofficial bidding war going on for Reynelda Goff's book.

This business was just nuts is what it was.

"Charlie, we had no proof that Marlin did anything illegal, certainly nothing we could jail him for. Didn't find any drugs on him, although like you I suspect there had recently been some in him. I don't know where he is."

She called the doctor for a replacement prescription—no wonder her mother seemed more in pain rather than less as time went on—that the doctor's nurse refused to grant. The doctor was at his Louisville office today. Louisville was a neighboring town that was becoming crammed with Boulder and California's overflow. Percocet must be good stuff.

After dealing with New York and Richard Morse, Charlie was not that easily intimidated. She gave the surgeon's nurse Detective Kenneth Eisenburg's office phone number. "And if you don't call him within the next half hour and call me back with that prescription, I will have him call you. He's busy too and having to take time off to call you will not make his morning."

Don't you just hate it when busy people treat you that way?

Sure, I do. But right now I don't have time to fudge around. Okay?

She should run over and tell Reynelda about her amazing good fortune—she might be able to afford to leave the good professor after all—but Charlie also needed to check out that screen leaning against Emmy's garage and whether Lita had gone to her shop or not. She wanted to see the news story about Boulder and the cemetery that had brought such interest in Reynelda's book, and she wanted to talk to Heather Tynne about just how much this place was worth and . . . well, the list was endless.

Instead, Charlie called the friendly skies to cancel the tickets home, knowing they'd bill anyway. Maybe she could get a note from Edwina's doctor or the Boulder Police Department. She could always resort to Richard's mysterious influence with the airline industry.

Next, she went out on the front porch and picked up the *Boulder Daily Camera.* The fact that a network news show had mentioned Boulder and all its fire, animal, and demon trouble could not chase off the front page the picture story of some basketball coach who had lost his home and pet dog to the conflagration in the mountains west of town. He stood, in living color, holding onto his weeping wife, the charred ruins in the background. The headlines blazed LOST TO MYRIAH. A subtitle did admit his was one of twenty homes and summer cabins lost to the wind-driven flames and at least thirty more were in deep trouble.

At home that would not have been so large a number. With all the immigrant infill, Colorado and Boulder County still seemed sparsely inhabited to someone used to Southern California. Of course, when it's your house and all you own, it only takes one to be important.

But, at the bottom of the page was ONLY IN BOULDER: CBS HIGHLIGHTS BOULDER'S NATURAL AND UNNATURAL TROUBLES IN SUNDAY NIGHT NEWSCAST. Charlie, sitting on the front step, could hear the hammers and staple guns over the slurry bombers and sirens. This was simply a very weird world, no matter where she went.

She stared across the street at the old Burrows house, once dark and now dark on one side only. Now inhabited by the Goffs, one a cranky professor, the other perhaps about to become a famous author. Probably for a very short time—few lasted long in an ever-merging publishing world fighting to downsize the number of books (product) and authors (vendors) and expense (editorial staff).

Who better than a professor of ancient religion to play the high priest, calling demons from wherever they dwell to the land of the dead in the heart of good old weird Boulder?

Could he be the only one of that "crowd" who was real and alive? The guy who crossed College past where Libby hid and brought with him candelabra and knife and stoppered bottle? Libby said that cloaked person passing her had been carrying something. And wasn't it a coincidence that his wife's book suddenly drew interest from a congealing industry frantic to keep a hold on its place in the sun?

Could the Goffs be together in this somehow? It all seemed so far-fetched. Maybe that was the clue to everything. Maybe someone who really wanted to get people to move away from this neighborhood knew they'd have to find something pretty fantastic to faze a longtime Boulderite.

But if Professor Goff was the high priest last night and the others some sort of illusion that only Charlie and Libby saw, why didn't the others see the high priest if he was a real person?

Because for a time, time stopped. Planes and cars and wind and streetlights didn't move.

Yeah, but, could the gnarly professor who can't really control his own wife have the power to stop time?

Let us not get carried away again. No one can stop time. Maybe create the illusion of stopping time. Maybe by hypnosis.

It wasn't possible to hypnotize both Charlie and Libby when they were so far apart. What were the conscious Fran, Kenny, and Mitch Hilsten doing during this supposed hypnotic period?

Charlie gave up, hoping a logical answer would present itself if she ignored the question. She went out to find the screen to Edwina's kitchen window.

It still sat up against Emmy Wetzel's garage. Charlie was about to pick it up when two things stopped her. The first was the possibility of messing up the "perp's" fingerprints with her own. And the second was the familiar beady red eyes of a lab rat crouching behind it. Its squeak was answered by another. Charlie turned to dark rat eyes in a dark rat, still chewing on the debris under one of Emmy's bird feeders. Charlie imagined there was longing in that stare.

When she carried the survivors into Edwina's bedroom, they didn't seem disgusted by any smell from the cemetery she hadn't managed to wash off. In fact, they appeared comfortable. Both had approached her before she bent to pick them up, and neither struggled once she did. "Hey, Edwina? Know these guys?"

Edwina was in the process of studying her face in a magnifying mirror. She looked over it dumbfounded. "Elmer? Louise?"

Charlie put on gardening gloves from Edwina's garage to pick up the screen that leaned against Emmy's, and she headed back with it. The phone rang just as she was passing the freezer on her way to the kitchen. Dr. Ringer's nurse had instructions for Edwina's refill. "But this is it. You'll have to wean her."

Edwina and two rodents looked up at Charlie when she entered, like they wished she wouldn't.

"Emmy's birdseed kept them going." Charlie pretended not to notice the tear her mother wiped off her cheek. "I wonder why the mountain lions didn't eat them."

"Probably hadn't gotten around to them yet. Where's Libby?"

"I was going to ask you the same question. She must have taken Missy with her. I have to run out and get you some pain medicine, okay? Be careful. I'll lock up. Don't open the door to good old Marlin."

"Medicine I got now isn't worth a damn. Why get more?"

"Somebody switched your Percocet for aspirin."

"Good old Marlin?"

"Who else? They called the prescription into Walgreen's. It'll be ready when I get there. Is it still in Crossroads?"

"Moved across Thirtieth. Take Arapaho to Thirtieth and turn north till you get to Walnut. It'll be on your right."

Charlie turned Howard's Jeep east on Arapaho and slowed when she came to Boulder High School. The cottages where volunteer saints cared for babies of teen mothers so they could attend classes had given way to parking lot. As had the greenhouse and florist shop on the corner where she'd bought a boutonniere for her one prom date before becoming what Libby dubbed a UM—unwed mother. Both had moved elsewhere, the UM program to the other high school, Fairview, at the south end of town.

Charlie felt again the sense of betrayal mixed with shame she'd covered with jokes and bravado when her friends went off to fun activities—sports, cheerleading, play rehearsal—the list of life that Libby's birth denied her seemed endless. Charlie went instead to one of the cottages to nurse her baby, learn how to care for it, and how to ensure she would not repeat her mistake. She had transferred the rage of feeling cheated to Edwina, just as Libby consistently did to her.

There was still no sign of Libby or Missy when Charlie returned to dose Edwina properly and bring her lunch. All her mother wanted was Campbell's Chicken Noodle Soup again with crushed crackers. Charlie worried they'd lost too much ground here with the switch in medicines. She found an old cage and bag of bedding material in a corner of the garage for Elmer and Louise and installed them on a low table in Edwina's room.

Odd how grateful the critters seemed, nestling under the bedding to scatter it in just the right heaps, washing their wiry whiskers.

Charlie went in search of some food for them, wondering if people were born and raised in a cage they'd grow to like it that way, remembering how the caged mountain lions next door had not been so happy. Of the way she and her daughter still fought the constraints of family.

She knocked on Emmy's door to see if she could borrow some bird seed, hoping Marlin wouldn't answer it. His rebellion had made a disaster of his life and his mother's too.

No answer. Where *was* everybody?

A distant cry for help turned her suddenly cold in the smokey heat. Although it came muffled, she recognized the voice instantly. It was calling for Charlie.

CHAPTER 32

———◆———

W HAT WERE YOU doing in the basement?"
"Call Kenny." Edwina had lost most of her noodle
soup down the front of her robe. She was pulling herself onto
the landing at the top of the stairs when Charlie had unlocked
the new deadbolt and swung open the door. "Don't go down.
Don't look."

"You were supposed to be asleep. I was only gone a minute."

"I thought maybe there were some food pellets left for Elmer
and Louise—never mind that, Charlie. Do something I tell you
for once. Call Kenny."

"What's . . . oh, God . . . Libby!"

"Charlie, don't. It's—"

But Charlie had already swung her mother out of the way and
up against the freezer. She was on the bottom step and feeling
nauseated herself at the sight and the smell that met her when
she registered Edwina's finish to the sentence.

"—not Libby."

It was what a gruesome death had left of Marlin Wetzel.

Charlie turned, breathing hard through her mouth, hanging
onto the railing as her mother had, taking one step at a time,
looking at the woman at the top of the stairs and seeing Marlin.

"Now will you call Kenny?" Edwina swayed.

Charlie had the presence of mind to pull off the soiled robe and put her mother into a kitchen chair. "Wait till I get you something to wear."

She dropped the sour garment in the bathtub on the way to Edwina's bedroom and grabbed the black peignoir with Missy's hair all over it.

Kenny was unreachable, a dispatcher assured her guardedly.

"Well, you sure as hell better get somebody out here. We've got a dead body in the basement." When Charlie gave Edwina's address, she was told to lock her doors and sit tight, help was already on its way. "It better be. My daughter's out there somewhere, and we got a dead body in the basement."

"You said that twice," Edwina noted.

"Oh, shut up," Charlie told the frazzled, sagging post-op patient in the mousy hair and sheer black lingerie who had just stumbled across a nightmare. The peignoir looked silly over a white nightgown that came to her knees. "I'm sorry. I'm just . . . You lost your lunch—would you like something to eat while we wait?"

Edwina thought some hot tea and dry toast might stay down, and she grew chatty while Charlie prepared it, probably an attempt to dispel the memory picture of the sight on the basement floor. Marlin had tossed his cookies too, major.

"I haven't heard a naughty word from you since we got here," Charlie said when the conversation lagged. "Not even when you were looped on morphine. Last month you were calling people dickhead and asshole and worse. What's happened?"

"Guess I'm not angry anymore—like you said, the lymph nodes were clear. Besides, I don't like swearing around Libby any better than you do."

"She knows and uses words worse than anything you or I could imagine."

"Not around me, she doesn't."

That was true. Edwina and Libby enjoyed a certain respect for each other that Charlie envied. But right now she'd settle for knowing the kid was safe.

When the phone rang, Charlie hoped it was Libby or Kenny instead of New York or California. It was Maggie Stutzman, friend and neighbor on the opposite front corner of the compound in Long Beach, who was caring for Tuxedo. Tuxedo had tangled with another tom in the alley behind Jeremy Fiedler and Betty Beesom, who owned the condos in the back corners.

"I took him to your vet for shots and stitching and am keeping him over here to watch for signs of infection. Meantime, Charlie, my carpet's full of fleas. What should I do?"

"Wait for fall. You could get him a new flea-and-tick collar too. I'll reimburse you when I get home, but we do tend to live with fleas in the summer."

"When will that be? How's Edwina?"

"Well, the lymph nodes were clear." Charlie didn't want to get started on the problem in the basement.

"That's wonderful news. Give her my congratulations and love. Take the time to appreciate her for once. I've also been hearing about wildfires and witchcraft or something in Boulder and your Keegan Monroe here. You tend to get in the thick of excitement wherever you go."

"Tell me about it."

"I must travel with you sometime. My life is so dull." Maggie was a lawyer stuck in workman's comp cases and growing sick of legal housekeeping.

"Listen, Maggie, I'll fill you in on everything in a day or two, okay? Right now things are a little tense here, and I have to get off the line. We should be home soon. I'll let you know. And I really do appreciate your keeping track of the damn cat for me."

"Hey, Greene, take a deep breath and settle down. I'm sure whatever it is, you can handle it. You're something else, you know?"

Somehow, Charlie didn't think she'd like this crazy world half so well if it didn't have Maggie Stutzman in it.

"Maggie says congrats on the lymph nodes and sends her love."

"You have yourself a very good friend there." Edwina put another slice of bread in the toaster and then shuddered. "How can I be hungry knowing *that* is still in the basement?"

"Maybe it's the Percocet kicking in. And why am I so worried about not knowing where Libby is, now that I know Marlin the Bogeyman will never harm anyone again?"

"Because there's obviously more than Marlin happening around here, but don't ask me what it is." Edwina put the kettle on for more tea and bent over the counter. "Did you put out ant poison?"

"No, but something got spilled that attracted ants and killed them." She put in a piece of bread to toast for herself. "There were spots of something that had dripped on the counter this morning. I wiped them up. The drips were circled by dead ants. I got so involved in the aspirin in your Percocet bottle and the sudden interest of publishers in Reynelda's manuscript, I guess I missed that one." Charlie reached for the dishcloth. "I don't know what you were doing when you got up last night but it was sure hard on the ant population."

Edwina threw her half-eaten toast in the sink and slapped the dishcloth out of Charlie's hand. "Don't touch anything more until Kenny gets here. Charlie, I didn't come in the kitchen last night. I used the bathroom but that was it."

"Which means I can't eat a piece of toast?"

"Those ants look poisoned, right? Well, so does Marlin Wetzel."

For once, Charlie did what her mother asked and left the toast in the sink. She remembered the vomit downstairs.

Charlie and Edwina Greene turned together to stare at the refrigerator. And Charlie didn't have to be psychic to know they both dreaded that Libby may have tried the same dish Marlin Wetzel had when he'd paused to dine from the neighborhood casseroles filling the refrigerator.

Charlie looked at the screen sitting up against the wall. Had Marlin come back last night to see if Edwina's prescription had been refilled, found it hadn't, and decided to snack instead? Charlie and Libby had come in late. What if they'd surprised him?

❖

Jennifer Tollerude escaped her police guard at Boulder Community Hospital when he left the door to go to a nearby water fountain. A few minutes later, when the next shift went in to check the patient, the bed was empty.

"We were on our way to the Tollerude house when we got a report of another body," Kenny said just inside the door. "Charlie, this is the third one you've found in a week."

"I didn't find it. Edwina did. It's Marlin Wetzel. He's in the basement."

"Poisoned," Edwina added. "Ate some of the food intended for this household, Kenny. And we don't know where my granddaughter is."

If Kenny noticed how ridiculous Edwina looked, he had the decency not to show it. She was unaware she resembled an ape in drag, scratching at her bandaged middle through the black chiffon.

Officer Darla came up from the basement looking put upon, as usual, but not particularly impressed. She and Kenny returned to the gruesome scene and then retired to the back step to discuss Darla's take on it in privacy. Someone else knocked at the front door. Charlie raced to open it, hoping to find Libby, but Mitch Hilsten stood on the step, his arms filled with books.

"Charlie, I think I've found the answer to everything."

"What, the meaning of life?"

"No, the strange ceremonies in Columbia Cemetery." He hurried past her and downloaded the stack of reading material on the dining room table.

"Mitch, we've got a dead body in the basement, and I don't know where Libby is and . . . and somebody poisoned Marlin, what if Libby ate the same thing?"

"Who's Marlin?" The superstar downloaded his look of triumph too.

"Well, if it isn't the big deal movie star." Kenny leaned in the kitchen doorway. "Just what we need."

The looks the guys exchanged were not flattering.

The phone's ring was not welcome. It was Pitman's, wanting to know where the bidding stood. Charlie, who hadn't thought she'd started it yet, could barely remember Braintree's latest unofficial offer, what with the press of current events. When she came up with the number, the voice on the other end said—

"Christ. Already? Okay, we're in." This was not Ellen Harm but Jerry Greenfeld, whom Charlie had thought was in sub rights. Had Boulder and Tom Horn hit national headlines again? She made businesslike noises and promised to accept no offers until she'd called him.

"We really don't need you here right now, Hilsten. We've got a situation. You are just a distraction."

"Kenny, he can stay with Edwina while I look for Libby, unless you and Officer Darla—"

"She's staying with Marlin Wetzel. I'm going after Jennifer Tollerude next door. We were wondering if anybody had told Emmy—wondering if you could do that."

Charlie took the assignment to get out of the house to look for her daughter, racing over to Emmy's first to fulfill her part of the bargain.

When she pounded on the back door, it opened all by itself. Silently. God, she hated when this happened in movies, but for real, it was *really* tough to take.

If this were a script written by a guy, I would walk in, shaking in my shoes and get hit over the head or knifed in the back by somebody behind the door.

Charlie pushed the door until it banged against the wall, but she didn't walk in. Even when she recognized the one totally out of place thing on the kitchen table.

---◆---

C HARLIE STOOD ON Emmy Wetzel's back porch, more of a semi-open lean-to. Room here for muddy boots and a few bags of birdseed, an old metal lawn chair to sit on in the morning sun with a cup of coffee, to watch the birds have breakfast.

But with the door to the kitchen fully open and by moving back and forth across this lean-to porch, Charlie could see the entire kitchen. Emmy did not lay dead on the polished floor tile, nor did Libby.

The room was decorated in Swiss chalet fashion, tiny flowers on ruffled chair cushions, knickknack shelves crowded with dust catchers, and at least six cuckoo clocks.

The odors of cooked cabbage and cinnamon. The arrhythmic clunking of wooden clocks slightly out of sync. Emmy had upgraded from the avocado stove and refrigerator. The table and chairs were a polished wood instead of the old Formica and plastic. Still, this room reminded Charlie of Disney's version of Pinocchio as much as it had when she was a child.

But for the one obtrusive difference—the notebook computer sitting on Emmy's kitchen table.

Charlie yelled Emmy's name, but she did not poke her head inside that door.

Right, somebody can't shoot you from the door to the living room? If Emmy is dead too, she can answer?

I am *not* stepping through this door.

You've seen too many movies.

Charlie left the door just where it was and turned away from it, denying the temptation to play silly, curious heroine. Lance Kelso stood on Lita's back porch, watching her.

"Looking for Emmy?"

No, Barbara Streisand. "Yes, and Libby. Have you seen them?"

"They're in here." He cocked a thumb over his shoulder at his mother's door.

Lance the millionaire watched her pass through Emmy's gate and cross the alley and his mother's yard with an unnerving disdain expressed simply by one raised eyebrow. When she came to stand at the bottom of the porch steps, he stared down his nose without lowering his head.

"I hate you too."

"I know." He still didn't blink.

"What's Libby doing over here?"

"Why don't you come in and see for yourself?"

Libby sat alive and healthy on one of Lita's low-slung chairs, tan legs stretched to the side of the man perched on a low chow table in front of her, dark eyes wide with disbelief.

"He has a right," Heather Tynne hissed at Charlie's elbow.

Lita hoisted herself up from the canoe couch. She was getting too old for this kind of furniture. "Come sit down, Charlie. I'll get you some iced tea."

"First, tell us what's going on over at your house," Lance said. "Look's like the police are back."

Charlie's ears were ringing. She stood just inside the door and refused to go further. One of the Dweeb brothers sat on the stairs. Emmy Wetzel and Twyla Clark, the cancer counselor, sat in other chairs along the far wall with Libby. And the guy in front of Libby turned around to stare.

Charlie started at the safest point, with Lita Kelso, her voice sounding far away over the ringing. "So this is where *my* daughter met up with Wiggims and the love child idea."

Lita stood in the middle of the room as if uncertain to go for tea. "Those two insisted." She gestured toward the millionaire and the Realtor on either side of Charlie. "And Twyla said it was for the best."

"And the young gentleman on the stairs?" Charlie progressed to the next least important item, hoping to be able to handle the hard stuff when her blood pressure lowered.

"He lives here," Twyla answered.

Lita said, "I always rent to a couple of students."

"Just like I used to, Charlie," Emmy added.

"I need to talk to you, Emmy. Privately."

"You haven't answered my question," Lance insisted.

"That's right."

"You don't need to talk to *me* privately?" Buddy MacCallister asked. He wasn't as dumb-looking nor anywhere as good-looking as Charlie remembered.

"That's right."

"Charlie, there is nothing unusual about people in the biz networking," Libby's biological father said.

"But there are ways to go about it, and you'll not find them in how-to books. And I am probably the last person in the 'biz' you should approach." I got the clout this time, Buddy-boy.

"You might need a favor someday." Buddy began to look and sound more like himself, just older and more plump.

"I needed a favor some years ago."

"Times were different then," Heather said, her eyes wide with phony shock. "Guys weren't supposed to do anything when girls got pregnant."

"I don't notice any guy offering anything now."

"One should always consider the danger of making enemies in the tight economy we now enjoy." Lance couldn't quite hide his delight at getting Charlie to spark.

227

"That's right, Lance, and he made one a long time ago. Emmy, could I have a word with you?"

But it was Libby who unfolded from the low seating first and stalked to the door, whispering to Charlie in passing, "Jesus, I thought you had *some* fucking taste. Wrong again, huh, UM?"

"I'll never allow my daughter to speak to me that way." Heather's righteous shock was convincing this time.

Wait till one wrong move on your part could push her over the edge in stupid decision-making that could wreck her life, and yours too. Just you wait, Heather Tynne.

Outside, a black-and-white followed an ambulance up the alley, both stopping on Edwina's garage apron, neither bothering with flashing lights.

"Your mamma?" Emmy looked up at Charlie, little round eyeglasses on a little round face reflecting the summer colors.

"No. Emmy—"

"I make coffee." Marlin's mom took off for the back door Charlie had left open. "You come."

"Is this your computer?" Charlie asked while Emmy spooned Folger's crystals into two gold-rimmed cups settled in gold-rimmed saucers. Charlie felt silly for earlier being afraid to enter this sparkling homey room.

"I don't know from computers."

"Emmy—"

"You want sugar?"

"This is my mom's computer, isn't it? Marlin stole it from her office at the University, didn't he? And broke into the house earlier looking for it there."

Emmy stood with her back to Charlie, staring out the window over the sink, her arms spread out against the counter, folds of sagging flesh hanging down over her elbows.

"He has hurt someone?" The breathless dread in this mother's voice tied a knot in Charlie's chest.

"Only himself this time." And you, as always. Oh, please don't turn around. "He's dead, Emmy."

After a long silence: "It is over, then."

"I'm sorry, but maybe you can finally find peace now." Charlie turned off the gas flame under the whistling kettle. "Want some coffee?"

Emmy just shook her head. "There is no peace for Emmy."

Charlie didn't want any coffee either. Marlin's mother didn't cry. She did let Charlie hug her. Charlie cried enough for both of them.

Finally, when Emmy pulled away, Charlie said, "Can I call someone for you?"

"No. They will hover soon enough. How did he . . ."

"He broke into our house last night, through the kitchen window, I think." You may always grieve, but don't feel guilty. Your son asked for what he got. And just so you should know that, "I found the screen leaning against your garage. He was looking for Edwina's painkillers and stopped to snack out of the refrigerator. My mother thinks he died of poisoning. We found him in the basement. It was probably one of the casseroles the neighbors had left."

"Not my schnitzel and—"

"No, that was gone. The only one we hadn't all eaten out of was Lita Kelso's."

Charlie turned at an odd noise and found Twyla Clark standing in the still-open doorway, her hand over her mouth.

Kenny Eisenburg loomed suddenly behind her. "Do you want to see him, Emmy? It's not necessary. Charlie, Edwina, and I have all ID'd him. It's not pretty."

Emmy just shook her head and reached up to wipe the wet from Charlie's cheeks. She whispered, "It's all right, liebchen."

"Better to remember him the way he was," Twyla counseled and then thought about the way Marlin Wetzel was, and added, "when he was a baby."

"It isn't necessary I should see him, Kenneth. I would like to be alone for a time."

But Twyla stole the stage by holding her wrists up to Kenny. "Arrest me, detective. I confess."

"To what?"

"You poisoned my son?"

"That poison wasn't meant for him, Emmy. Twyla, you were trying to poison my mother because she wouldn't counsel with you? You didn't bring us a dish, did you?"

"I made the goulash Lita brought over to Edwina because Lita didn't have time and it called for a little meat. It takes thirty-six hours to cook. But I didn't put any poison in it."

CHAPTER 34

———❖———

"TWYLA CLARK DOES odd jobs to make ends meet and fill in for what counseling doesn't," Charlie told Edwina, Mitch, and Reynelda Goff as they munched on Kentucky Fried. Kenny and cohorts had cleaned out the refrigerator, and chicken was what Edwina wished for when Mr. Wonderful offered her anything she wanted.

He saved some face by pointing out, "You know this stuff isn't good for you, don't you?"

Charlie remembered him eating yogurt with granola and fruit for breakfast while she had huevos rancheros a lifetime ago in Moab, Utah, last month. But he was making a fair dent in the Original Recipe, mashed potatoes and gravy, coleslaw, and biscuits in Boulder, Colorado, this afternoon.

And so was Edwina. She'd had her Percocet, gotten rid of Marlin in the basement, and was looking better.

"Yeah, but fat is so comforting," Charlie said. "The last time I had KFC was two years ago in Oregon when I went up to see Keegan's dad."

"About Twyla," Reynelda prodded.

"Oh right, well she boxes mail orders for Lita's shop on the mall and cleans houses—"

"That's not news to us, Charlie. Twyla cleans for me," Reynelda said.

231

"She even cleans for the hot-snot widow next door." This was Edwina, with grease on her chin.

"Hot snot? Edwina Greene," Reynelda chided, "bet I know where that came from."

"My granddaughter." Edwina nodded. "Got more goodies for you, if you ever decide to write something modern and with-it."

"Excuse me?" Charlie broke in. "Anything else you know about Twyla Clark you haven't told me?"

"She lives just up the block on Ninth. The old Clayton mansion on the corner, made over into apartments. She rents there. Husband dumped her when she got breast cancer."

"Regular Newt Gingrich." Mitch reached for the container of gravy perched atop a stack of mail-order catalogues and junk mail on the dining room table. Journals, papers, and books, including those Mitch had brought, covered the rest, so they ate off paper plates on their laps.

"From what I hear about Twyla, he may have had other reasons." Edwina fixed the superstar with a less than friendly eye. "It's possible Mr. Gingrich did too."

Mitch looked surprised. He had forgotten Edwina's conservative bent. She sided with the liberals only on specific environmental issues.

"What else haven't you told me? Like the Dweeb brothers living with Lita?"

"I don't know you want to know something unless you ask me," her mother said patiently. "Yes, there are students over there, Ron and Lyle, I think—Libby knows them."

"They're not brothers," Reynelda added. "Ron Robertson, and I don't remember Lyle's last name. George hired them to help with restoring the flower beds after the renovators this spring. They're good workers."

"Seems awfully coincidental they'd meet Libby at Juanita's when they live right across the alley." Charlie didn't know that's when they'd met. Could have met earlier here in the neighborhood, and Charlie and Kenny had simply assumed they'd picked her up that night. Libby was fully capable of setting up a meeting from a public phone in the hospital without mentioning it. "And what was Marlin doing in the basement?"

"Maybe he was trying to get to the toilet down there to throw up. Didn't quite make it," Edwina said. "My guess is he panicked and chocked on his own vomit, by the look of him."

Charlie decided against another piece of chicken. "How would he know there was a toilet down there?"

"If he's the one that's been breaking into the house, he probably knew it pretty well."

He might have gone down in the basement when he heard Charlie and Libby come in late. "I think he's the one who broke into your office in Ramaley too. There was a notebook computer on Emmy's kitchen table. Kenny's confiscated it for the time being. Toshiba Satellite?"

"Sounds like it. I can see Marlin Wetzel going after the Percocet, Charlie, but what would he want with my computer?"

"Maybe he thought he could sell it and buy more drugs," Mitch offered.

"I think somebody hired him to break into the house for it. And the first time he found only a couple of backup disks, so he broke into your office. Edwina, what could he or whoever hired him hope to find on your hard disk? Think."

Edwina gnawed at the gristle on the end of a drumstick. "I hadn't put much new on it since I came back from Utah. I knew the lump was there and went right to the doctor. My life progressed from bad to horrible. Couldn't concentrate on much of anything. Hope I had everything backed up, what with Marlin and now Kenny messing with it. Since I'm probably not going to die tomorrow after all, I'm going to need that stuff."

Charlie didn't have the heart to tell her mother the shambles left of her office. Backup disks might be hard to find. "What 'stuff'? You had personal as well as work related 'stuff' on there, didn't you? Did you think on the computer—you know, like, noodle problems?"

"Charlie"—Mr. Wonderful could contain himself no longer—"I've been waiting to explain what I've learned about the meaning of life in Boulder's Satanic circles." He thumped one of the stacks of books he was responsible for, but before he could go on, the phone rang. Being an agent and living with a teenager Charlie was used to ringing phones, but she could see this was becoming an irritation to Edwina.

Charlie happened to be looking at Reynelda when Roger Tedesco at Braintree informed her they had heard informally of the informal offer by Pitman's and would up their own. She hadn't even let the perpetrator of all this madness in on what was happening.

Here Charlie was in the middle of a murder or three and looking at an about-to-be wealthier lady who had no clue she was even going to sell a first book to a New York publisher. First books normally earned a tiny advance, to which the author had to add a year's wages at a real job for self-promotion. This to make at least a blip on the sales chart/report cards of the corporate world.

Charlie might be looking at the first star book author she'd ever handled who wasn't dead. Reynelda Goff plastic-spooned coleslaw and stared back in sweet innocence.

"Certainly worth considering, but I'm assuming your legals don't plan to hit us with boilerplate on electronic, and that there will be a nice escalator for film."

Mitch started in again the minute she hung up. "Wait, I need to talk to Reynelda, who's soon to become a published author."

Reynelda took the astonishing news with little show of excitement. She did set down her coleslaw, pull a string of white meat off a chicken breast, and slip it to Missy Tollerude, who had appeared from nowhere, stretching and yawning.

"What did I tell you?" Edwina wiped greasy fingers with glee and one of those alcohol soaked paper things that come in a foil packet with the chicken. "If anybody could do it, Charlie could. Can't wait to see old George's face when he hears of this."

Everyone took startling news in different ways and would be hard pressed to predict a reaction in advance, but Reynelda rather seemed like she could wait.

"I'm grateful, Charlie, really I am."

"You realize this will probably be a two-book deal. If the ceiling keeps rising, more like three? And that you are an incredibly lucky lady?"

"I wouldn't have written it if I hadn't thought I could sell it to a publisher. What would have been the point?"

Charlie's mouth was still hanging open when Mitch congratulated the new author and then went right on to insist they discuss the demonic rites carried out in Columbia Cemetery.

"I've decided it's all a hoax," he said, surprising Charlie almost as much as Reynelda had. "I think someone is trying to scare the people of this neighborhood."

"Scare them into selling their homes and moving out?" Charlie'd had the same thought, but what about the high priest and the cloaked crowd only she and Libby thought they saw?

"That's a possibility."

"Something in all these books leads you to this conclusion?"

"More like the nothing in all these books. Listen." He grabbed one, opened at a bookmark, and began to read silly stuff. Mitch repeated these actions with at least four of the books. "See what I'm getting at? No reference to mountain lions nor to any of those symbols on the altar next door that Edwina described to me."

One of them did sound a little like that graveside performance with the knife and candles last night, though.

"What, you brought all these books over to show us they didn't have anything in them pertinent to the present problem?" Edwina asked, confused. "That's negative research. Not to say it isn't valid, but—"

"What about blood?" Charlie asked, watching Missy stretch her neck up to beg more chicken from Reynelda, who focused on Charlie instead.

"According to George, blood and wine or mead form a part of most rituals and religions since ancient times," the author said. "And house cats sometimes, if not mountain lions."

"What I can't figure out is how they got the mountain lions into those cages in the Tollerude basement," Charlie said.

"They baited traps with house cats." Edwina snapped her fingers. "That's what they wanted with my computer too."

"To bait a trap for a mountain lion?"

"No, I remember now, seeing odd cages under that atrocious waste of precious redwood next door the Tollerudes call a deck. That's one of the things I was keeping track of on my computer. I was hoping to keep my rats alive with sneak feedings in the alley, and I came across these traps. In fact, I let several cats out and logged that in my computer. Cougars couldn't have got to them the way the cages were rigged, but it could frighten the house cats to death just being that close. The Tollerudes probably saw me back there and thought I had more on them than I did."

"Mountain lions eat house cats?" Mitch asked.

"And dogs. They prefer to kill their own. In the mountains, they eat deer. But once in the city, it doesn't take them long to figure out that household pets don't have that gamey taste. One day it's going to be a human child left alone in someone's yard. It'll be a disaster for that child and that family, but it will be Armageddon for the resident wildlife."

Mitch nodded. "Man is ultimately the cruelest of creatures."

"I still don't understand why you were logging cages under the deck next door on your computer," Charlie said. "You didn't tell me you knew what was happening to the missing cats."

"You didn't mention missing cats, and I was keeping track of any strange goings on in or near that house, planning on filing suit, nagging my neighbors into action, and blitzing the city council and the zoning and planning departments with complaints and irritations such as letters to the "Open Forum" in the *Boulder Camera*. Oh, I lay awake nights planning revenge on the powers that be and those intent on forcing me out of the only life I had left. I was becoming an activist. Then I discovered the lump and didn't care about the neighborhood. Went on my trip to Utah as an expert for the documentary, all the time aware of that lump. Aware that I had not seen a doctor about it. Feeling so cheated in so many ways."

"I don't remember what kind of symbols were on that supposed altar next door," Charlie said, embarrassed to be changing the subject because she couldn't deal with it at this point.

"I thought there was something familiar about them, but I was so sick yesterday I couldn't think straight." Edwina found a pencil and some empty space to make hen scratches on a piece of paper. She passed it to Charlie, who'd paid more attention to Marlin Wetzel and caged mountain lions than the altar cloth.

"Looks like cartoon swearing."

"Does even more so if you turn it right side up. Only on the altar cloth they were upside down and sideways."

~!@#$%^&*( )__+<>?":{ }

CHAPTER 35

IT TOOK CHARLIE a moment to see what she was looking at, knowing she knew what it was but unable to access it. Access. "It's like you held the shift key down and hit all the keys on your computer keyboard that have signs instead of letters or numbers on top." Charlie handed it to Mitch.

He nodded. "Somebody's playing a big joke on somebody."

"Three dead men is no joke." Three so far—one shot, one poisoned, and Andy stabbed. Andy, who'd had the altar and captive lions and cats in his basement, had bled to death. Charlie pulled meat off a drumstick bone to lure Missy away from Reynelda. "The mountain lions had wounds on their necks, and even Missy here has a scab. Edwina, if you were going to draw blood from an animal, would you do so from the neck?"

"No more than I would on a person. Too close to the heart. Neck arteries pulse. It'd frighten animals more, people too. And it's a lot harder to puncture the arterial walls than you think, would cause more pain."

"But you could get blood from the neck?"

"Oh you could get more blood than you bargained for. . . . Andy Tollerude."

"Stabbed in the neck."

"You think somebody was just after his blood? Seems pretty drastic. . . . Most of it ended up on his front sidewalk."

"What if that somebody was an amateur? More interested in

238

a ritual than in a professional drawing of blood?"

"If you puncture the carotid, maybe. I don't see a needle doing *that* much harm."

"What if this amateur used a ceremonial knife?"

"That would do it." Edwina put a finger up against the place on the side of the neck where you'd feel for a pulse on somebody you weren't sure had one. "Make the hole too big in the carotid, and you might as well cut their throat."

"How long would it take Andy to lose consciousness if that's what happened to him?"

"I'm no medical doctor, but I'd guess two to three minutes."

"Time to get from his altar to his front yard." Charlie studied her new about-to-be-famous author.

"Here, kitty." Edwina enticed Missy to the other end of the table with more chicken but couldn't bend over to pick her up.

Mitch grabbed the cat and placed it on Edwina's lap. "I've seen that look on your face before, Charlie. You're detecting."

"Just noodling. Like you've been doing, except with all those silly books."

"It's possible somebody used a needle to draw blood from this cat and the others. I don't remember the wounds on the cougars but, like I say, I wasn't much use yesterday. Now that you mention it, there was a bandage on the floor of one of the cages. All we have to do is ask Kenny. But Charlie, why would somebody take a knife instead of a needle to Andy Tollerude? Why would anybody need that much blood? Especially if it's all a hoax, like Mitch thinks?"

Charlie was too busy watching Reynelda, who looked like she'd lost all *her* blood, to answer. At least all of it in her face.

"Even a hoax can have serious intent," Mitch offered. "Doesn't mean it's harmless."

The phone rang again, a distracted Charlie reached for it and looked up to see Detective Kenny Eisenburg appear in the kitchen doorway with his little cellular. He did not look happy.

"Who is this?"

"Charlie Greene. Who is *this?*"

"Jennifer from next door." Jennifer sounded like she'd gotten into Edwina's Percocet too. "I just wanted to tell you—your friend, Kenneth, has my daughter? Well, I have *yours.*"

The line went dead with Charlie staring at the mouthpiece, trying to digest the message. She stared at Kenny. "She has my what?"

"Your daughter."

"Somebody has my granddaughter?" Edwina stood. Missy made a leap for the table. Mitch grabbed the gravy. "Who?"

Kenny flicked his shiny forelock to the south. "But don't worry, I have a SWAT team on the way."

"You've been watching that house all this time and didn't notice a girl that size being kidnapped?" Mitch was wearing his *Deadly Posse* look again, but the gravy bucket nullified the effect.

"Just what is that supposed to mean, Hilsten?"

"I think it's pretty obvious."

"Jennifer Tollerude is holding Libby hostage next door?" Edwina interrupted. "What with, a gun?"

"The body in the alley was shot," Charlie said in a sort of dream trance and barely registered Reynelda Goff slipping out the front door. Edwina's best friend was not that helpful when the going got rough. "Kenny, a SWAT team could be a lot more dangerous than Jennifer Tollerude."

The men in black pants, shirts, boots, and tight hoods—which covered everything but the white oval of their faces—would have been harder to see at night. In broad daylight, they kind of stood out.

Charlie couldn't tell how many there were. They kept running and changing places and ducking between shadows that didn't hide them because the afternoon shadows were a light gray and these guys were black with white ovals. There was one spread out on his stomach on the roof of Howard's garage and another on Lita's, both of which Charlie figured Jennifer could pick off from Deborah's bedroom window pretty easily. But she couldn't point that out because Kenny wouldn't let her talk.

He was pissed because she and Mitch wouldn't stay with Edwina in the house. They crouched behind a black-and-white in the alley, Charlie between two heroes who were not getting along. She was close enough to Mitch to feel him tremble. He was supposed to be getting into the role of a train engineer at the turn of the century. She suspected he was fantasizing the mindset of a modern SWAT team instead.

She didn't know why she couldn't talk. Everyone else was.

Sharp commands came from all sides—some whispered, some aloud, some on radio phones, all very alarming, few she could translate.

Libby must be terrified. It had taken the SWATs at least a half hour to get here.

Officer Darla tried unsuccessfully to whisper someone back into the house behind Charlie, the one next to Lita's. Charlie turned to see a SWAT guy with a rifle on the roof and poor Darla on the balcony just below him with a crowd of people who must have come from several lots around, knowing where the best view would be.

Charlie didn't know how much longer she could hold the squat position. It was putting her feet to sleep.

When she heard a faint *psst,* she turned again, this time to see one of the dweebs motioning to her from the corner of Lita's garage, the SWAT above him on the roof unaware of his presence. Charlie was about to motion some silent secret response when . . .

"Jennifer Tollerude, the house is surrounded." Darth Vader's voice came from somewhere Charlie couldn't see. "Release the hostage, wait five minutes, and exit the house with your hands on your head!"

Charlie forgot all about the dweeb as Darth repeated the

message again and again, with very little variance in pitch.

Apparently nothing encouraging happened at the Tollerude house, because Darth was replaced with a kinder, gentler voice.

"Jennifer, this is Twyla, and I know how terrified you must be. Deborah is safe and well and waiting for her mommy. Don't disappoint her by doing something so unnecessary. Listen to me, Jennifer, put the gun down and walk out the kitchen door with Libby Greene. I promise you'll be holding your darling Deborah in your arms in less than an hour. She needs you, Jennifer."

If Charlie had been wearing a hat, she'd have had to take it off to Twyla Clark right then. How could any mother not respond to such reason?

But Twyla repeated the message of reason three times, and Charlie, growing restless, turned to see Ron or Lyle still trying to hail her with silent motions. She gave him a sidehanded "wait" gesture, but he straightened suddenly. So did the guy on the roof above, and the sharp commands around her became a cacophony.

Charlie tried to straighten too, to peer through the black-and-white's windows at the Tollerude back door. But so did Kenny and Mitch on either side of her, each with a hand on her shoulders to keep her down.

So she backed out of their hands and stood up straight to look over the top of the police car.

In a way, she wished she hadn't.

"Shit," she let out in a sigh. The guys, too late to protect her, stood too.

"Hold your fire!" Kenny yelled to the entire state.

"What is this?" a SWAT yelled from the next police-car barricade.

Edwina Greene stepped out of the sliding glass door and crossed the long redwood deck, her black peignoir dragging along behind her, the ruffles on the end of one sleeve not quite concealing the hand gun.

"Edwina?" the cancer counselor said from some remote speaker.

"Throw down your weapon," Darth Vader added.

"Oh, give it a break." Charlie raced into the fray before her two companions could grab her.

The world caught up with her at the Tollerude gate, where rough arms stopped her just as a weary Edwina looked down from the top step of the deck. "Charlie, there is nobody in there. I've been all over the place. Nobody."

———————————◆———————————

CHAPTER 36

K ENNY HAD BEEN so sure he had Jennifer trapped in her house, he hadn't traced her call to Charlie. And the superstar wouldn't let it rest.

"I know she was in there," Kenny insisted, rage darkening the skin along his cheekbones.

"Somebody has been," Edwina said. "The milk glass on the sink still has a damp coating on the bottom, and the jam on the table knife in the sink is sticky."

Everyone looking at her in surprise made her testy. "Well, I *am* a scientist."

"She said she was Jennifer *from* next door," Charlie remembered belatedly. "Not that she *was* next door."

Kenny held out a bag with the Ziplock open, and Edwina dropped in the weapon. "You didn't tell me you had a firearm."

"You didn't ask me."

"How did you get in that house without being seen?"

Kenny and Mitch had been duking it out with verbal bluster in the dining room and Reynelda had just disappeared out the front door when Edwina dragged herself off to her bedroom— Charlie had assumed because of exhaustion and worry over the fate of her granddaughter. But her mother grabbed the gun that two police searches had not discovered. She climbed out her bedroom window when Charlie and Mitch moved their argument with Kenny about refusing to stay in the house to the back step.

Edwina had motioned Reynelda earlier to leave, and she crossed directly to the Goff house after exiting the window. "Rey drove me around the block and pulled up in front of the monstrosity. I slipped through the gate, which is practically on the sidewalk, long before the guys in black arrived."

The motion detectors weren't set to go on in daylight, and the lights wouldn't have been that noticeable if they had. Edwina'd moved quickly to the south side of the Tollerude house and ducked into a large basement window well, broke the glass with the butt of the gun, and crawled inside.

"How could Reynelda let you do that?"

"She has grandchildren, Charlie. She understands."

Charlie had to admit this wasn't the first time she'd noticed simplicity and speed outsmarting deliberation in emergencies. She also knew the consequences for her mother and daughter could have been devastating. But Charlie hadn't been comfortable with the idea of the SWAT team either.

"Edwina, that was foolish in the shape you're in. What if Jennifer Tollerude had been holding a gun to Libby's head and pulled the trigger when she heard the glass break?"

"She'd have been one sorry female." Charlie's mother hiked up a dragging end of the ridiculous chiffon and tried to straighten her posture against the pull of the dressings. She winced. "Now, unless you plan to arrest me on the spot, Kenny Eisenburg, this surgical patient is headed for her bed. I suggest you find my granddaughter post haste."

Charlie should have held a wilted Edwina as she had Emmy Wetzel earlier, and she did follow along behind her mother as if accompanying her like the good daughter she wasn't. But when she heard the ire level rising between Mitch and Kenny again behind her, Charlie swung off for Lita's house.

He waited for her on the wooden swing on Lita Kelso's porch and acknowledged her with a nod. "How's it goin'?"

"Are you Ron or Lyle?" This was the guy sitting on the stairs when Libby met her biological father this afternoon.

"Lyle, Lyle Dean." He handed her a huge sweaty paw. "Careful," he eyed the exposed skin left by her shorts as she sat beside him. "Whole place is one big sliver."

He wore the latest summer fashion for young guys. Libby called them "droopy drawers." They looked like baggy knee-length boxer shorts and usually bore silly designs. These had brown-and-yellow fish who appeared to be attempting to mate with forked tongues. The analogy escaped Charlie.

The ensemble was completed by a clean black muscle shirt, filthy shredded baseball cap worn backwards, and sandals that may have been rescued from the landfill too late.

"I hope you wanted to tell me where Libby is," she led the conversation when Lyle didn't rush in with anything. Charlie had the sinking feeling she and Libby didn't have a lot of time.

"Up there." He gestured in the general direction of the Flatirons and Flagstaff Mountain.

"That's kind of a big area, Lyle." Charlie tried to swallow a gelatinous mass of phlegmy goo that wanted to clog her air intake when she drew in breath. The swing stilled, they watched an ancient bomber drop slashes of red slurry at the crest of the horizon, instead of on the other side as before. Two news helicopters vied for position, fighting updrafts, smoke clouds, and a clearly rising wind, as well as the ungainliness of another slurry bomber lumbering in behind the first. "Could you be a little more specific?"

The red in the sky was too early for sunset.

"Mr. Kelso's cabin." Good old Lyle confirmed Charlie's worst fears.

"Who's with her, Lyle?"

"Mr. Kelso and that Heather chick." An endless scream of sirens on Ninth turned the wrong way on Baseline. Boulder was gearing up for serious trouble, as Charlie should be.

"Why are you telling me this?"

"Because I don't want them to hurt Libby. She's a good kid."

Charlie had to backtrack a moment in her turmoil to register that he was probably nineteen or twenty. To him a sixteen-year-old was a kid and he wasn't.

Are we kind of avoiding the issue here?

Charlie was infinitely more worried about Libby in Lance Kelso's hands than in Jennifer Tollerude's. He wasn't a mother. "Did they force her?"

"I don't know, I wasn't here. Mrs. Kelso told me they'd all gone up to the cabin."

"All? Did that include Jennifer Tollerude? And where's your friend Ron?"

"I don't know where he is, and I'm worried."

"I'd better talk to Lita myself."

"She went down to the shop. She's not here."

"With all this excitement in the neighborhood, she left?"

Lyle nodded, watching the flames lick up behind Flagstaff. "She's crazy, but nothing like him."

Charlie tried to fight down panic long enough to discern how much of what he told her was true. "Where is that black van that was parked next to Lita's garage on the other side?"

"Up at the cabin. Mrs. Greene—"

"Charlie."

"Charlie, I want to go with you. Make sure Libby's all right? By the looks of things, we might have to put on some ruggeder clothes."

"Kenny!" Charlie stood and waved and ran down the steps, but the detective didn't even look her way as he and Darla and the black-and-white shot down the alley, Darla driving. Charlie turned around to glare at Lyle. Why was it there was always a hero underfoot until you needed one? "Tell me about the blood," she demanded.

"Now? We have to hurry."

"Okay, run change clothes and meet me over at my mom's house. Do you have a car?"

247

"Yeah, I'll be there in five minutes. We've wasted too much time already. Pick you up in the alley."

"How much do you trust your buddy Reynelda?" Charlie yelled as she raced through the house.

"Implicitly," Edwina yelled back from her bedroom. "What's happening?"

"Tell you in a minute," Charlie tore up the stairs just as Mitch came out of Edwina's bedroom. God, he was wasted on super-starism. He ought to be a nurse. "Call her now."

Mitch walked into the guest room just as she dropped her shorts and pawed through packed, unpacked, and repacked luggage for the one pair of jeans she'd brought, lightweight and comfortable from too many washings.

"Where the hell have you been?"

"Talking to Lyle Dweeb. He says Libby's up at the cabin."

"What cabin?" The superstar grabbed the back of the jeans and gave her a snuggie, helping shake her down into them. Then he came around in front to hold them together so she could zip them. "I don't see how women breathe in these things."

"You don't know Lance Kelso has a cabin in the mountains?"

"I don't even know Lance Kelso."

Charlie kicked off her sandals and reached for her trusty Keds. "He's a millionaire."

"That's nice." Mitch knelt to shove the other shoe on her foot while she tied the first.

"He's got Libby." Charlie grabbed a lightweight jacket—the only one she'd brought—and stopped to pick up a sweatshirt and jeans for her daughter.

"Why has he got Libby?" Mitch asked behind her as she raced back down the stairs.

"That's what we're going up there to find out."

"We? You mean me too? You don't want me to stay home and do the dishes or anything?"

"Edwina, did you get a hold of Reynelda?" Charlie turned at the door to her mother's bedroom, and Mitch ran into her. "Don't get huffy on me now. This is serious."

"Huffy? Who's huffy? I'm honored to be included."

"Listen, I finally need a hero, okay? Looks like you're it. Do you mind?"

"But what about Jennifer Tollerude?" Edwina asked behind her.

"All I know is one of the Dweeb brothers over at Lita's—"

"They're not brothers."

"Lyle says Lance and Heather have taken Libby up to Lance's cabin. He apparently knows where it is. I don't."

"You're not going up there alone with him?"

"I'm taking Mitch. That's why I wanted Reynelda to take you to the closest shelter. The fire's coming over the mountain. You and this house are too close. Listen—"

Sirens and slurry bombers, wind and thrashing tree limbs. Charlie and her mom stood staring at each other.

"My granddaughter and my data," Edwina actually had tears on her cheeks when Reynelda Goff walked in without knocking.

"Mom, your data is safe on your computer in Kenny's office."

"You called me Mom. . . ."

"Now stop that." She turned to Reynelda. "I need to get my mother into some decent clothes and out of here. I need Howard's Jeep. Do you have your car?"

"George just left with it, I don't know where he's gone. We only have the one because he can walk to the University."

"The fire's coming over the mountain. I have to know she can get out of here."

"So *we're* going to drive into it?" the hero said but handed Reynelda his keys. "Take the Bronco parked out at the curb. I get to go with Charlie."

"Now you stop it too." Charlie ran for Edwina's medicine.

"Grab some clothes," Reynelda said. "You can put them on in the car."

"But Elmer and Louise . . ."

"We have room for Elmer and Louise." Reynelda rushed into Edwina's room and picked up the cage. "Now hurry."

CHAPTER 37

I CAN'T REMEMBER ever seeing Edwina cry before, not when I told her I was pregnant, not when my dad died. . . ." Charlie and Mitch raced around, closing up the house. "Now I know things are really bad."

"God, you're beautiful when you get upset."

"Will, you *puleeeze* stop?" She locked the back door and pulled him into the shadow of the garage just as a pickup pulled onto Howard's garage apron and beeped. "Now here's the plan. I don't trust Lyle or any of them. I don't know what's going on." She shoved the keys to the old Jeep at him. "You've got to follow us. Don't lose us, okay?"

"Why can't the three of us go together?"

"Because, if you're with me when something goes wrong, you won't be able to rush in and save the day because you'll be in the same fix I am." Heros could be so dense.

Charlie jumped into the truck beside Lyle and he took off with a squeal before she had the door closed.

Not that it did them much good.

They were turned back at the end of Ninth Street by a row of cars jamming Baseline and a private security rent-a-cop who was helping out with crowd control in the crisis. His uniform looked official, but Centurion Guards was embossed on a sew-on badge above his left breast pocket instead of Boulder Police. He informed them Flagstaff Road was closed to all but emergency traffic and advised them to head for shelters being set up at Centennial Middle School and Crestview Grade School out in North Boulder.

Buddy MacCallister lived close to both, and Charlie experienced the inappropriate reflection that it was ironic she should be sent to Dog Patch in an emergency.

Lyle swore professionally, whisked the pickup around, and headed them back down Ninth in the other lane, passing Howard's Jeep and a startled Mitch Hilsten in the jam-up.

"What do we do now?" She couldn't help looking out the back window to see if Mitch turned around too. It didn't seem he could. A solid stream of the bottleneck traffic on Baseline had been diverted to the lane behind her.

"Find another way."

"There isn't another road up Flagstaff."

"Not from this side." The truck was one of those high-wheeled things and definitely rode like a truck. In spite of the seat belt, Charlie bounced above the traffic, hanging onto the door handle.

"But where are we going?" And how will Mitch find us?

"I'm counting on them not closing off Boulder Canyon yet." They ran a light on Arapaho and turned left on a yellow at Canyon Boulevard. "Most of the fuzz is going to be busy tonight. Keep your fingers crossed we don't cross one." He stepped on the gas. "I'm going to get you to Libby. Don't you worry."

And they were in the canyon, the cars coming at them with lights and fast like they were evacuating Nederland? No, too far away. Maybe the citizens of Nederland were on their way down to watch Boulder burn.

Lyle hooted like a cowboy on Nickelodeon. "We made it."

"What if Lance's cabin is in the path of the fire?"

"That's what's got me worried."

"Lyle, why is that black van up at the cabin? Whose is it?"

Car lights flashed on sheer rock walls. They took the curves with squeals, and Charlie had another ill-timed reflection. This

252

used to be the most hazardous road in Colorado, as far as volume of traffic, dangerous curves, and fatal accidents. She just wanted to live long enough to see that Libby did. Was that too much to ask? And poor Mitch was long gone, and here she was alone with this kid who might or might not mean her and her daughter good.

She longed for the security of merely having to worry about Keegan Monroe's every mood in Folsom Prison.

"Ron's," the kid finally answered the question she'd nearly forgotten she'd asked.

"And Ron's van is up at the cabin because it smells too bad to be left in the city, right?"

He'd changed into shredded Levi's, solid hiking boots, and thrown a jacket over his muscle shirt. He was a big kid, emanating an energy that almost made heat in the truck cab. "How'd you know?"

"The dead man in the alley."

"Ron didn't have nothing to do with that."

"How did that man get in the van? How did he get shot, and who dumped him in the alley, Lyle?"

"I just know it wasn't Ron. I got a suspicion though."

"Lance Kelso."

"He's the mover and shaker over at Mrs. Kelso's, let me tell you."

"Why? Who was the dead man?"

"Somebody's husband. I don't know whose, honest, Mrs. Greene, so don't ask. Hold on. . . ." And the truck swung off the road, narrowly missing the car in the lane it crossed, bumped down toward Boulder Creek, over a bridge, and through the graveled parking lot of the Red Lion Inn, famous for its setting and for its wild game that didn't taste gamey— That last according to Edwina, who used it to entertain guests from out of town rather than face clearing off the dining room table. It was also where Charlie had gone to dinner the night of her only prom.

The old lodge stood shuttered and dark, except for security lights at the doors. Only a maintenance truck in the graveled parking lot.

"Why did we turn off here?" Charlie panicked and made no attempt to sneak the look she sent out the back window. No Mitch Hilsten in Howard's Jeep had turned off behind them. She was truly alone out here with this guy.

"Just passing through."

"Through what? There's no road."

The Red Lion Inn shared a wide curve in the canyon with the most dangerous highway in Colorado and Boulder Creek. Once across the parking lot, they met up with a small stretch of rock and weeds and then a wall of mountain. Just when Charlie thought the kid was going to send the pickup climbing over the wild terrain and bash them into the mountainside he swung the wheel to the right and gunned them through a gate.

"Is too a road. Just private is all. Used to be an old mining road."

They dragged wire for twenty feet, but the wood part of the gate lay in splinters behind them. It was twilight up at the top of the canyon, night down at the bottom. Charlie kept hoping to see lights following them. But the only ones she saw were on the highway, and after the first switchback they were gone too.

This was more of a track than a road, and boulders had pushed up through it over the years. Forest soon crowded in close to each side. Grassy weeds grew down the narrow track's center, reminding Charlie of the alley behind her mother's house.

"Now tell me about the blood," she demanded.

He pretended to concentrate on his driving. Which made Charlie suspect he was trying to make up lies. "Ron and me," he said finally, "didn't swipe the blood. Just the dead cats."

"From Lita Kelso's basement mortuary? Why?"

"Yeah, it was a joke, you know? Every time we'd put one of 'em in the cemetery, we'd read about it in the paper the next day, even see it reported on TV news. Kind of a kick. Until old Emmy catches me running through her yard and comes after me, threatening to shoot. I didn't know it was a water gun."

"So somebody else stole the blood?"

"Mrs. Tollerude said it was us, but it wasn't."

"Who do you think it was?"

"I think it was old man Goff. He's into some pretty strange stuff."

"Did you know Mr. Tollerude before he died?"

"Yeah, you know he wanted us to shoot a deer? That's against the law. Offered to run one over with my truck. But no, I had to shoot it so there'd be a lot of blood left. Not illegal to run over the town deer, but you shoot one and you've got every animal-rights type calling the police with your description and videotaping you hauling the carcass away."

"To the Tollerude basement."

"They needed the blood for the ceremonies and the meat for the big cats."

"Why do you think Professor Goff stole the blood?"

"He's damn near as weird as Mr. Kelso. Voluntary donations, jeez. Cat blood wasn't good enough. He didn't let you pretend either."

"Did he have some role in the ceremonies?"

"He took them over right away. Mr. Tollerude couldn't control things once Professor Goff joined."

"Did Mrs. Goff ever come to a ceremony?"

"Not that I saw."

"What does Mr. Kelso want with my daughter, Lyle?"

There was a long thinking-time silence here too, and long dark places between the trees. "You know, they put live kitties in traps to try to lure the mountain lions? I wonder if Mr. Kelso's using Libby as a lure to get you."

CHAPTER 38

CHARLIE WAS STILL trying to assimilate the unconnected pieces of information or hastily made-up lies Lyle Dean had told her when they bounced up a gully and onto a real road—gravel but two-lane. In the growing darkness, burned tree skeletons and a chimney—all that remained of a house—stood out against the sky.

What would Lance Kelso want with Charlie? His only apparent interest seemed to have been to introduce Buddy to her daughter, and that he'd accomplished on his own.

If Edwina's home was in danger now, so was his own mother's. You'd think he'd be worried about that.

"Tell me about Mrs. Tollerude, Lyle. Where does she fit into this? It was Jennifer who called threatening Libby, not Lance."

"She works for Mr. Kelso."

"Doing what?"

"Don't ask me. But that's where she gets her orders. So did her husband."

"And Lita, what say did she have in any of this?"

"Oh, she never questioned Mr. Kelso. You know mothers."

"So the body in the alley, this somebody's husband—how did it get from your friend Ron's van into the alley yesterday?"

"We pushed it out. Smelled really bad. Drove it around front, ran in and asked Mrs. Kelso what to do, and she said to take it up to Mr. Kelso's cabin and leave it. The van I mean. Ron set out to do that, and I haven't seen him since. Okay, I'm worried about Libby, but, Mrs. Greene, I'm worried about Ron too."

"I thought you said you and Ron didn't have anything to do with the body in the alley?"

"We didn't kill him is what I meant. And we didn't know he was in the van till we opened the door. We wigged, okay?"

"But I saw that van turning into the alley last night. How could it if Ron brought it up here yesterday?"

"Probably saw Mrs. Clark's van. In the dark it looks like Ron's, but it's maroon instead of black. She lives up at the end of the block in that apartment house, and they park in back."

"Twyla Clark, the cancer counselor?"

"She's also a cleaning lady. Keeps her vacuum cleaner, mops, and stuff in the van."

"Does she clean Lita's house?"

"Nobody cleans Mrs. Kelso's house. That place is just one big lint, dust, and hairball—perfect for a couple of grubby students." According to Lyle, Twyla offered to clean Lita's house free last week to repay the kitty mortician for preparing her recently deceased cat for burial but withdrew the offer when Lance snuck it out of the back room and put it in the store window. "She really got her panties twisted over that. But the guy for sure has a mean streak."

"Why would Lita have the last remains of Twyla's cat down at the Shop of Mystery if Twyla lives right in the neighborhood?"

"She wanted to show it to a customer who was going to have to put her cat to sleep. City people are silly about cats. At home, we have them just to keep down the mice and snakes."

"Isn't Lita vegetarian?" Or had Lance lied to Charlie about that too? "How do you handle the cooking arrangements—are you and Ron vegetarians?"

"Hell no, we're from the western slope," he said with pride. And he didn't mean this side of the front range but the *other* side of the Continental Divide.

"Brought up on steak and potatoes, beans and eggs. My dad's a rancher and Ron's manages a peach cannery. No, we eat out a lot, and Mrs. Kelso, she lets us grill stuff on the back porch. We can bring it in to eat it. My folks just have a conniption fit when I tell them about it. My mom says Boulder's screwier than television. Like, we have to use our own utensils and dishes. Other than that it's been a cool place to live until Mr. Tollerude kicked off."

"Could the man in the alley have been Twyla Clark's husband? The ex-husband?"

"I don't think the dead guy was that old."

Charlie didn't either. So where to go from here? "Why does Mr. Kelso—Lance—need all this blood for ceremonies? And what are these ceremonies supposed to accomplish?" What would a millionaire businessman with his own plane and pilots need with a scam like such a bizarre ritual?

Could Charlie's nemesis even now be draining the lifeblood from Libby Abigail Greene? The kid sitting next to her was right about one thing—Lance Kelso did have a mean streak.

"Beats me. I never even seen him until after Mr. Tollerude bled all over his front walk. I don't think Kelso was even in Boulder then. I didn't know about this cabin until a few days ago. But I still think he's the man pulling the strings behind those who get to take the fall. And Mrs. Greene, Ron and me don't plan on taking it. That's why I've put so much trust in you tonight. Our folks couldn't handle it if we got in any real trouble."

"I appreciate your candidness, but somehow this doesn't all add up." This wasn't the first time Charlie wished she really were psychic.

The wind wasn't as violent on this side of the front range. But the fire had been here. In patches, leaving other places untouched. Whole swaths of still-smoking tree skeletons stood next to an unburned meadow with healthy trees on the other side. As if the wind had driven the fire ahead of it so fast it flared in streaks, stopped at a wall of rock, and flared up again some-where else.

Embers glowed red in places, and there was no one here beating them out with a shovel or pouring water on them. Most of the professional forest-fire fighters had boarded planes at DIA.

"What exactly were the Tollerudes doing for Mr. Kelso, Lyle?"

He snorted impatience with her incessant questioning. "I don't know. Holding blood ceremonies in their basement."

"What part did you and Ron take in those ceremonies?"

"None after Mr. Tollerude died. Christ, my folks didn't want me to come to Boulder. Wanted me to go to school in Gunni-son. Wait till they hear about all this."

"Was Mr. Tollerude murdered?"

"It was an accident. And things wouldn't have got so out of hand if that's all that happened. I mean, it's too bad, but we knew it wasn't murder so that made it—"

"Made it all right with your consciences?"

"Well, what were we supposed to do? We're just kids."

"The man in the alley had a bullet hole in his head, Lyle. Mar-lin Wetzel was murdered by poison. I'm not too sure it was meant for him, but poisoning the wrong person is still murder. So, we have one fatal accident and two murders you and your friend Ron are involved in."

"And I don't want there to be any more. That's why we're hurrying, Mrs. Greene."

"I've never been married, Lyle. No matter how you cut it, 'Mrs.' doesn't apply. And you know that. You were sitting there snickering on the stairs at Lita's house when Libby met the man who helped create her and never offered further help. What would your parents think of that? Of Libby and of me?"

"Libby's special. She's different."

"No. She's just very pretty."

"Look, I'm trying to help you and Libby, but all you do is throw questions at me, Jesus." Lyle pulled over to the side of the road and pounded a fist on the dash. "What do you want?"

"Libby may be pretty and special to you. She's next to everything to me. I have to know what I'm facing here. If you can't understand that, Lyle, you're not leveling with me."

"You women think you're so smart nowadays, getting to be a pain in the ass."

"Your mother's a woman, is she . . . ?"

"You leave my mother out of this. She's—"

"Special because she's your mother. Like Libby's special because she's pretty. Rest of us are just a pain in the ass."

"No, it's not . . . women just know how to turn everything around to make a guy feel guilty. Well, we don't like it, okay?"

"So you and Ron drank this blood—"

"Tasted it is all. It was like church and the Holy Sacrament sort of. It just wasn't grape juice."

"So what did you use for the flesh part? Paper wafers? Raw meat from the freezer?"

"That was for the mountain lions. Only I wouldn't shoot them any deer, so somebody went to the store and bought beef. Can you believe feeding a wild animal aged sirloin? Only in Boulder. My folks'd have a herd of calves if they found out about it. Ron and me were just sort of experiencing university life and—"

"What year are you two in?"

"I'm a second-year senior and Ron is a third-year, but he switched majors twice. Well, let's go." He opened his door and slid a long way down to the ground, went around to lower the tailgate, and crawled into the truck bed.

Charlie sat, stunned. Go? She watched him unlock a metal box under the back window and lift the lid, which hid what else he did from her view. She turned to look at the surrounding night. No lights from buildings anywhere in sight. The only light was a glow in the sky where the fire still burned at the edge of the city, the twinkle of the ubiquitous passenger airliner overhead, and the red wink of live embers stretching up a hillside to the left of the road. Go where?

CHAPTER 39

❖

THE ROAD, LYLE explained, went up over the back of Flagstaff Mountain and would be blocked off to keep sightseers from sneaking in from that direction. "It's quicker to walk over this little rise here anyway. Cabin's just on the other side, and they won't see us coming down the lane."

"This little rise here" was fairly steep and largely burned over. Charlie watched for embers and watched her white Keds blacken. She could feel the heat still in the ground through the thin soles.

She didn't like this whole situation. Lyle carried a battery lantern in one hand and a rifle in the other. Charlie remembered Edwina taking along a handgun when she went on field trips to the desert, but she'd never seen so much firepower so casually displayed when she lived in Boulder.

They reached the top of the rise without having to shoot anybody and without Charlie's canvas shoes catching on fire and burning her from the ground up. They looked down on the roof of a dark building, light streaming out onto the ground at each end to limn its size. It was huge.

The light at one end revealed several vehicles. Neither this side of the rise nor the building below appeared to have suffered fire damage. Lance Kelso not only had a mean streak, he had a lucky one.

Lyle switched off the lantern and started down. With the rifle and his boots and the outdoor exposure, there had been a subtle change in the authority apportionment here. To prove it, she'd stopped badgering him with questions. She was too worried about immediate dangers.

Charlie skidded on loose rock and sat down hard, biting her tongue. Lyle caught her by the wrist to stop her, then sat beside her. They waited in silence to learn if someone in the house had heard the rocks she'd loosened tumble down this side of the rise.

She tasted blood and was sickened by the reaction of her taste buds again. Charlie was not reassured by the rifle either. Like with the SWAT team, in an exchange of gunfire the wrong people could get hurt. Lyle explained the stupidity of going into something like this unarmed, pointing out the death toll so far.

They stayed in this position for a long while, and finally Charlie leaned over to whisper in the kid's ear, "What now?"

"I've been trying to think of something."

"Should we maybe peek in the windows? See what they're doing? Or figure out whose cars those are so we know who's inside?"

"That sounds good." But he didn't move. "I'm sort of waiting for something to happen to give me a hint, you know?"

"No." *I think you've lost your nerve. Or else this is some kind of trap you know of that I don't.*

Charlie was about to take charge of this expedition when a scraping came from the shadows below. Then a grunt, a giggle, a "shushing," and a whispered string of profanity.

"Lyle? Is that you up there?"

"That's my mom. What are they doing? She'll ruin everything."

More shushing down below and some consternation on the rise above. Lyle turned to Charlie. "That's Ron."

"And Libby."

"Get down here right now, you two." Ron's whisper was angry. "You stand out like fucking beacons up there."

"Mom? You'll ruin everything."

Charlie followed Lyle meekly down the rest of the slope and into the shadows. "I thought Lance was holding you prisoner."

"You've got it all wrong, as usual." Libby's disgust was palpable. "You were supposed to stay with Grandma."

Charlie had a brief appreciation for Mitch's feelings. "But Jennifer Tollerude called to tell me she had you."

"Least you brought your rifle." Ron took the weapon, not much happier with his friend. "Hope you didn't leave the ammunition in the truck again."

Lyle produced a rectangular box—like staples come in— and the other kid loaded the gun.

"I'm not so sure that's a good idea," the only real adult in this crowd ventured.

"Do you have a clue what's going on here?" Libby stood shivering in shorts and somebody's jacket.

Charlie remembered the clothes she'd left in the truck. "Not really."

"Then stay out of the way, okay?"

The boys led the strike force to the end of the cabin with the lighted parking, then ran and squatted from shadow to shadow like SWAT guys. Libby performed similarly. Charlie ran in a straight line, figuring it would be faster. Her cohorts glanced at each other, embarrassed, like Charlie was the only one on the floor who couldn't dance.

"How did you get up here, Libby?" They stood in the shadows of a balcony overhang at the corner of a porch that disappeared off into the night, deciding what to do.

When Libby left Lita Kelso's after finally meeting her "dad," she returned to her grandmother's house to discover the police there again, removing Marlin from the basement. "And I couldn't find Missy, so I went looking for her next door. That Jennifer bitch forced me into her car and made me drive it up here."

"I'm glad you didn't try to be heroic and drive into a ditch. She might really have shot you."

"Tell me about it. She said she shot the guy in the alley with that gun and would be happy to use it on me if I gave her an excuse. Poor Deborah, having a mother like that. I think *I* have problems."

"Gee, thanks." Charlie hadn't given Missy a thought when she ushered Elmer and Louise, Edwina, and Reynelda out the door in such a hurry. Now was not the time to mention it. Something about that situation left Charlie uneasy the way it was. "When Jennifer called to tell me she had you, we thought she was next door."

Jennifer Tollerude had called from her car phone on the way up here. "She called a bunch of people. I thought she was going to shoot me by accident, trying to hold the receiver and the gun and punch numbers with only two hands."

It had been too far for Ron to walk back to Boulder after delivering the smelly van and no other vehicle was available, no traffic on the road to hitch a ride home, the phone lines and electric service cut off by the fire. An automatic emergency generator restored power to the house, but Ron found the fuse box and shut it down when Jennifer Tollerude forced Libby into the house at gunpoint. The outside lights were controlled from someplace he hadn't discovered.

Ron gained entrance to the house to spend the night, via the same improperly fastened kitchen window he'd used to sneak Libby out when Jennifer sent her to rummage for food. She was unaware of his presence in the house, but Lance spotted him peeking around a doorway and motioned him to remain hidden.

"What did Jennifer want me up here for?" Charlie wanted to know.

"She just wanted to make Grandma miserable. She hates Grandma and the people still inside."

Jennifer had enticed Lance by offering to set fire to the cabin if he didn't come. Heather tagged along. "And there's this scrawny old guy who talks through his nose. We have to help them, Mom. She's wigged enough to shoot somebody."

Two things happened at once to end this interlude of quiet indecision—the crack of a gunshot from within the house and the sudden dramatic appearance of Mitch Hilsten around the corner of the garage. He was as surprised to see them as they were him, and Ron came very close to shooting the superstar in the belly.

He'd decided Ron had fired that shot, and Charlie had to get between them to keep Mitch from committing suicide. She explained about the very real danger to the people inside and turned to see Libby slithering along the front of the house, peeking in a window, and then ducking back.

Charlie swallowed her motherly panic, and Ron whispered that Libby was certain no one had locked the front door after the last, George Goff, had arrived.

Mitch followed them from Boulder after all by forcing Howard's Jeep into the traffic crush in the other lane on Ninth. "Nobody was willing to take on a battered old Jeep with their expensive BMWs, so they let me in in self-defense."

By this time, Lyle's high-wheel was far ahead but it stuck up above traffic, so Mitch could see the fancy light bar on top of it when Lyle braked. "You weren't ever that far away in the canyon. I couldn't follow when he turned off to cross the creek, so I drove on until I could turn around and come back. Saw that light bar heading up a road on the other side. Stayed way back after that, came across the parked truck, followed the footprints in the ashes, and here I am. You always did underestimate me."

Charlie'd looked away long enough to miss her daughter's disappearance. The door yawed open and empty. She started after the miscreant and was halfway to the dark hole when two black-and-whites and several other vehicles came barreling down the driveway. And behind her, Mitch ordered in his *Spy of Wall Street* voice, "Give me that gun, punk."

Fudge, it was probably Kenny on the spot, and Mitch had the rifle by now. Jennifer was already armed. And Lance Kelso the Mean was in there too.

It's my kid who could get caught in the crossfire.

Charlie had to admit later that she lost it just then. But she raced for that open doorway, was inside, had it closed, and felt it up and down for bolts and locks. There were plenty.

"Mom, what are you doing?" Libby's harsh whisper brought Charlie close to losing control of her motherly bladder.

"There's one gun out there already and three heros. One gun and a crazed woman in here. Hear the traffic out there?" By now it was the slam of car doors. "There're more guns and heros arriving by the minute. Think about it."

"What are the two of us supposed to do?"

"I don't know. Maybe I can persuade her—"

"Jennifer? She's crazy. She's not going to listen to you."

The kid was right. Charlie had acted on the panic of the moment rather than logic. "Okay, but we're both leaving together. I don't want you here when the posse rides in."

She'd turned to undo the locks and bolts when a huge double door in the wall to her left opened wide, spilling light on wood flooring the color of gold.

Jennifer held her hostages in the game room. They sat around a pool table holding lighted candles instead of billiard balls. Lance Kelso looked relaxed, in control, and amused, as usual. Heather Tynne appeared ready to check out under the table, and Jennifer looked like a wax dummy replica of herself with a gun in one hand and a glass in the other.

"Step back in the room and don't goniny farther," she warned George Goff, who'd opened the doors. "And Libby, you get in here. Took you long enough. Did you find us shome food? Who's that with you?"

The gun in Jennifer Tollerude's hand wavered in Charlie's direction and fired.

CHAPTER 40

*T*HAT WAS AN incredibly stupid thing to do, locking your-self and your daughter in there with us." Lance Kelso's lean face wrinkled slightly as he bit a plump perfect strawberry off its stem. "Monumental, really," he said around it, and then contemplated a mango. "But I must thank you."

Charlie, trying not to implode, bit down on an even plumper grape and into her tongue again, but this time tasted crow. He was right about the stupidity. "You're welcome."

While he masticated a bite of mango, Lance spread brie on English wafers, handing one across the aisle to Charlie and another to Libby, who sat smirking in the seat facing her mother. "I think I should repay you in some form. Your magnificent fool-hardiness may have saved us all."

Charlie hid her groan in a throat clearing that caused him to pour her more champagne and Libby to snort behind her hands as she had when her grandmother discovered her absence of eye-brows.

"Flying us home is more than enough repayment, believe me." The last thing she needed was another guy who felt he owed her something, especially this one. She took a gulp of champagne before it occurred to her that her nemesis was feeding her.

When Jennifer shot at Charlie, Libby gave her mother a violent shove. Charlie's tailbone still ached from the fall, and she couldn't be sure if she was alive because of the shove or the fact Jennifer Tollerude was stewed at the time. She'd already taken a shot at Lance and missed, the one they'd heard when Mitch appeared, messiahlike, out of the dark.

Lance plied Jennifer with insults and scotch, gambling that he could incapacitate what was left of her self-esteem as well as her coordination before she killed him or George Goff or Heather Tynne. When she took the shot at Charlie, it gave Lance the opportunity to grab her and the gun and hold her down until Mitch, Kenny, and the rest of the posse could get in the front door Libby and Professor Goff unlocked for them.

Lance's Star Ship had first-class seats in soft buff leather, broad and comfortable and only one deep on either side of the aisle. The passenger compartment sat nine, with a small potty in the back on one side.

The pilot and co-pilot, who had seen to the catering of this flight, were now discreetly hidden by the cockpit door.

Jennifer had been taken screaming from the house and proceeded to do her best for the next few days to implicate Lance. The ironic part was, Lance *was* the man pulling the strings, as Lyle had thought. But he was going home, after dropping Libby and Charlie off at John Wayne Airport in Orange, and Jennifer was going to jail, although her lawyer would surely cop an insanity plea. She and Andy didn't own that house blocking Edwina's sunlight. It was owned by one of Lance's investment companies. He had traded it with his father for the retirement condo on Kauai.

This company had bought up several properties in the area, and Jennifer was certain that Edwina, in her snooping, had come across the fact and would ruin the scheme. It was Jennifer who hired Marlin to find and destroy Edwina's computer.

He'd obeyed only the first part of the mission before his run-in with the thirty-six-hour goulash.

Lance built the "monstrolith" and rented it to a seemingly normal upscale family, admittedly hoping to boost property values and taxes in the neighborhood and force the old-timers out. There was nothing illegal about that. The fact that it was a rental was hidden by Andy's office of "director" in the corporation.

"No reason to take it personally," he'd assured Charlie when she at first refused his offer of a free ride home. "It was simply a business decision."

Charlie changed her mind when yet another frantic call came from California. Keegan Monroe had "frozen" in Folsom Prison and couldn't write a word. The bidding on Reynelda's book had topped out at well over a million, and Charlie had to get back to her own business decisions.

Lance acknowledged the blood cult was an attempt to make selling out and moving elsewhere a more palatable position to homeowners, but he steadfastly maintained it to be the creation of an overzealous Andy Tollerude and carried on after his death by Jennifer.

Jennifer admitted this was true but charged Lance with encouraging Andy to find ways to frighten the neighbors. Which charge Lance denied, and she could produce no evidence to prove it.

Authorities established the wildfires were started by runaway campfires, the work of street people—Marlin Wetzel and the dead guy in the alley among them. It's a popular activity when the weather's nice, and wasn't the first time disastrous fires had been set in this manner close to Boulder's backdrop and wouldn't be the last. It's difficult to keep the homeless informed of burning bans, and questionable whether they'd respect them.

There was no provable connection between the two panhandlers and Lance Kelso. Their connection, again, was with Andy and Jennifer.

Business or no, Charlie knew the owner of this airplane was directly responsible for more than could be proved. She even felt sorry for Jennifer, and more so for little Deborah. At least the child's grandmother had flown up from New Orleans to claim her and Missy.

Heather Tynne's last salvo to Charlie was—as a minor official in this perfectly legal company of Lance's—that the homeowners would make enough on their property to move up. In the process the neighborhood would move up with more upscale people moving in. "Everybody wins this way. The only way is up."

Mitch Hilsten's last salvo was a really personal look, like he gave Sally London in *Bloody Promises* just before he got out of bed to go off to be slaughtered in the trenches of World War I. "See you when I get back from Canada."

Kenny Eisenburg's last salvo was, "Hilsten's too old for you, you know that, Charlie."

But, of course, Edwina's parting shot was the most memorable.

The three generations of Greene women stood in the living room of the house that hadn't burned, waiting for Lance to come take them to his Star Ship, the fire having been stopped on the ridge you could see from the front step.

Charlie gestured toward the stucco wall shading the sunroom for eternity. "You must envy your friend Rey's sunny new addition."

And Edwina, breathing easier, able to stand straight with her dressings removed and half of the drains gone, managed to guffaw and cough in reasonable comfort. "Nah, if I really need sun, all I have to do is pack my bags and move out to Long Beach and in with you and Libby."

Charlie's mother had watched the blood in Charlie's face drain to her ankles. "Gotcha!"

Lance Kelso's final salvo, when his pilots landed the Star Ship, was, "Almost everything is a business decision in the modern world. Just be glad you're not important enough to be a major target. Much better to be a victim of chance."

CHAPTER 41

"I't's the getting started," Charlie told Keegan Monroe by phone. "Once you get going, you're fabulous. You're a pro. Just relax and it'll come." She glanced fondly at a real community sitting over coffee cups in the booth seats of her breakfast nook, shamelessly listening to every word.

Jeremy Fiedler was currently between bimbos, so interested in the gossip and "his ladies" in the compound. Presently a landscape architect with a trust fund, he worked out of his home when he felt like working.

Beside him, white-haired Betty Beesom, one arm resting on her protruding stomach, licked a finger to pick crumbs off the table. She'd brought over fresh-baked cinnamon rolls.

"Start anywhere. You can redo what's wrong, but you'll loosen up by making a beginning. I'll be there in a few days and hope you'll have something to show me. Even a page or two, or a sketch, or an outline, anything."

"You have to do this every time he starts a project?" Maggie made room for Charlie to slip in beside her. Hair Irish black, skin pale cream, smile welcoming—Maggie Stutzman was sanity in an insane world.

"He usually needs little or no handholding. Prison life must be getting to him. Not surprising." Charlie hoped it wasn't the big money.

"You still haven't told us who put the ant poison in the

goulash." Jeremy went to the stove for the coffee pot. "Or who killed the man in the alley."

"Jennifer Tollerude again, on both counts. Except her name isn't Tollerude. It's Steinmuller, and so was the guy's in the alley. Andy was a boyfriend. She was still married to Chris Steinmuller, Deborah's father. I remember Deborah referring to Andy as 'Mr. Tollerd,' but then things got crazy and I forgot about it."

Steinmuller, a drug addict, had traced his family to Boulder and demanded money. He moved his panhandling business with the seasons and knew Marlin Wetzel from Seattle.

Jennifer desperately wanted a safe, normal home after the horror of living with an addict. Andy needed a family for his part of the bargain with Lance Kelso and promised to protect her.

"Andy cut an artery in his neck during a ritual in the basement. According to Ron and Lyle, they'd been drinking this weird beer and weren't particularly sober. Those attending managed to stop the flow by applying pressure long enough to get him outside where remaining construction debris made it faster to get him to a car at the front curb than into one in the alley. The plan was to race him to the hospital. It was obvious there'd be no time to wait for an ambulance."

But he died in the front yard, leaving the others in the middle of all this blood that must look like a murder. Kenny was still sorting out who those others were beside the boys, but Lita Kelso, Heather Tynne, and George Goff were mentioned prominently.

Jennifer and Deborah had returned from a trip to California to find only bloodstains left of Andy Tollerude.

George Goff had suggested planting the rest of Andy on top of Tom Horn immediately. Lyle and Ron helped him do it.

Jennifer's real husband, Chris, hadn't shown up yet when Andy was supposedly murdered, and she fixated on Edwina as the source of all her problems, until Lance Kelso blew into town. Jennifer wasn't convinced that the crazy old woman next door was really in Utah at that time either. She was growing increasingly paranoid about the turn of events, enough to stir ant poison into the goulash Twyla Clark left simmering on Jennifer's rangetop while cleaning her house as part of its thirty-six-hour cooking schedule. Twyla would take it to Lita afterward, but explained it was destined for poor Edwina Greene, who had undergone surgery for breast cancer.

The blood spots in front of the freezer in the basement were identified as those of Jennifer's husband. She'd paid Marlin Wetzel to strip the body of clothes and identification and get rid of it. He'd dumped it in the handy black van in the alley, where it cooked on the ribbed, uncarpeted floor in the intense heat of an enclosed automobile, passing through the rigor stages faster than expected.

"You know," Maggie said, her upper lip wet with coffee, "maybe I don't want to travel with you after all."

"That George Goff sounds highly suspicious to me," Jeremy insisted, and all the heads around the table nodded in agreement. "You know I've seen your name twice in *Variety* in the last week, Charlie? This George is the husband of your new celebrity author, isn't he?"

"Yeah, I thought at first he was a harmless old crank. But he worries me." Charlie was thinking of the crowd of cloaks that never existed around a high priest in Columbia Cemetery. "Just between us, I'm not that comfortable with my suddenly successful author either."

Mrs. Beesom leaned over the table to squint knowingly at Charlie. "Is it your psychic sense, do you think?"

"I don't have a psychic sense. It's just that she's a lot smarter than she looks." It was George Goff who was in jail at the moment. I can't believe she was unaware of her husband's connection to the phony blood cult. And the sudden attention her book received was influenced by media attraction to Boulder's strange troubles. Could that weird beer the phoney cult was drinking with their blood the night Andrew Tollerude slit his own throat have been mead?

According to Libby, Jennifer enticed George Goff up to the cabin with the offer of free blood. "I was scared that the free blood was going to be mine. Do you think he's the guy nobody but us and the other freaks in hoods saw in the cemetery?"

"Libby, somehow you and I imagined the same thing at the same time."

"How do you figure that?"

"Because nobody else with us saw it, it's the only explanation that makes any sense."

"You think that makes sense?"

Libby strolled into the kitchen now, fresh from the shower, hair wrapped in a towel, body in a robe short enough to make Betty Beesom cluck. Charlie could only hope the kid wouldn't bend over. Libby popped the ring on a diet Coke and reached up to scratch Tuxedo under the chin. He lounged atop the refrigerator, a shaved patch on one shoulder where another cat's bite was undergoing treatment for infection.

Ignoring her rapt audience, Libby said, "Hey, Tux, you know Mom can talk to the animals like Dr. Doolittle? Why don't you go over and have a chat?"

It was late the next night when Charlie made it home from the office after failing to catch up with the delayed workload but enjoying the attempt.

In the small sunken living room and the light from a streetlamp, Tuxedo sat next to the blinking answering machine, his tail wrapped around his feet.

Charlie kicked off her pumps and sprawled in an easy chair next to the cat and the machine, allowing herself the pleasure of the moment. It *was* nice to have a place to come home to.

The message was either from Canada and Mitch Hilsten or

from Libby, explaining why she wasn't upstairs in her bed as she'd sworn she would be. Charlie wiggled her toes in the dark, glared back at the unblinking cat eyes, and punched the button on the blinking machine.

She was wrong again. Imagine that. The message was from Edwina.

"Thought you'd like to know that Rey ratted on her husband." Edwina sounded delighted. "She told Kenny, George had been collecting blood and burying it in the flower beds. She even showed him some of the unusual bottles he stored it in and a robe and other crazy paraphernalia he kept in a locked storage closet in his study. Looks like she won't have to share her advance with the old goat after all. Didn't I tell you, you underestimated her?"

The next and last message was also from Charlie's mother. "Sorry I forgot to thank you for coming home when I needed you. I'm doing it now. Good night."

So the high priest was there, explaining the candle wax and a few other things, but the cloaked crowd was some kind of illusion like the time standing still. I can live with that.

Tuxedo's eyes glowed like Mitch Hilsten's in the light bars coming through the grated window.

Very tired but buoyed by being back in her own world—and just for the crazy hell of it—Charlie leaned forward so they'd be eye to eye. She told the cat in her mind about the wonderful mountain lion on Mitch's deck in Boulder and about Wiggims the Mostly Lovable.

So what do you think? Can we be friends? At least call a truce? Can I communicate with kitties? In English?

She reached a finger out to scratch him under the chin like Libby had that morning. Without a word, he bit her hard enough to draw blood and tore off up the stairs.